The Journal

Robin Stevens

Matador
9 Priory Business Park,
Wistow Road, Kibworth Beauchamp,
Leicestershire. LE8 0RX
Tel: 0116 279 2299
Email: books@troubador.co.uk
Web: www.troubador.co.uk/matador
Twitter: @matadorbooks

ISBN 978 1788039 642
British Library Cataloguing in Publication Data.
A catalogue record for this book is available from the British Library.

Printed and bound in Great Britain by 4edge Limited
Typeset in 10.5pt StempelGaramond Roman by Troubador Publishing Ltd, Leicester, UK

Matador is an imprint of Troubador Publishing Ltd

Cover artwork by Sasha Otto Mataya
www.sasha-mataya.co.uk

With loving thanks to Alice for her patience and understanding

Assuming that Truth is a woman - what then?

Friedrich Nietzsche

Part 1

1

My sister Charlotte used to say that if you had something on your mind you should write it down. She never said why, but I never asked. Wherever she went, she always carried a small, scruffy notebook or a scrap of paper.

When we were younger, she would pause right in the middle of something, take a pen from her pocket and begin to write. It never took long – only time enough for a sentence or two – but that didn't matter. It impressed me. And it frustrated the hell out of me at the same time. I didn't think any of my thoughts were important enough to note down.

Whenever I noticed her reaching for the paper and pen, I would look at our surroundings and try to guess what she might be writing. I wanted to imagine what it might be; to be a thought in her head for a while. But I never managed it. I didn't know where to start. We could be walking to the shops, playing with leaves in the garden, or lying on the grass counting the clouds. The world seemed so complicated. It was all so *in depth*.

That's the phrase my Geography teacher at school had once used, when we were looking at poverty as a global problem. They always made us study depressing stuff in that subject. We saw countless pictures of starving children and swollen stomachs and flies and weeping grey eyes and cracked brown mud. When someone in my class had asked why we couldn't solve poverty by getting people to be a bit nicer to each other, Mr Miller had laughed and said that it wasn't as simple as that.

'The problem was a bit more *in depth*,' he had said.

He had said it in the way people do when they think they know everything and everyone around them is an idiot. I couldn't stand his face in those moments. The way he looked twisted something inside me and made the dark place grow. It seeped into my stomach and made me feel sick. He was a liar – one of those people who walks around like they know the truth – when he didn't even know about the statue.

I don't think he even knew what *in depth* meant. It was a fake-out. It certainly wasn't an answer. He hadn't known any more about how to solve the global hunger problem than we did. He just had more *wrong* answers. And what was the use of that?

The only thing I took from it was that the more I thought of these depressing problems the more complicated everything seemed.

I hated Geography. The world and its global problems were more and more all over the place every time I learned about them. If *depth* is the number of wrong answers out there, there is too much of it if you ask me.

On one occasion, as Charlotte and I lay on the grass in the garden and she scribbled on one of her pieces of paper, I had asked her what she was writing. I hadn't expected an answer. My sister was private with these things. She had a look on her face that said, *Really? You think I'm going to answer that?*

However, on this occasion I had been surprised to see her turn and announce that she was writing an *aphorism*. I say announce because often with my sister she didn't simply say something. Saying was for when she talked about the small things, while announcing was for when something interesting was involved. In these instances she would speak with importance in her voice; with an invisible weight hanging off each word.

On hearing her announcement, I had nodded and looked down, pretending to examine the blades of grass in front of my feet. I remember feeling something tiny crawling between my toes. The sun shining on my cheek. A warm gust of wind tugging at my shirt. I remember having the feeling that everything around me seemed okay. As if there were no *depth* at all. Sometimes the global problems out there disappear and I'm only left with the ones in my head.

After a minute or two, I had asked her what an aphorism was. She had raised her head and announced that it was a short phrase that made a point or revealed some sort of truth. Friedrich Nietzsche had written them when he wasn't getting his headaches, she had added.

I didn't know who Friedrich Nietzsche was, but had pushed on and asked what her aphorism was. She had sighed and said that I probably wouldn't understand because I wasn't old enough to be an *attempter* like her. A true *free spirit*.

'Attempt to do what?' I had asked.

5

She had smiled and said, 'Precisely!'

I had always hated it when she did that. I remember clenching my jaw and my anger solidifying into a wall of cast-iron silence. It had been my best weapon; its strength fuelled straight from the dark place.

Ten minutes had gone by before Charlotte had sighed and pushed me on the shoulder. I had wobbled backwards onto the grass and she had laughed. She would tell me this once, she had said, but only if I never asked her what she was writing again.

My sister often made these secretive deals with me. She called them pacts. It usually happened when I had asked her a question to which she had, not only an answer, but an *answer*. She loved this kind of answer. They were the only ones that mattered, she would say. The big ones. The ones that switch your whole head around.

The reasons *why*.

If she were to give me something that important, there had to be a clause in the contract to balance it out. Something that made me appreciate the significance of the whole thing.

I hadn't minded these agreements. They had made me feel special because, even though I didn't know much of Charlotte's inside world, the agreements we made meant that I knew more than anyone else. And I had liked that idea.

So she had shown me the piece of paper she had been writing on. I can still picture it: the torn edges with the words messily written and not sitting on the lines as they should have. That had annoyed me. I remember frowning and leaning in.

It said:

If God exists, why wouldn't one day of evil a year be enough for us to tell the difference between right and wrong?

I had read it once and read it again. I hadn't known what to say. I had looked around the garden and back up at the clouds, but still had no clue as to where this aphorism had come from. This had lost me for a minute and I had got stuck on the idea of thoughts. How do thoughts happen? Do I think them or do they think themselves? Sometimes I feel like I'm a thought delivery system. They arrive and I pass them on, but they're not really *mine*.

After showing me, Charlotte had folded the piece of paper away into the pocket of her cardigan and gone back to lying on the grass. I had wondered whether she thought her aphorism made a point or revealed some truth, or if an aphorism could do both. I hadn't been able to work it out either way.

True to our agreement, whenever Charlotte got out a pen and paper after that I had never asked what she was writing. Instead, I had developed the habit of trying to create an aphorism myself. Not to imagine her thoughts, but to *attempt* my own. I had the right to try it, at least. I would look around me, as she did, think and try to settle on something. I would let my thoughts happen for long enough to turn themselves into a truth. I would say the aphorism aloud in my head, feeling pleased with myself.

If my attempt produced something, that is.

I had never fully understood why Charlotte said

aphorisms were supposed to reveal *a* truth and not *the* truth, or if there was even any difference. I guess it had something to do with perspective, as she had once said, but I had never got that either. It must have been about the statue, I had deduced; the one she used to explain to me.

But didn't there have to be *the* truth, at least about some things? Otherwise, what was the point of anything?

Never knowing how good my ideas were, or whether there was such a thing as a *good* aphorism, I had kept them to myself. Some of them were definitely better than others, but they were at least worth something.

Now, as the engine of my Joy Liner bus clunked its way out of the terminal, I looked out of the window and tried to think of something that was true. It comforted and calmed me to do so. Took my mind somewhere else. Settled my nerves.

Made the mess go away.

Once my thoughts had settled on a phrase I said it aloud in my head.

A beautiful world means nothing if everything you care about gets ruined.

I thought this was quite a good aphorism. I was pleased with it in a strange way. Even though, deep inside in the place that I kept buried, I knew it was just more darkness.

2

The bus continued on its journey and I let my eyes lose focus on the passing scenery. The complexities of the world reduced themselves to a single blur. The *depth* became a simple layer of changing shapes and colours. A mixture of the world's countless ingredients that gradually became rhythmic in a strange way; a display turning on a reel in front of my eyes. As if reality were a flicker book that pretends to make things move.

I was aware of bright greens, deep blues and dusty oranges. Giant leaves, tumbling shacks and cloudless skies. Everything seemed so bright, so real. What would it be like to experience the world if everything I saw was a constant blur? That was a question that needed an *answer*, but I wasn't the one to give it.

Comfortably settled in my aphorism, my questions and my blur, I had stopped paying attention to what was happening outside of me: the humid heat; the noisy, bustling people; the bright, bright sunlight; the sticky, cramped seats; the thick, choking exhaust; the complexity of it all. It was too much. I had retreated into my self-preservation mode, ignoring everything around me in an attempt to avoid interacting with it.

Self-preservation was one of a number of modes I had developed during my childhood, and one that, if I'm honest, I employed whenever possible. My default setting. It seemed to make things so much easier. I had too many distracting thoughts inside my own mind, let alone outside of it. Dealing with the world, I found, was often difficult.

And I wasn't good at dealing with difficult things.

As usual, self-preservation mode was proving successful. So when a question came at me and all the lines and shading and precision and colour of the world zoomed back in at once, I didn't know what to say.

'Hello. Do you speak English?'

3

All the waiting and queuing and pointing and confusion and standing and sitting and moving and picking up of bags and putting down of bags and apologies and frowns had led to this. A conversation. As if squeezing into the correct hot, sweaty seat on the Joy Liner bus from Phnom Penh airport wasn't awkward enough. The name of the bus was a lie.

Already my English-weather trousers were stuck to the burning black leather beneath them. My legs were slowly swelling inside. By my head there were smudged sick stains on the window. The catch that slid it open refused to budge in spite of my efforts. It was so hot that each breath was a tiny bit like choking.

The heavy bulge of the person in the seat in front of me was crushing my knees. A small girl was staring at me from a seat diagonally across. She had giant brown eyes and looked at me as though she knew *the* truth. Everyone else was talking and gesturing and interacting successfully.

A thin, wiry man was climbing down the aisle trying to sell pictures of Jesus. In the picture, Jesus was smiling. He had perfect hair and white teeth and there was some gold writing I didn't understand. He was pictured as self-satisfyingly happy; it didn't seem fair.

I had been assured by another thin, wiry man that my bag was tied to the roof, but he didn't speak much English so I had no idea whether or not this was true. The stifling air inside the bus had a kind of thickness to it. It was obviously everywhere, in a way that I hadn't experienced air being before. There was a solid nature to it, as if it were as real as me.

The young man who had asked the question was sitting in the seat next to mine. He looked a little older than me, but not by much. Perhaps nineteen or twenty. His voice sounded excited by the idea that I might speak English, eager for it to be true. His hair was blond, short and shaven. Dark, rough skin suggested he had been out in the heat for some time. He was somewhere between burnt and tanned. Blue eyes shone out from his face, colourful and confident. He was succeeding on this bus in a way that I wasn't.

What's more, he had a *presence*. I have never had a *presence*. I immediately judged him to be superior to me. Placing in relation to others is always important, I have found. Equality is a lie invented by people like me to make ourselves feel better. That's a truth. It feels like *the* truth, to me at least. It only took going to school to make me realise this.

When he smiled at me, his perfect white teeth gleamed out through the stubble around his chin. Initially, all I could do was try to smile back. Doing this bought me enough time to gather my thoughts and put together an answer to his question.

'Sorry, yes,' I said, unsure of what else to say.

I've found that it's always a risk to commit yourself to saying too much when you first meet people. You don't know where it might lead.

'Fantastic! I thought you would. Have you come from the airport?'

Leaving the tiniest of pauses, he carried on before I had time to answer. 'Where did you fly in from today?'

'London.'

'No shit! Wow, so you're, like, just arrived and everything. I thought you might be. You're pretty white, dude. No offence! So what's the dealio? You out for a long time or...'

He left a pause for me to fill in my own answer, but I didn't want to reveal the truth. I didn't want sympathy, and I didn't want to talk about Charlotte. Not yet.

'I don't really know, to be honest. I'm going to see how it goes.' Which was *a* truth, even if it wasn't *the* truth.

'Nice. You're gonna love it here, man. There are so many places you've gotta go. Angkor Wat, you know that place? Big fucking historical monument.'

I nodded my head.

'Yeah, that place is awesome! It's like one giant, *archaic* meal you've simply gotta chow down on, my friend!'

Things continued in this same vein for the next half-hour. I sat and listened and spoke occasionally, usually to offer a 'yes' or 'no' when an answer to his questions was needed. I was trying to concentrate and keep up, but I kept falling back into self-preservation mode. Default settings are hard to shift. People don't have reset buttons; how great it would be if they did. I often spent times in my dark place wishing I could change who I was. Become something new. Start again.

The longer the conversation drew on, the more I longed to get back to my blur. A blur offered no surprises and asked nothing of me. A blur couldn't reveal that I was hopeless or lost.

A blur would leave me alone.

4

Jon-Paul told me his name after telling me that I had to go to Thailand once I had finished in Cambodia. Apparently it had the 'sickest beaches in the world'. The badge sewn onto his backpack told me he was Canadian. I had never met a Canadian before. Or anyone with a national badge on their backpack.

He had been travelling for five months on a round-the-world ticket and seemed to have been drunk in every destination. I didn't mean to, but I thought of another aphorism while he went into detail regarding a Swedish girl he had picked up at a beach party in Sihanoukville, a town on the Cambodian coast.

Sometimes it's how much people talk, not what they say, that tells you the most about them.

I read it aloud in my head a couple of times and was satisfied that it revealed *some* truth. My sister might have liked it. I was pleased for a moment, before I realised Jon-Paul had continued to talk while I was formulating my truth and I hadn't heard any of what he had said. I tried hard to get into my focused-alert mode and stick with the conversation. The trouble was this mode never worked well when other people were around.

'Okay,' Jon-Paul said, leaning over to the aisle side of his seat and staring intently out of the front window, 'we're nearly here. You ready for the ride?'

'What ride?'

'The rip-off ride! Jeez! You never heard of it?'

'No.'

'Shit! You *are* green! No worries, I'll educate you, buddy. God knows I wish someone had educated me before I got taken on my first ride.'

He paused as if he was gathering his thoughts. 'Okay, you're white. I mean *really* white. You're young, you're polite and you look nervous. What this means to a Cambodian at a bus stop – shit to any Southeast Asian at a bus stop – is that you're rich, soft and easy pickings. No offence buddy, that's just how it is. You don't yet have the look that says, "I've seen this before and I'm not buying it."'

He took a breath and continued. 'If you're not careful when you get off the bus, you could end up changing money for a rate that's so bad you start doubting your ability to add up, taking a taxi ride for the price of the car itself, staying in a hotel that will rob the belongings you leave in their "safe"' – the quotations marks were made in the air with his fingers – 'and having your rucksack carried for you until you pay them twice the price of your belongings to give it back. All in the space of five minutes. Seriously! And you'll be left sitting on your lice-infested bed in a smelly room with fake money, no passport and no bag wondering what the hell happened!'

Jon-Paul's head turned as he finished talking. He was becoming preoccupied with what was going on outside the bus. The Joy Liner began to slow and pulled off the road into what looked like a bus station, but without the organisation. The way this country functioned confused me. I could see the heads of hundreds of people crowding around a large number of brightly coloured buses that were parked wherever there seemed to be a space. My swollen, sweaty leg muscles tensed. I noticed the sick on the window again.

'Listen, buddy, you look like you're in big trouble so I'll help you out. Stick with me. Make straight for your rucksack and don't bother saying, "No thank you". You got a hostel booked?'

'No,' I said. 'Should I have done? I just thought I'd sort of turn up.'

'Oh, that's cool, man. Listen, if you want you can come with me. I know a fun place to stay. Good crowd, decent food, cheap as the rest. You up for it? No worries if you want to do your own thing.'

I hadn't thought where I would stay at first. Everything had happened so quickly I hadn't had time to research. I had decided it didn't matter as long as it was close to the tourist centre.

'Is it fairly central?' I asked.

'Yeah, bang by the lake. Right in the thick of it.'

'Okay. If it's all right with you that would be good. Thanks Jon-Paul.'

'No worries!'

The bus pulled to a high-pitched halt. Jon-Paul stood up and looked at me with a strange amount of seriousness in his eyes.

'Just tunnel-vision it, and if you've gotta be polite, say no. I'll sort us out a ride. See you by the bags!'

He pushed himself to the front of the bus and stood by the doorway, ensuring that he would be first in the queue to get off.

I followed suit after grabbing my small pack and stood waiting in the sweaty queue to disembark. A large woman was leaning against me from behind and I could feel her soft, warm breasts pressing against my lower back. A trickle of sweat emerged at the base of my spine and stayed there.

There were problems everywhere, not just in my mind.

My knees were no longer being crushed by the seat, but were instead digging in to a holdall that was blocking the aisle in front of me. A gentleman with a moustache and a stained beige suit got up from his seat in the row ahead of mine. He flicked me a nod of recognition as he grasped the holdall's handle and began to drag it towards the exit. Above the driver's steering wheel, a plastic statue of Jesus praying with his hands together was blue-tacked to the dashboard. A faded air freshener in the shape of a pine tree hung from the rear-view mirror, its scent all but gone.

I could hear a stadium of people outside, all trying to talk at the same time. The tiny bells that trimmed the edges of the curtain by the door began to jangle together tunelessly as people swept by and out. I approached the steps of the bus and sucked up a deep breath of the warm, sticky air that hung around me. I don't know why I did this because I hated it. Outside of me, it made me feel wrong. The funny thing was that, when I held it in, it was like I somehow existed more.

I walked out of the bus into a world that was much more real than usual.

5

The bright sunlight brought with it a melee of tuk-tuk and motorbike, or 'moto', drivers, touts and tourists. They were all crushed on top of each other tightly around the exit to the bus. As if a piece of meat had been thrown into a pack of hungry dogs, each tourist was targeted and jumped upon by the stronger members of the crowd at first and then the weaker ones. There seemed to be an unspoken ranking order among the touts and drivers, each taking their position at their accepted places in the queue. As I said, placing is important.

When I made it onto solid ground I could see Jon-Paul ahead of me. He was striding through the crowds making straight for his backpack, which was in the process of being picked up by a local gentleman with thin, greasy hair who was wearing a tattered red waistcoat. I edged my way into the frenzy, attempting to appear confident and experienced as Jon-Paul had suggested, but I wasn't pulling it off. I didn't have a mode for this. My pretence was easily detected and I was clearly a target for the crowd. Faces were angling my way from all directions.

'Hello, my friend! Where you go?'

'You need moto? Hotel?'

'I know very many nice hotels for you! Cheap, my friend. Cheapest in Phnom Penh!'

'What you need? My friend? Hello?'

As several people spoke to me, grabbed my arm and called me their friend at the same time, I tried to refuse each one while attempting to get near my rucksack. Fighting my way through the crowd I saw my bag sticking up, half in the air.

'Hey! Is this yours?' Jon-Paul was wrestling a bag off the shoulders of a young Cambodian boy. The boy couldn't have been more than seven or eight, but he was obviously stronger than he looked.

'Yes,' I replied, shouting through one cupped hand because the other was being held by three different people.

'Excellent! Follow me, my young Padawan!'

With a final, forceful tug of his arm he tore my rucksack from the struggling boy, and strode away from the tussle.

After many more refusals and as many angry faces, another bus pulled in across the track from us. The pack moved with absolute fluidity. A shoal of fish, a shiver of sharks perhaps, hunting down their next prey. They swam around me and reformed seamlessly on the other side in order to repeat the process again.

'Thank God we're through that!' I said, thinking out loud. My heart was beating fast and my field of vision had narrowed to almost nothing. I took a moment to breathe and become aware of more than my immediate surroundings.

We were in a dusty clearing, the buses ten or twenty yards behind us. All I could smell were exhaust fumes and dust. They were in my eyes and my hair and my mouth and my lungs. To my right were lines and lines of motorbikes, hundreds of them sitting there in a jumbled order like a swarm of colourful insects, jostling and huddling around something sweet. Their metal wheels and chassis were shining in the midday sun. I wondered how hot they must be.

'Pretty intense, huh? You made it through, though!'

As he spoke, Jon-Paul was busy putting his bag on his back. He had two guys waiting beside him. They looked at me as though they had seen me before.

'These guys'll take us to the hostel. Nine hundred riel each to go on their bikes, okay?'

I nodded my head, glad to be given any kind of deal that didn't involve having to make it myself. I couldn't remember how much nine hundred riel was worth, and I tried to calculate it. A piece of certainty would have been nice. But before I could work it out one of the drivers smiled at me and nodded his head.

'Hello, my friend! Come this way!'

We walked across the track and I followed my driver to his moto. It was skinny and yellow with blue writing on the sides. As he kicked the stand, its handlebars glinted in the sunshine. I forced my mind from the exchange rate and focused. The style of the bike was close to that of something you might see in the movies. It was an old-fashioned scooter, similar to a Vespa, except that it was smaller and had a much longer and flatter seat. The seat was black, slightly padded and oblong. It reminded me of a rubber brick, the kind people dive into a swimming pool for in their pyjamas.

21

I remembered doing that to get a swimming badge when I was younger. I had thought it stupid at the time.

'Who goes swimming in their pyjamas? What's the point?' I had said to my father as he drove me home from the swimming pool, but he had been too busy making calls to give me an answer. He had still been too busy with work to turn up and see me awarded my badge the following week.

Despite the length of this seat, it seemed barely big enough for two people to sit on due to the size of the bike itself. I looked down at my bags and back at the moto. The driver saw my look of uncertainty and smiled.

'It's okay!' he said. 'Plenty of room for us. I am very good driver. Fast and comfortable, my friend!'

He climbed on and revved up the engine, and I saw Jon-Paul jump onto the back of the other moto and speed off in a cloud of dust. I clambered on slowly and proceeded to hold on as tightly as I could. Me, my two rucksacks and my driver veered out onto the track and we scuttled our way up towards the main road.

6

Through the centre of Phnom Penh I clung on tightly to my driver and my bags as we wove our way through endless traffic that followed no discernible road laws. Motorbikes swam through the roads like barracuda, moving together as one as we were pulled into the flow and got swept up with them. I tried and failed many times to calculate the cost of the journey. My mental arithmetic was usually reliable; a reassuring source of answers. A way to make sense of a little bit of the *depth*. But I couldn't keep my focus with all the stopping and going. There were too many distractions.

We rode so close to other bikes, tuk-tuks and cars that I could smell their engines and taste their exhausts. I was brushing shoulders with their riders. My danger-survival mode was taking over. This mode was rarely engaged, but it was one over which I had no control. Once it locked in, my ability to concentrate on anything else evaporated. It was one of those moments when my thoughts and modes occurred whenever they wanted to, rather than when I chose. I was merely a competition between different things and there was no me apart from or beyond the winner.

As though there was thinking going on and a mode was delivered without the need for me at all.

Adding to the confusion, there was the endless noise of horns and beeps. They came from every direction. It was expected of anyone riding on the road. As if somehow, by not making any noise, no one would know you were there. My driver used his horn every other minute, though I couldn't see that it made any difference. I thought how bizarre it would be if everything, all the horns and beeps and engines and screeches and cries and clatters and roars, fell silent.

I soon learnt that almost anything could fit onto the back of a motorbike: wobbly, wooden crates full of eggs; battered boxes bursting with brightly coloured fruit; mounds of tattered clothes tied together with tarpaulin and a washing line. Seeing the astonishing practicality of a scooter being used for five people, an entire family, made me feel embarrassed for my earlier concern that my bags and I wouldn't fit on. I watched those bikes intently, scared for the littlest children balanced in baskets attached to the handlebars. They seemed so unaware of the dangers around them. So *free*.

By the time we pulled off the main streets and into a side road I had loosened my grip a little around the driver's waist, just enough to enable me to twist and turn my head freely. Looking around, I could see that we were heading towards a dusty, unpaved street that seemed to lead into another world.

We slowed right down as we entered the street. It was bunged up with tuk-tuks and motos, with people bustling all around. There was a different feel to this part of town and I noticed other foreigners for the first time since I had left the bus. There were large numbers of tourists milling around, casually chatting, laughing, eating, ambling, arriving and leaving. Everybody appeared to know exactly what they were doing or where they were going. To not be amazed by what was happening around them. To not be at all scared or lost. To be relaxed and happy. To not seem at all alarmed or concerned.

To find this whole experience *normal.*

7

The beeps issued by my moto driver continued as he tried to navigate his way through the static, dusty crowd. Street food stalls, money changers, cafes and guest houses surrounded the road. The buildings were made from a ramshackle collection of faded wood, tarpaulin, corrugated iron, plastic and concrete.

It was a real surround, because they weren't only along the sides of the road but within it as well. Little islands floating in a sea of tuk-tuks and motorbikes. Every shopkeeper beckoning us towards them. Staring. Shouting. Gesturing. A full-on assault of the Phnom Penh service industry. I wondered what the shopkeepers would make of the streets of London; so grey, cold and reserved.

We eventually pulled up and stopped outside a guest house on the right-hand side of the road. My driver kicked up the stand on the bike and I climbed off my rubber brick. The cool wind from the ride had gone and as I stood up my shirt instantly stuck to my body. Sweat began to crawl nervously out of me, afraid of what might happen to it. I looked up.

A searing sun in a bold blue sky.

'This is it, buddy. Don't you just love that smell?'

Jon-Paul was rifling through the pockets of his linen trousers as he looked at me with a giant grin, which I instinctively copied without knowing why. He pulled out a crumpled wad of notes, peeled off a couple and handed them to the moto drivers. I tried to decipher the smell he was talking about but couldn't work out exactly what it was. The best way I could describe it was a dusty, hot, chilli-infused exhaust smell with a hint of sweat.

'This ride's on me. Right, let's get ourselves a room,' he said pulling his bag onto his back and turning towards the guest house.

'You're gonna love this place. I mean, it's not much and to be honest all these places along the lake are pretty much the same, but the crowd who stay here are way cool. Totally chilled out and into life, you know what I mean?'

I didn't know what he meant, but I nodded anyway.

'Where's the lake?' I asked.

I had heard there was a lake in the middle of the city, but knew nothing beyond that. The police report had mentioned that Charlotte had stayed by the lake in Phnom Penh, so it was my only real starting point.

'Oh, it's right over the other side of the hotel. Awesome for sunsets, but you wouldn't swim in it unless you were looking for a little typhoid and a spell in a Cambodian hospital. Which I really can't recommend, by the way!'

He laughed and, wanting to be polite, I did the same. I tried to imagine what having typhoid would feel like, but couldn't. Mainly because the only thing I knew of typhoid was that it was something you could catch if you swam in Cambodian lakes.

We briefly collided with our heavy bags before regaining our balance and walking into the entrance hall of our guest house. The multicoloured, hand-painted wooden sign above the door of Happy Sunshine Guesthouse led in to its main structure. The building frame was made from smooth, thin poles of wood, which created walls and rooms that had little separating them.

The front doorway was small and, as we entered, the low ceilings formed a dark, humid hallway with rooms leading off either side. There was a large, round mirror at the end of the hallway a few metres away. To one side I could see daylight coming from a shared open space at the back of the guest house. As my eyes were adjusting from the bright sunshine outside, a man appeared from a room to my right and greeted us.

'Hi guys, how's it going? You looking for a room?'

I disliked this man the instant I met him. He had a pseudo-American accent and was pretending not to be Cambodian because it wasn't good enough. He spoke in a slightly condescending tone, as if we were unable to find a room on our own.

I often found that I was capable of disliking someone after only knowing them for a short period of time. My sister used to say that it was difficult to get to *know* someone. She would say that the whole process takes so much time and effort that most people give up or don't bother trying.

Hardly anyone knows anyone, she had once announced, right before running upstairs and slamming her bedroom door.

I had thought to myself later that if what Charlotte had

said was meant to be an aphorism, it wasn't a good one. Sometimes, for me at least, getting to know a person was easy. Occasionally people give themselves away when they aren't trying: a movement, a frown, a particular expression, a tone of voice. Some people I could know straight away. It was easy.

'Hey, Frankie! How's it going?' Jon-Paul grabbed Frankie and gave him an *alternative* handshake.

'Jonny! You're back again! Good to see ya!'

Frankie turned his head and looked down the corridor as Jon-Paul began speaking. I liked him even less.

'Back again! Absolutely, buddy. Love this city! This is my buddy, Ethan. He's fresh off the boat and looking for a place to stay. I told him there's only one place to crash in Phnom Penh and brought him straight here… Sunshine Happy Guesthouse!'

Jon-Paul beamed at me and put his arm around my shoulder.

'Hello, my friend,' Frankie said, turning to look at me.

He shook my hand the *traditional* way, and there was a brief silence as neither of us spoke. What was it that made me the kind of person who always received the *traditional* type of handshake? I looked at my feet and tried to make up an aphorism about getting to know people while we all stood there, but none of them sounded right.

Instead, my mind began to question why I hadn't brought a pair of flip-flops with me. I was puzzled until I remembered that it was because my last pair had been lost a few years earlier, though I couldn't think where. Maybe at the swimming pool. I pictured them drowning at the bottom of the pool with the rubber bricks. Perhaps I could have got hold of some nearby.

At that point, I looked up to see Frankie staring at me. He had an expression on his face that was easy to read. I had seen it on many other people's faces in the past. He thought I was *odd*.

Thankfully, he broke the silence. 'So, uh, I have a twin room free for you, my friends. Follow me; I'll take you there now.'

We picked up our bags and followed behind Frankie as he shuffled off: Frankie, Jon-Paul and then me. We reached the end of the corridor and turned right past the mirror, cut left again before stopping outside a room that was in an even darker part of the building.

'Here you go,' Frankie said, pushing open the door and ushering us inside. The room was a box shape and just big enough to fit two beds, a mat and a table. There was a small wooden cubicle in the far corner that looked to contain a toilet and a basin. It was hot and sticky inside and there was a ceiling fan that rotated at a pace that was incredibly inefficient.

A faded picture of a lake hung on the wall, which I guessed was the one behind the hostel. The lake in the picture was a pale turquoise. Old age seemed to have taken away the richness of colour the paint had once had. It lay still behind cracked glass.

Charlotte had once knocked over one of Mum and Dad's vases. She said it had been an accident, but I was there and it hadn't seemed as though it was. This painting of the lake was the same colour as that pale, old, broken vase. It was as if the shatterings had been swept into a frame.

'Looks good to me,' said Jon-Paul, throwing his bag onto the bed. 'This okay with you, buddy?'

'Uh, yeah. Great.'

I wasn't going to go anywhere else at that point. I took my eyes off the picture and put my bag down. My back was cool with sweat as it came off.

'So,' continued Frankie, 'you want anything? We got a good price on weed and I can get you pills or mushrooms for tomorrow if you like? How much you need?'

Frankie lingered by the door as he asked this, leaning on the frame and scratching his elbow as he spoke. As if it was no big deal.

'Just an eighth for me, Frankie. I've still got some really good shit from Laos. You after anything, Ethan? You wanna get a little crazy tonight?'

Jon-Paul looked at me in a similar way to when we had first met. There was no sense in his voice that this was anything other than normal. I was getting to know him a bit better.

'Not for me, I'm… er, I'm tired from the flight. I'll leave it for today, thanks.'

Panic mode had set in. I busied myself with opening the top of my bag as I replied. Fumbling with the clasp I caught my finger in the zip and breathed sharply through my teeth.

'Okay, my friend. No worries. I'll get it to you later on, Jon Paul. Laters, my friends.'

And with that Jon-Paul offered up a salute and a grin as Frankie left the room.

I sat down on my bed and nursed my finger. The sting of the pinch stretched up my arm. I made my excuses when Jon-Paul asked if I wanted a beer. I needed some time to myself.

As he left to see if any of his friends were in the hostel, I turned to lie on my bed, my eyes gazing at the slow piece of rotating metal on the ceiling. Had it been the right decision to come here? How was I going to do this?

I shut my eyes and the heat and the air filled my lungs. Tiredness took hold as my mind slipped out of the world around it. Sleep was easy. I could deal with that.

The doorbell rang. Amid all the noise coming from the living room I heard my sister shout.

'I'll get it!' she yelled, almost all in one word, as if she were speaking a foreign language.

There was a thumping series of steps and the click of the latch on the door.

'Hello Charlotte. Happy birthday!'

A calm, adult voice came from the other side of the door. The sound of it floated over the mayhem, unfussed by it. She wasn't excited by Charlotte's birthday, but I wasn't surprised by that. Adults never get excited by anything.

'Are you having a nice day?' the voice asked.

'Yes, it's great, it's great!' There was another thump and I pictured Charlotte jumping up and down, her ponytail wagging like the tail on Buster, the dog from next door.

I wished we were allowed a puppy, one that we could play with and throw sticks for, but Daddy didn't like mess and he said puppies made far too much of it.

'Is your mother here?'

'She's in the kitchen. Hi James.'

Through all the noise there was a little quiet. James must have been one of Charlotte's friends from school.

'Come on, James. Say hello,' floated the voice. If it were a thing, it would be a bird. A tiny one with pretty wings for gliding.

'Hello.'

I could just hear James from my hideout position. I racked my brains to work out if I knew who he was. I had only seen a few of Charlotte's school friends and didn't remember any of them being called James. Faced with a blank in my head, I invented a picture of a boy to fit the voice. He was short and funny-looking, with a floppy mop of hair. He had a pair of glasses with a felt patch sellotaped over one of his eyes. One of his legs was shorter than the other, so he had to wear a chunky shoe on one foot, which made him walk in a wonky way.

'Come on inside, everyone's in the living room! Come on!' Charlotte was speaking in her foreign language again.

The thumping doubled, its noise echoing up through the hallway towards me as Charlotte and James went into the living room.

I was kneeling a few steps outside my room, just far enough away to hear what was going on downstairs. I had kept my bedroom door open in case I needed to quickly hide. As I gripped on to the banisters, I counted in my head how many people had arrived at the party. Twelve. How strange! I felt a little funny, sitting there at the top of the stairs knowing there were twelve people in our front room. I couldn't imagine how it must look. What were they all doing? They would have to be careful. I hoped they were being grown up and responsible. Daddy had worked very hard for the nice things we had in the living room. He didn't like it when we forgot that and got carried away with being silly.

When I had found out at the dinner table the week before that Mummy and Daddy had decided to let Charlotte have a birthday party this year, I hadn't been able to finish my cauliflower cheese. I had been sent to my room without any pudding as a result, but I didn't mind. I couldn't have eaten anything else anyway. She had never had a party before, neither of us had. Each time Charlotte had asked for one, Daddy had always said no. I hadn't even asked when it had been my birthday.

Daddy never said why we couldn't have a party, he just said no. When Charlotte kept on asking he got cross with her and sent her to her room. Each time Daddy got cross, Mummy and I would sit in silence and not say anything. If we did that for long enough it seemed to make Daddy better.

I heard the floating voice again. It sounded a little quieter this time, as if it were further away. She must have gone into the kitchen, I deduced.

'Hello Jane,' the voice said.

'Hello Rosemary,' said Mummy. Mummy's voice didn't sound normal. I listened harder, pushing my ear through a gap in the railings.

'James has gone into the living room with Charlotte.'

'Oh good.'

I heard some clinking and clanking noises coming from the kitchen. I heard the oven door open and shut with a whoomph.

'How *is* Charlotte? Is she enjoying her day?'

'Fine, fine. She seems to be enjoying herself.'

'She's very excited.'

'Oh, that's just who she is. She gets excited easily.'

'Yes, yes. Quite. And she hasn't had any other *episodes*?'
A little stretch of quiet as cold as the fridge sunk into the kitchen. The oven opened and whoomphed again.

'No, she's fine.'

'It's just that she got herself into a real state that time at sports day. I remember having to come in and help out…'

'Well, we've moved on from that. Charlotte's fine. She's doing well,' Mummy interrupted. She never did that normally.

'Well, good good. That's nice to know.'

A loud whoop came from the living room, followed by a cackle, which I knew was Charlotte's.

'How's Richard?' Rosemary asked.

'He's fine.'

'Is he here today?'

'No, not at the moment. He'll be back from work soon, though. You're more than welcome to wait if you would like to speak to him.'

'Oh no, I shan't intrude.' The floaty voice stopped.

For a minute, no noises came from the kitchen. I pressed myself against the banisters as hard as I could. If only I could magic myself invisible, I could go down and stand next to them and they would never know I was there. I'd stand next to Mummy and jump and wave and dance in front of her as much as I wanted and she'd never know I'd even done it.

'Well, I must be going,' the floaty voice said, unaware of me in the form of an invisible brown bear, growling and snarling in front of her.

'Very well, Rosemary. I wouldn't want to keep you. Would you mind seeing yourself out?'

'Not at all. Shall I pick James up at six?'

'Yes, that will be fine.'

'Okay, see you later.'

'See you later,' Mummy said as I did an invisible Red Indian war dance around her. The latch unclicked and clicked again as Rosemary stepped out of the front door. The oven door creaked and whoomphed once again.

I realised I could smell vanilla and lemon and butter. Scrummy wafts of warm cake air were travelling up the stairs towards me and they made me feel hungry. Mummy and Charlotte had said earlier, when I had first gone up to my room, that I was invited to the party, but I had said that I would stay upstairs. I had said that I was in the middle of something important that couldn't be interrupted. However, with all the yummy smells and exciting noises and my tummy starting to rumble, I thought I should maybe go down and join in after all.

I kneeled and tried hard to hear what Charlotte was doing.

In my listening I heard the key enter the front door. I could make out the individual clicking of each of the metal shafts inside the lock as they fell into place around the shape of the key.

I pictured, in my head, a book I had read about how a Yale lock worked. Its pictures and diagrams had made me smile. They had shown a team of tiny men pushing an enormous key with all their might into an even more enormous lock. Another team of men had been making sure that each internal shaft slid perfectly into place in order for the lock to turn. With real locks, the book had said, there weren't any tiny men monitoring these things; they happened on their own. This was what made me smile the most when I thought of it.

When it came to our lock, I knew it was Daddy who was making it turn. As he pushed open the door a little tingle of cold air come up towards me. All the rest of the noise in the living room carried on and I wished it would stop.

Daddy wiped his feet on the mat by the door, a series of rough scrapes; four or five times for each shoe. I didn't hear him put his briefcase down and hang up his coat, but I knew exactly how he was doing it.

After a minute, which felt like forever, I heard Daddy's voice in the kitchen. When my teacher at school had first taught me how to read a clock I had asked him how it was that everyone told the time the same way. He had looked at me strangely and asked me what I meant. I had said that sometimes time was fast and other times it was slow, so how could it be that everyone told it the same way?

He had smiled and said it was because, in reality, time was always the same even if it seemed different. I remembered asking how anyone could know that, and he had said because we *just do*. I hadn't believed him, and had asked Charlotte about it when I got home later that day. She had told me that I needed to learn how to read a clock, but that it didn't mean that I was wrong, which had just confused me more.

'Hello,' Daddy said.

'Hello,' Mummy said, still sounding different.

'Is everything going well?' Daddy asked, opening a cupboard and sounding as he always did when he was busy with something else.

He often sounded like that when he was asking me how school had gone, or saying well done for getting ten out of ten on my maths test. He was a typical adult. As I said, he never got excited by anything.

'Yes, I believe so. Charlotte seems to be having a nice time. She's very excited by it all.'

'Not too excited, I hope? I don't want her getting herself into a state again. That won't do.' I heard the hiss of the tonic bottle that Daddy wouldn't let me touch. It fizzed and gurgled as it was poured out into a glass. I imagined the piece of lemon bobbing among the bubbles like an upturned boat.

'I think she's fine.'

'You think, or you know?' Daddy asked, in the same way he did when he told me he liked the desk tidy I had made for him at school.

'Well, if you go in and see her you can determine for yourself.'

'No, you know I won't be going into the living room. I still have work to do. I'll go into the study.'

'It *is* Charlotte's birthday.' Mummy's words shortened. 'I'm sure she would appreciate you going in and wish her happy birthday.'

'I have no desire to go and see a group of badly behaved children ruining my living room. I think I've done enough by agreeing to this event in the first place. I will speak to her afterwards and wish her happy birthday then.'

'But the cake's nearly ready. Will you at least come in to see her blow out the candles?'

'No.'

Mummy's voice quietened. 'She'll be upset if you don't, Richard.'

'That may be true, but I'll speak to her later, Jane. Just make sure she doesn't wind herself up again, for God's sake.'

I heard the back door of the kitchen open and close. The oven whoomphed again. A kitchen drawer slammed.

A thunk came from the living room, followed by several more and fits of laughter.

I was on my haunches and my legs were beginning to feel stiff and sore. I sat back down on my bottom, feeling the blood rush into my thighs, my shins, and then my feet. My hands were still gripped around the banisters. I had spent a great deal of time on that landing, listening to Mummy and Daddy downstairs, trying to understand them. If ever it went quiet during those times, my mind wandered and I often thought about the landing itself. In all that time, though, I hadn't been able to think of anything small enough to *land* on our landing, apart from maybe a bird, but they don't fly around indoors. I concluded that the name must be one of those silly adult things.

My mother called out to Charlotte and asked her to come into the kitchen. The thumping began again.

'Yes Mummy?'

'The cake's ready. Round up your friends and we can all sing happy birthday together.'

'Oh good, oh good, oh good!' Charlotte said in her special language. 'Is Daddy back from work now?'

'Yes, he came back a few moments ago.'

'So he'll come in and sing happy birthday too?'

'Your father's in the study, Charlotte, and doesn't want to be disturbed.'

'So he won't come in and sing happy birthday?' Charlotte's language returned to normal, her words all slow and separated.

'No, I'm afraid he won't. He'll come and wish you happy birthday when it's time for everyone to go home.'

'But why won't he come and sing happy birthday to me now?'

'He's tired from work, Lottie.'

'He's always tired from work, Mummy. It's my birthday! Why won't he come and sing happy birthday to me?'

I recognised Charlotte's new voice. I had heard it before when things had gone wrong and Mummy and Daddy had got cross.

'Because he won't, Lottie. He's busy. Let it go so we can cut the cake and all have a piece. I made you a lemon drizzle cake especially. It's your favourite.'

'No, I won't let it go! I don't want any cake if Daddy won't come and sing happy birthday.'

'Lottie, don't be difficult. Your father will speak to you after the party. Don't ruin what has been such a nice day.'

'Me don't ruin anything? Me? I'm not ruining anything, Daddy is! He always ruins everything!'

'Charlotte Willis, you mind your tongue! Don't talk about your father that way!'

'No! Daddy ruins everything! I hate him! I don't want him to say anything to me and I don't want any cake. I hate stupid lemon drizzle cake. I'm not a baby anymore! And I don't want to have a party anymore either. I'm going to my room!'

'Don't be rude, Charlotte, you have guests! You must stay and entertain them!'

'I don't care! I don't want a birthday any more. I never want another birthday again!'

Charlotte thumped her way towards the stairs. I quickly sprung to my feet and darted back into my room, closing my door just in time to hear her footsteps on the landing.

My mother shouted. It was a sound that I couldn't remember hearing before. It made me clench my toes up into a funny sort of ball, like monkeys do when they hang from trees.

'Charlotte, get back down here!'

'No!'

Her door slammed. My ear stayed pressed against my door, but after that all I could hear was silence. The noises from downstairs had stopped. What was everyone doing? Maybe they were all stood around, statues listening, the same as I was. I pictured a whole room of people standing with one ear pointing towards the stairs, time passing slower for them than for the clocks.

More footsteps came up the stairs. They were softer than Charlotte's, and more regular. They stopped on the landing. It was Mummy. I knew because if it had been Daddy he would have said something by then.

'Charlotte,' Mummy said sternly, still standing on the landing. 'Come along now. You were having such a nice day. Let's enjoy the last few hours of your birthday and then we can cut the cake with Daddy later when he's finished his work.'

'It's not my birthday any more. Daddy can finish his work for as long as he likes. I don't want to see anyone. None of them understand, anyway. No one does.'

'Understand what, darling?'

'Nothing. Leave me alone.'

'If you don't come downstairs now, we won't go to the effort of doing anything like this for you again, Charlotte Willis. I can assure you of that.'

'I don't care! I don't ever want another birthday party, anyway! LEAVE ME ALONE!'

'Fine. Don't think your father and I will put ourselves out for you in future, young lady. Your ungrateful behaviour won't go unpunished!'

Mummy thumped down the stairs. Her voice upset me. The noises began again in the living room once she reached the bottom. I looked at my wristwatch. There were still two hours left before everyone was supposed to go home. It didn't matter how quickly time went, that was too long.

I climbed up onto my bed and sat still for a moment, thinking of what might happen to all the people downstairs. Of what would happen to Charlotte once they had gone. What my Daddy would do when he heard what Charlotte had said and done.

Charlotte's bedroom door opened and slammed shut. Before I could have even tried to get to the landing, she thumped down the stairs harder and faster than ever before. I heard the front door do exactly the same as her bedroom door had done, only even louder. I leaned to look out of my window and saw Lottie with a small, pink bag running down the street, her hair streaming out all loose and wavy behind her.

On that occasion it was seven hours before we saw her again.

8

'Life's more than just living, you know?' Leah passed on the glowing joint and carried on speaking as she exhaled. 'It's more basic, simple. It's easier. Just allow it to be. Stop worrying so much. Learn to feel, not think. Your feelings can reveal something about the world you might not have known was there.'

She relaxed back against the stained, patterned cushions and stretched her legs across the wooden floor. I was in awe of her at that moment. It was a kind of fearful admiration, an inflicted respect that left me desperately wanting her approval and acknowledgement. I didn't know what these feelings she was describing could reveal, but I wanted to. She talked as if she *knew*, and I almost believed her.

Disorientated after falling asleep in my sweaty clothes, I had woken up in my room from a dream in which I had been lying on my bed at home. In the dream, I had been staring out of the window at the trees when I had started to sweat. Water had begun pouring out of me, and the trees I had been staring at had turned to orange dust as a giant sunray swept past them and into the room. The burning glow of the sunray had sped across the room towards me and I had only just managed to leap out of its way before it hit my bed. It had melted everything.

I had heard the sizzle and hiss of blistering plaster and paint. An acrid, bitter smell had made me gag. The walls and my bed had started sliding towards the floor and the liquid had quickly begun to turn into a lake around me. The lake had been turquoise, its surface cracked and broken. I couldn't remember why I had recognised it initially, but soon enough I had realised it was the one in the picture on the wall. I had remembered that I was in Cambodia.

At that instant everything had dissolved beneath me and I had felt myself panicking. Confused awake and confused asleep. Gradually the world had crept into my dream, replacing it bit by bit until it was gone. When I finally sat up, it took me a couple of minutes to settle myself and adjust to where I was.

I got up to find something to drink. There had been nothing in the room. I had heard that you shouldn't drink from the taps, so I had splashed some cold water on my face and wondered, with my head feeling clunky and slow, where my best option to find water might be. For five minutes I had paced, trying to think of somewhere.

The conclusion I had reached was that the common room was my only option. I had breathed out slowly through my nose. I hadn't known if I could deal with that kind of place. How would I *approach* it? My social mode was never a reliable one, especially in situations like that, and it had a tendency to slip back into self-preservation mode at any opportunity. But it was either that or venture back to the road outside, where everyone knew what they were doing apart from me. And I definitely hadn't been ready for that.

I had peeled my sweat-soaked shirt off my back and replaced it with one from my backpack. It was clean and good on my skin. Its smell had been familiar and it had helped me steady myself before I headed out of the room. As I walked past the mirror in the corridor, I had caught sight of my appearance. I had looked tired. And incapable.

I had lingered briefly, trying to turn my hair into something I was happy with. After three attempts I had heard someone coming down the corridor. I had quickly looked away, taken a deep breath and walked into the common room. I had stood in the doorway, trying to take it all in.

There were several seating areas made up of either bamboo furniture or kaleidoscope-coloured cushions scattered over the wooden floor. There was a small bar in one corner, which was lit up by fairy lights that stretched all the way along the far end of the room and wrapped around a green palm tree in the other corner.

A pool table sat to one side.

Two white guys with dreadlocks had been playing, cues in hands. In the corner nearest me there was a TV with a DVD player, where a couple had curled up together on a beanbag to watch a subtitled European film that I hadn't recognised. Manu Chao had been playing on a CD player and there had been a strong smell of marijuana in the air.

As my eyes had taken in the light I had seen that the far end of the room was open and, with a shimmered reflection of the fairy lights, the lake had revealed itself to me for the first time. The slightest of breezes had come in off the water, which had felt sublime after the solid heat of my room.

Annoyingly, Jon-Paul had noticed me before I noticed him, which meant my brief control over the situation had been lost. He had beckoned me over to sit on one of the collections of cushions and I had had no choice but to obey. He had been sitting with a group of seven people, all of whom he had quickly introduced and I had nodded my hellos: Elodie, Leah, Jacob, Manuel and Christina – who were a couple – Amelle and Jon-Paul. Together, they had had one of those *things*, as if they all somehow knew something I didn't, so I had quickly judged them to be superior to me.

Leah had been speaking as I sat down and had continued to speak for a while afterwards. She looked to be in her mid-twenties and fully aware of her potential. She was somebody I could know very quickly. Almost everything she did gave her away. She was intelligently, unattainably attractive, and when anyone first met her, including me, she somehow managed to draw them into a clear acknowledgement of that fact, without ever doing anything explicit.

There was this sense in the space around her that you were privileged to be spoken to by her. It was a telepathic awareness of the fact that you should be grateful for the time she spent with you, which, as I soon learnt, would become infrequent and brief if she didn't find you sufficiently interesting.

I was not sufficiently interesting, which I had already suspected to be the case. This wasn't news to me. The strange thing was that even though I knew all this I still wanted her to like me. I still enjoyed being around her. And even though I knew what my sister would have made of Leah, I still listened to her as she imparted her wisdom. And I still agreed with her, even though I didn't really know if I agreed at all.

'I don't understand why people worry so much, you know?' she continued. 'This force that keeps things moving – nature, life, energy, God, whatever you want to call it – it's fundamentally *good*. Why else is the world such a beautiful place?'

She had her eyes closed and wasn't addressing her questions to anyone in particular. Jon-Paul and I stayed quiet, as did the others sitting in the den, many lost in their own haze of marijuana.

I wasn't in any position to answer her question. Everything had gone a bit fuzzy. Delayed. Shuffled sideways. My mode selection was all mixed up. My eyes were working at a different shutter speed. For some reason I had taken a few drags of the joint being passed around. I could feel a strange sensation. Fingers of smoke beginning to clasp and tighten around my brain. I'm not sure why I did it; it wasn't something I would usually do.

I suppose I thought that smoking some that evening might encourage my hesitant social mode to hang around and develop for a while. That it might help me *fit in*. That maybe it would relieve the suffering and confusion for a brief moment; make this little piece of life better. Actually, all it did was give me a fluffy, dry mouth and a desire to sit in silence and admire Leah, while all the time fighting the urge to write an aphorism about her.

As I reached for my water bottle, Jacob raised his hands – which I soon learnt he was prone to do – and readied himself to speak. I gave up on the aphorism and the question about Leah's last comment that had fizzled into my head ('How does she know what *good* even means?') and listened in.

'Yeah, I mean it's like, life is this *thing*, this *thing*… put into the universe and it pushes everything on in this pursuit of perfection. Everything getting better and more and more complicated and intricate as it goes. That push, man… for me that's God. What else could it be?' Jacob gesticulated in a careful, gentle way with his hands as he said this, but didn't once raise his head from the cushions on the floor.

As I listened to Jacob my mind selected again, and I thought back to a time when I was thirteen and had tried to read a book by Proust that I had taken from my father's bookshelf. I had once heard my parents have a conversation about him at one of their dinner parties. This particular party had been attended by friends of the family, only known to me as Mr and Mrs Carstairs.

I had always been intrigued when they came around. I had often listened in to their conversations from the landing after I had been sent to bed. The Carstairs were educated and enlightened in a way I had never thought my parents were. I had enjoyed hearing them discuss things. They spoke precisely, logically and rationally, never leaving any room for misinterpretation. They never used words that didn't seem to serve a *purpose* one way or another. Everything they said had some kind of point. Most of the things I said weren't worth much at all. As I sat leaning on the banisters at the top of the stairs, I had vowed to read Proust the following day.

The next morning, I had waited until I knew my father had gone out to the garden and quickly adopted my stealth mode. I usually used this mode when I needed to avoid people, or to try and find out useful things I wasn't supposed to know, like where my Christmas presents were hidden. But that day it had taken on a special purpose. An *honourable* purpose: the quest for knowledge.

I had opened my door a crack and peeked out, looking both ways. The coast had been clear. Walking quickly, I remember sneaking into my father's study and surveying the bookshelves. Often his study was locked, but when I tried the door on that particular day the turn of the handle had brought a smile to my stealthy face.

He had a whole wall full of books, running from the floor to the ceiling. I had enjoyed standing there, looking at them. Their many colours, shapes and sizes had formed a patchwork of jumbled stories and clever people's knowledge. I had scanned the shelves laboriously, all the while listening out for my father's footsteps from outside. My heart had been beating unusually fast. After a few minutes, I had found the book. On my tiptoes I had leant up towards it, prised it carefully from its slot and made sure I would remember which spot I had taken it from. I had hidden it under my jumper and run to my room.

Once I had closed the door behind me, I had switched off my stealth mode and relaxed. Lying on my bed, I had opened the book carefully, treating it as though the truth were buried in there somewhere and handling it incorrectly might make it fall out and be lost forever. I hadn't been able to imagine being clever enough to write a book that other people would read.

I had looked at the small, black and white words on the first page and read them intently, thinking they would make me wise and philosopher-like. Perhaps even placing me on the same intellectual level as Mr Carstairs, meaning that everything I said would be logical and serve a *purpose*. I remember thinking that the next time they came over for a dinner party I would be able to drop something from Proust into the conversation before I went to bed, as if it were something I would say. I was sure that would impress them. I might even have been invited to stay up and join them at the table for dinner.

However, I hadn't been reading for long before I lost interest. Each day I had read a little less until one day the book hadn't been opened at all and had begun to gather forgotten dust under my bed. It was a *long* book.

I do remember reading one thing, though. Proust thought conversation was the worst form of communication, because you never had enough time to think through what you wanted to say. I remember thinking how strange this seemed. What did it mean for my parents and Mr and Mrs Carstairs to be having conversations about Proust when he thought so little of them?

Conversations, according to Proust, involve instant reactions and an exchange of poorly formed ideas. He thought letters were the purest form of dialogue. They were considered and intentional. However, as I thought of it more, I always thought there was something endearing, something honest about someone forming ideas out loud in front of you. They were allowing others to share in their thinking; to be a party to their mental processes. They were happy for me to see little pieces of their consciousness. As though they were offering a brief insight into the mysterious castles and cathedrals – as Charlotte called them – that they had built in their minds that are only usually for one.

'I don't think God exists,' said Amelle as though she really meant it. 'This whole concept... it's so vague, so unnecessary. Why can't you have a beautiful world without God in it? It's like saying you can't appreciate something without attributing it to something else. I know that chocolate tastes good no matter how it was made, who made it or where it came from. I just appreciate it for its goodness. Why can't you do that with the world?'

There was a pause during which time had slowed down, and the room was silent. Briefly, nobody seemed to be aware of the external world as they all retreated into the cathedrals in their heads. Charlotte used to say all the elaborate cathedrals in people's minds were built on *dogma*, but I didn't know what that meant. She said people needed the detailed constructions of layers upon layers of beliefs and values and rationalisations so they could get lost and hide from the things they were afraid of. In the silent pause, I wondered what my cathedral was built from and whether or not I could keep hiding from the dark place.

'Mmm, chocolate is sooo good,' said Jacob, his head lifting from the floor for a moment. 'There isn't enough chocolate in this fucking country. I think we should get some chocolate.'

Everyone laughed and the nature of the conversation changed immediately. The serious tones disappeared and I could sense that everyone had relaxed, switching their topics of thought to something less taxing. It always amazed me how the atmosphere in a room could change so swiftly, as if a member of the group had stepped out and left.

My shuffled mind imagined two atmospheres having a conversation.

'Popping out for a while,' says serious atmosphere, 'won't be long. You – relaxing atmosphere – take over for a bit, would you? And do it properly this time. Stop being so damn lazy.'

I laughed to myself for a moment before stopping abruptly and checking that nobody had seen me do it.

Leah got up and changed the CD. She twirled and glided away from the hi-fi with her eyes closed as the electric beat, staccato and strings of Björk melted out of the speakers and gently nestled in my ears. I thought of Charlotte again. She adored Björk. I knew this album better than anything I had ever owned myself. She had played it constantly on repeat one summer until my parents had asked her to turn it off, which she had taken great offence to. Music was integral to her life.

'Great music is the importance of life,' she had said once. 'Any emotion you feel can be expressed through it and life improves in its presence. Truly great music fills every part of you. It flows through you and touches parts you didn't even know existed. It exaggerates every emotion you could ever feel and makes it the most important thing that you can feel. It can solve all your problems, if only

53

for a brief moment; long enough to make everything else disappear. Great music is beauty, available on tap.'

As I listened to the music I looked out onto the lake towards the horizon. The sky was blue with smudges of orange and grey, and the sun floated hazily over the lake. The collection of corrugated iron roofs surrounding the lake stuck together, with different levels forming a mini skyline in silhouette.

The lake itself was a rich, deep green colour, almost too green, and it was spattered with rubbish, which had been thrown in haphazardly. It was a nice view, but not entirely beautiful. There was something *wrong* with it. Sometimes I look at things and they seem *wrong*. I can't always explain why, but on this occasion I think it was because the lake lacked the natural charm I imagined it had once had, before all the rubbish and the people and the noise and the shit.

I wished the world could go back to the way it had been before it got ruined. Before it all got so messed up.

9

'Hey, did you know that for around thirty bucks you can fire an ex-revolution AK-47 at a firing range outside of town?'

'What?' Amelle asked, incredulous.

'Yeah, thirty bucks gets you a lift to some field somewhere and thirty bullets to fire. Apparently, they've got all sorts of weapons down there, even rocket launchers. I met a guy the other week who said he'd paid fifty bucks and they'd let him blow up a cow! Can you believe that shit?!'

I didn't know what time it was. I had been out in the area by the lake for a while and it had grown dark. Jon-Paul was drunk and stoned, his eyes glistening and his smile wide. He was even more talkative than usual. He announced his exploding cow story to the group and was met with several nods of recognition and a mixture of discerning frowns and wide grins.

Leah was lying across from me, engrossed in a conversation with the guy next to her. She kept touching her leg as she spoke. She was wearing baggy linen trousers, but I could tell she was amazing beneath them. I stopped myself picturing how she might look naked and dragged my heavy body from the floor. I needed to escape.

Everything was still fuzzy and skittery, only now it was making me feel on edge. As if something I couldn't identify wasn't right. I had to concentrate hard to get out. I focused as much as I could and made my way through the collection of bodies lying between me and the bedroom.

I had just made it through the last pair of legs, relieved to be near the exit, when Jon-Paul called out.

'Hey! Ethan! Where you off to, buddy? Not leaving already, surely?'

A collection of heads turned to look at me as Jon-Paul spoke. I froze. My social mode was nowhere to be found. Too disjointed. Too tired. Not that it was ever terribly successful anyway. If I could have disappeared into the air and floated away, I would have done.

'Just off to… Off to bed, actually.' I looked down at the floor. The angles of the rugs on the floorboards looked wrong.

'Bed?! The fun hasn't gotten started yet! We've got a big night planned, my young Padawan! Come on, stick around! Hey, look! You can sleep when you're dead.'

'Oh no… I don't think so, thanks.'

I wobbled slightly. I hadn't disappeared. 'I'm really tired. I need to get some sleep.'

'He's tired! Ha! Stoned, more like! Anyway, we can fix that.' Jon-Paul pointed to the bar. 'Find this man some Red Bull! Or some uppers! Listen, Ethan, go hard or go home. That's how it runs around here. Am I right or am I right?'

Jon-Paul appealed to the crowd as he spoke. There

were several knowing nods from faces that appeared to have heard this speech before.

'Come on. Cut him some slack, J-P. He only arrived today.'

I couldn't work out where the voice had come from initially, but I soon realised it was Jacob. He still hadn't lifted his head from the floor, but his words spared me.

'Let him go. See you in the morning, Ethan. There's always tomorrow night, eh?'

'Yeah… Yes, always tomorrow. Always tomorrow. Thanks Jacob. See you in the morning.'

I quickly walked down the corridor before anything else could be said. Jon-Paul groaned as I left, but soon joined in a new conversation about something or other. Always tomorrow. Was there an aphorism there? I wasn't able to work one out if there was.

As I closed the bedroom door behind me the room felt hotter than ever. I stripped everything off bar my boxer shorts. It didn't make much difference. Digging out my washbag, I brushed my teeth and collapsed onto the bed. There was so much to prepare for; so much to think. But all I wanted to do was sleep. If I could get up early the next day, I reassured myself, I could start properly. Get a map. Plan a route. Find something that might help.

Closing my eyes, I began to feel worried. My teeth clenched. The dark feeling was creeping in. I tried to distract myself, but I was too tired for aphorisms, and I couldn't concentrate on any calculations. I did the one thing I had left at times like these. I tried to meditate. I turned my body to lie as flat as I could.

Charlotte had taught me about meditation. She had

told me it had great potential, creating untapped time for reflection. It was a clean way to empty my head, she had said, to get in touch with my *spiritual* side. It would help when I got scared. Help stop me worrying so much. The simplest trick, she had said, was to imagine a point between my eyes and hold my concentration on it. Avoid all distractions. Any time a thought entered my mind, I had to ignore it and return to the point. Put away all the worries whenever they appeared.

Stop the darkness.

I imagined the point and did my best to focus. She had been trying to help and I had wanted to be able to meditate. It had seemed so mystical. So incredible. Perhaps there was something more to being a person. Some kind of spiritual side. More than the physical me. More than this. I had wished there was.

I had tried meditating for years, whenever I got desperate. But I had never got anywhere with it. It simply didn't seem possible for me to only think about one thing. I couldn't see how anyone could do it. I wanted to know how Charlotte could.

Maybe she had something I didn't have. Maybe she had more than me. Maybe she *was* more than me. As I tried and failed one more time, a single thought crossed my mind and comforted me. I gave up on the meditation and thought of that.

I'd made it. I was in Cambodia.

That was something at least.

*

All evening the night sky had been untouched; clear and clean and uncomplicated. I remember lying on my back and staring up at the stars. Millions of them. Pinholes of light from years ago, shining through from another world.

We had talked and thought and laughed and been silent. I had always listened whenever my sister had taken the time to tell me something. Those moments had been our secrets. Truths no one else knew or understood. Answers and questions I had never considered. They climbed into my mind, settling and changing things. They restructured the rooms in the cathedral; my thoughts, my ideas, my life.

If only I could have sat everyone else down and explained. They would have appreciated her the same way I did.

She had spoken in worlds. She would create them out of nothing and set them free and allow them to evolve. I would dive in and get lost. Sometimes she would guide me through, picking apart her creation piece by piece. Other times she would let me get lost, watch me struggle and say nothing until I found my own way out. I had visited places I had never known in those worlds. I had questioned things I had never seen.

An owl had sounded out into the night. I had turned my head to look at her lying on the grass next to me. Her eyes had been distanced, focused on the sky above. I remember the way she had looked. Still but poised. In the moonlight, her face had been porcelain. She had twisted around and looked at me.

'I want you to hold on to something, Ethan. It's an

important question you have to think about. You've got to promise me you won't forget it.'

'Okay.'

'It's a question you have to ask yourself. One that will make you remember.'

She had paused and looked right into my eyes with her pupils wide open.

'Why are the stars so beautiful? Why, when there could have been nothing, or chaos, is there something ordered and amazing and wonderful and *beautiful*? Don't forget that question, Ethan. Don't forget it. Don't lose your wonder. Life will try to take that from you, but you can't let it, understand? They'll try and drip you dry, make you forget. The world is an amazing place. Don't fall into the black holes that suck that out of you. Okay? Promise me that, Ethan. Promise me.'

She had looked at me sternly and frowned. I had heard her frown. It had sounded like a tree falling.

'Okay.'

'Say it, then. Say you promise.'

'Okay, I promise.'

'Good. I won't let them take you, Ethan, not you... Not you.'

She had rolled away and looked back up at the sky. The owl had sounded out again and I had been sure that the sound of the insects buzzing around me had briefly stopped. I had wrapped my arms around my middle and opened my eyes to the stars. She had been right; they *were* beautiful.

We had stayed out until sunrise, together on the grass. As the darkness had begun to dissolve we had watched the sun spread across the sky. A new day beginning in a series of tiny, imperceptible moments. Today had become tomorrow in front of me. I had closed my eyes and fallen asleep.

When I had awoken, sticky and dry in the hot sunshine of a new mid-morning, she was gone.

10

I awoke the next morning with a headache that clung to me. My head was thick with it and it slowed down my thoughts. Everything was stuck together. I tried to untangle myself, rubbing my head and turning to see Jon-Paul asleep on his back. His mouth was open and his head was tilted towards me. He was snoring. I didn't know what time he had come in the night before, but it had been after me and I wasn't sure how late I had stayed up. The whole situation was most unusual.

I sat up and slowly turned my neck, trying to ease out some of the tension. The headache bit into me, consuming my full attention when it was the last thing I wanted to focus on. Standing slowly, I walked over to splash some water on my face. I leaned on the basin and stared at myself in the mirror. The dark feeling leered a little before I tried to shut it out.

Maybe there was nothing more to me than this.

After showering and changing I ventured out of the bedroom and its timeless capsule of sticky, smelly heat. Closing the door carefully so as to not disturb Jon-Paul, I walked past the mirror. I turned away from the common area and strode through the corridor towards the main entrance. I could hear voices that belonged to people I had met the previous night out by the lake, but I kept walking and stepped out into the bright sunlight of Phnom Penh in the early afternoon.

I didn't know. My self-preservation mode was calling. Was I ready for this? I was scared. I didn't have a mode for anything right at that moment.

I surveyed the dusty street in front of me. Its movement and intensity. The number of people. The depth of expectation and disappointment that lay within it.

At that moment, as was often the case, I thought of something I wished I hadn't. I wondered what would happen if everything went wrong. But then something even worse, a far greater fear, entered my mind.

What if everything turned out as I had hoped and it still wasn't enough?

I lingered on the pavement, pretending to search for something in my pocket that I knew wasn't there. Looking up at the sky, I squinted hard in the sun's warm glow and rubbed the side of my shoulder. I bit some of the skin from my bottom lip.

In the emptiness of that busy street a decision arrived.

Now was the time. It had to be. I had to be strong enough for this. I had made it this far; it was no good giving up now. I wanted so badly to get her back. I wanted so badly to feel whole somehow. I wanted so badly to be *more*.

I stepped out into the street and turned right.

11

One small message governed my future from that point.

A few words on a piece of paper.

The last thing I knew my sister had done was see a poster advertising a place where English speakers could volunteer to teach. Apparently, the Cambodian police had no idea where this place might be. They also had no idea whether Charlotte had gone there, or whether it even existed. They didn't even know where she had stayed in Phnom Penh. So much for a just and efficient police force. Hostels were supposed to take your passport details when you arrive to stay with them, but we found out quickly that this is rarely done. Failing to ask a few legal questions when there is so much illegality going on doesn't seem to pose much of a problem.

The last time Charlotte had been proven to exist was the final time she had emailed me. It's funny how she needed proof to exist now; that her existing on her own without anyone knowing wasn't enough. I often wondered whether that was how God feels. If he exists. I thought there might be an aphorism in there somewhere, but writing aphorisms about God felt strange somehow.

I still remember that last email now. It was typical Charlotte.

Dear little brother,

How are you? I hope you're happy and well and enjoying life. How are you feeling? Do you know what you want yet, in life I mean?

I'm in Phnom Penh and everything is beautiful. I've made friends with a group of people from all over. They're really helping me see the world clearly, see it right. Helping me shake my head free and see the connection and philosophy in everything. God, it feels good! Do you know what I mean?

Seija, a Swedish girl who is pure beauty through and through, is going to do some volunteer teaching with me at this little school in the middle of nowhere. I feel so selfish for my travelling. It appals me that I lived just for myself for so long. When I saw the advert in that cafe I knew I had to go. It was there on the wall, like it was destiny. Life is too valuable to spend it on yourself.

Anyway, I hope you're happy and that one day you'll visit me. Don't worry for Mum and Dad, I'll contact them when I'm ready.

Must go, the moto driver's waiting for me. This is going to be so great!

Much love a thousand times over,
Charlotte

I had often received emails from Charlotte. They had usually been sent when she was happy. This made me happy to read them and, every day I could, I checked my email account whenever she was away, hoping for something from her. They were irregular, but I never waited more than two weeks for a message. For two years she had emailed me at least once a fortnight. I knew I could count on her for that.

And then they had stopped.

Before they had stopped, her messages had always been short, flitting between points and lacking any real detail; a stream of consciousness. Her personality captured in words on a screen. She had never emailed Mum or Dad, and had only written them letters every few months. I think she had thought they wouldn't understand. She had known they would reply to her emails asking her to come home. I had agreed with her and kept her emails secret from my parents thinking it wasn't for them to know. Charlotte had contacted me; only me. Why did they need to know?

Looking back, I wished I hadn't kept those emails secret. Maybe things would have been different.

Maybe they could have convinced her to come home.

It had been a month after that last email that I had first told my parents I thought something was wrong. It had been six weeks before they had started to take me seriously. It had been two months before they eventually contacted the police. It had been six months before they had given up.

I tried to draw the thoughts out of my head as I ran my fingers through my hair, trying to convince myself of some kind of thought osmosis.

Looking up, I realised I had been walking for some time without paying attention to anything around me. I had reached the far end of the main street my hostel was on. How many cafes had I passed already?

The only real idea I had for finding Charlotte was the one that had been pushing around inside my mind ever since she had gone missing.

I've got to find that poster.

The one on the wall in the cafe.

It must still be up somewhere. It had to be. If I could find that I could go to the school and maybe she would still be there. At the least they might be able to tell me where she had gone next. In some sense, knowing the poster was real would be enough. At least something of her disappearance would be true.

It was lunchtime and the street was as busy as ever. I looked around for the nearest cafe as a starting point for my search.

The trouble was, it was hard to know what a cafe consisted of. There didn't seem to be anything that fitted a definition I would have given for the word 'cafe'. Apart from the occasional interspersed shopfront, most places that served food and drink were nothing more than small, covered areas with stands and a few tatty tables and chairs. The stands usually consisted of a removable cart, a handwritten menu and a gas-powered hob that kept a battered kettle steaming on top.

The dusty areas of the cafes with the low, wobbly, plastic chairs were only just kept in the shade by strips of tarpaulin or corrugated iron. Young, messy tourists sat on these chairs in their loose-fitting clothes, chatting and drinking a coffee or Coke. Some appeared to be smoking joints. Some were consulting guide books. All of them were glistening with sweat, the beads glinting in the sun.

The women behind the stands sat staring into the

middle distance or counting their change. Sometimes they got up to wipe down their work surfaces or tiny plastic tables, only to return to their original positions. They all wore patterned cloths over their built, stocky frames. Small, portable televisions with aerial ears balanced on top of the stands kept some of the women occupied. None of them appeared to be sweating.

From this standing position, I turned my head and could see four different 'cafes'. God knows how many others I had passed on my walk there from the hostel. And that was only one street.

'Hello, my friend! Do you need help with direction? Where do you want to go today? We take a trip somewhere, yes?'

A nodding face appeared in front of mine. *Directly* in front of mine. It was the face of a young man, who looked no more than seventeen. He had a toothy smile and shiny brown eyes. He was shorter than me by some way. His faded blue Yankees cap had a curved peak and sat on top of his head at a jaunty angle, as though he had thrown it on and didn't care. Little tufts of greasy black hair poked out from underneath. He rubbed his small snub nose and waited a split second for my response. There wasn't enough time for me to choose which mode to employ.

'I, uh…'

'You want to go to S-21? Prison camp. Very sad place, my friend. Difficult but important, yes? How about the killing fields? No? Ah! I know what you want! How would you like to shoot some war guns, my friend? Cows go kaboom! Ha! Not for you? Okay, I can take you on tour of Phnom Penh. All day private tour just for you! See all the sights. Maybe find nice lady after for you. Cambodia has most beautiful women in the world. Yes sir! You a handsome young man! Handsome men deserve beautiful ladies! Myself is included in this, yes!'

His broad smile was replaced with a serious frown. He put his hand on my shoulder and leaned in close. The index finger of his other hand started pointing at nothing in particular. His grip was gentle and I found myself leaning in, as he had.

'But Phnom Penh dangerous place, my friend. You don't want walk these places on your own. Many bad people here. I can guide you, give you pieces of mind, yes?'

My initial surprise didn't feel too startling. Compared to the usual, I mean. I was calm enough to wonder which pieces of his mind he might give me. He didn't scare me and he seemed easy to know. The *placing* between us was okay.

A tour of Phnom Penh might be good, I thought. It would help me see what was out there, get a feel for the place and get my bearings. It might be the sensible thing to do. Let me know how much of a grand task I had on my hands. This trip needed to have a level of sensibleness to it. The rest of my life had involved attempting to achieve this.

Sweating in the sunshine, I was strangely comfortable until I noticed a man who had been standing at the corner next to us creep up close to me. He was much older than the boy in the cap and his face was hard and creased and sun-beaten.

The boy also noticed the man and sighed as he turned towards him. They immediately became embroiled in a heated debate. Hand gestures were made and the discussion drew looks from tourists as they walked by. I could feel their eyes on me as I stood there, rubbing the back of my head, unsure what to do. I imagined melting away back to my room at the hostel. My mode – whichever one it was – was telling me to run. I thought of my parents. Were they were worried yet about where I had gone?

After a brief animated discussion, the boy in the cap turned and walked away, throwing his arms up in the air.

The older man watched him intently as he left, before turning to me and saying, 'My friend, come, come. I will give you tour of Phnom Penh.'

He ushered me towards a waiting tuk-tuk. 'We go now, yes?'

He put his hand on my shoulder and tried to walk me towards his tuk-tuk. His grip was uncomfortable. As he began to move me, I turned to see the boy wandering off. His head was shaking and he was kicking the dust up from the road.

'No, I er…' I said.

The man sucked his teeth as he waited for me to finish my sentence.

'I'm fine, thank you,' I continued. 'I… I don't need a tour.'

'My friend, I will do you good price. No problem.' His tone had changed to a subtle plea that wasn't *delivered* in a menacing way. His eyebrows were raised and his head was tilted slightly to one side as he tried to usher me to the tuk-tuk once more.

I thought of my father.

'No, really. Maybe another time.'

I turned away from him and walked quickly down the street, feeling his gaze piercing me as I walked away. The hairs rose on the back of my neck and my blood rushed through my veins. I was in a mode that I frequently employed, but always resented doing so because it was never deliberate. My *flight* mode.

My sister had once said that humans have evolved to deal with difficult situations by either fighting or running away. I didn't know if it was true – could it be that simple? – but she had *announced* that the world was divided into those two types of people and that she felt sorry for those who didn't have the guts to stand up and fight. I knew she had been talking about me when she said it, and had been cross with myself because I knew she had judged me correctly. But I didn't think people chose to be one type of person or the other. I couldn't do anything to change it. It seemed to me that it was one of those things that just *happens*.

Walking quickly, I headed back towards the only place I knew and hoped Jon-Paul would still be there. Perhaps I could talk to him about finding popular cafes in the area. Surely, he would have been to a few. I crossed the street and tripped over a stone, momentarily stumbling before regaining my balance. I clenched my teeth as the pain shot up from my toe.

I let out an angry 'Shit!' and pinched the bridge of my nose with my fingers as I stood in the middle of the road.

It took me a minute to get moving again. As I approached the hostel, I saw the boy in the cap leaning over a cafe stand across the street. He was talking and laughing with the woman working behind it. Her face was tight with laughter and she looked at the boy with real affection. I moved a bit further down the road and watched them for a while. They seemed so happy. Seeing them together gradually calmed me down.

After a minute or so, the boy turned his head in my direction as he put a bottle of Coke to his lips. He spotted me across the street. Our eyes met and before I could look away he had waved hello and beckoned me over. My first instinct was to turn and walk back towards the hostel; to run. But the picture of my sister telling me about evolution came back into my mind. I didn't want to be that person any more. I was fed up with being disappointed in myself. Maybe there was *more* to me. If it *was* a choice, maybe I should try and make it.

I crossed the street and said hello. The boy reached out, shook my hand and said that his name was Tee. He held his other hand up and gestured towards the young woman behind the cafe stand.

'This is my sister, Davi,' he said.

'I am very pleased meet you,' she said, looking directly into my eyes.

She smiled at me in the way only a big sister can. I felt genuinely comfortable for the first time in a very long time.

*

If you were to ask any of my friends or family when it was that Charlotte disappeared, I think they would say they didn't know. You would get a vague, questioning look followed by a swift attempt to change the subject. The realisation that Charlotte had disappeared wasn't something that had happened overnight, they would say. In most cases, I suppose, disappearing had been a slow process for my sister; her life fading away along with the memories we had of her. Memories that I held so dear.

The memory of her smile, the slight dimples in her cheeks; of when we had dug the flowerbeds, our hands covered in earth, planting our own pieces of creation; of the sun shining on her hair as we had swum in the lake, fish dancing around our feet; of fresh cut grass in our hands as we built a new home for our latest crawly captive; of the hidden glisten in her eyes when we had buried Charlie, the only pet we had ever had; of the firmness of her grip as we had crossed the road on my first day of school; of her convincing, guilty face when she had taken the blame for my mistakes. All these memories were fading, rusting, peeling and fraying at the edges.

A whole life slowly disappearing.

But I don't think my sister went slowly. For me, there was a single day when I knew my sister had disappeared. Of course, my memories of her have faded now, no matter how hard I try to hold on to them; most of them reduced to glimpses of my personal version of the past, which are less pictures and more *feelings*. But when I think back to one moment that has shaped and changed my life enormously, a moment that has stuck with me and I can't forget, I think I could tell you exactly when it was that my sister disappeared.

It was a Thursday in April and the grass still wasn't green. April had been cold that year and had clung on to winter with a stubborn intensity that I didn't know seasons could have. It hadn't wanted to let go. Grey had tainted everything and winter had kept spring coiled so deeply it might never be released. The dark feeling had always been close to me at that time. Whenever I was on my own it had been there at the back of my mind.

I know it was a Thursday because we had been sitting around the dining table, my mother and I, eating pasta, as we always did on Thursdays. My father had gradually taken to eating his dinner in the extension at the rear of the house. This was an acknowledgement of the awkwardness the table possessed with only three of us around it. It was an incomplete set with the key piece missing.

I had always tried to sit in Charlotte's place when we were younger. It was a game we would play, rushing to the table when Mum had called us for dinner, trying to get there first. As Charlotte was three years older than me, sitting in her place had made me feel grown up. And even more, it had meant that I felt part of her grown-up life. I had become part of all those things she used to do that I had never understood. As though I was somehow on the other side of her closed bedroom door; a key in her lock that had been impossible to pick, even then.

My father always used to tell us off for running to the table, his disappointed glare meeting our eyes as we tumbled into the dining room. I remember Charlotte being sent to her room on the odd occasion when she had made fun of me for beating me there. I never used to mind. It was her right for being the winner. I had gazed at her empty placemat on those occasions and wondered whether she resented me for not being sent to my room.

Since Charlotte had left, the empty chair and place mat had consumed my father's stare whenever he entered the dining room. It had been uncomfortable for a while, seeing this at every mealtime we shared together. I think it had hurt my father the most, this empty space. This simple *lack* of my sister. I can't remember a time when I had seen my father hurt before then. It had shocked me. He had eaten with us until he hadn't been able to bear looking at that empty space any longer. He had taken up a place on his favourite worn-out leather armchair by the window in the conservatory, looking away from the house and its memories.

Pasta was what my mother had prepared for dinner on Thursdays. We had steak on Tuesdays, pasta on Thursdays, fish on Fridays and a roast on Sundays. There was no set dining rota or cooking timetable in the house for what we ate and when, it simply, as with so many things in my life, *happened*. Falling into a routine for me was the same as falling in love. I didn't expect it to happen but it did, and when it did I found it almost impossible to let go of it.

I used to hate routines. I had always had so many of them, and this had made me hate myself. I mean, they helped me exist and yet they stopped me from *being*. To be precise, it wasn't the routine itself I hated, but the lack of freedom that accompanied it. Living out your life doing the same things day after day, week after week. Limiting your choices and possibilities. To me, it meant you weren't alive; you lacked any passion, any drive to find something better. That you were finding ways to pass the time, not *living*.

My sister always used to say that 'people only repeat the same things because they are afraid of doing something new' and I fed that aphorism, as with any others she had *announced*, into my mindset and my vocabulary, convincing myself they were my own beliefs. But deep down I knew that I needed routines. No matter how much I resented them, I couldn't function without them. And that's why I hated myself so much.

But in those days of April that year I had gained a newfound respect for routines. I had come to appreciate them in their small, comforting ways and to see that that they had real human origins. It wasn't always fear or lack of passion. It was the way that they could carry a life on that was struggling or floundering and give it stability; a solid, reliable core of support. The way they could give certainty. There could be something positive in them. They added structure to my life. They faked things just enough to make them bearable. They added another layer to my cathedral that meant I could hide a little longer. So I had hated myself a little less.

At that time our lives were being driven on by the clockwork of routine, forever giving me something to do, giving me a focus and reminding me of what needed to be done next. Without that clockwork, that focus, I think our lives could have fallen apart, piece by piece. My mother had not been in a frame of mind where she could have created something new, got excited by a new pastime or even decided on what we should eat for dinner on any particular day.

And so, as always, it had been pasta on Thursday. That day I remember sitting in my own thoughts as I ate, something that I have done for as long as I can recall, but that I had started to do even more since Charlotte had gone missing. It used to annoy my parents, my slipping away. They would snap at me to bring me out of it.

More recently, my mother had found her own way of dealing with it. She had simply continued to talk at me across the dinner table. I had tried to engage her in the conversation when this all began, to join in with talk of the dragging winter and the chrysanthemums in the garden to comfort her. We would talk about anything small; news items, next-door neighbours, roadworks. While my father had become detached, insular and withdrawn, my mother had pushed her concern outwards, trying to divert her attention.

For all their similarities and seeming love for each other, my parents were very different people. Seeing them divide as they did, so cleanly and simply after all their years together, made me realise this. I didn't know whether they had never loved or understood each other, and that Charlotte's disappearance had simply brought this into my view, or whether it was her act of disappearance itself that had driven them apart. They had always merely been parents to me. Rigid constructs, inflexible and beyond human. I had never known them as *people*. And when they had let their guards down, when their personalities had begun to show, when they couldn't spend time in the same room any more, it had been one more thing I didn't know how to deal with. It was more *depth* at a time when I was already struggling to stay afloat.

I had gradually given up engaging in conversation with my mother over the dinner table. Partly because making conversation was never something I had been good at and partly because it didn't matter whether I responded or not as my mother kept on talking. But mainly because I had lost the will to try and keep up with my mother's desire to avoid the subject. I couldn't keep talking about weather and shopping when my sister had been missing for more than six months. I couldn't.

Each time she spoke it was a lie. A lie of omission. A deliberate avoidance of the truth that, honestly, though we never said it, was cutting into each of us so deeply that it hurt in a way I didn't think a feeling ever could. And I understood that was what she had to do to try to cope with this truth, but I couldn't do it. The pain had settled too deep and, because of this, the dark place had become too big and wouldn't stay buried anymore.

The only hope that had flickered and lit up each dark April evening was the eight o'clock phone call my father used to make. Every evening for four months my father had made a phone call to the police. This was an agreement that had been reached with an officer on hearing the determination in my father's voice after it was announced that the police would no longer be contacting my parents on a regular basis. Every evening at eight o'clock my father would call the Cambodian police station and somebody would be there to answer and give him any information that might have surfaced that day.

There had been a brief, tiny moment of hope and

anticipation whenever my father had picked up the phone and dialled that international number. Although it was never said, it was the one thing that had meant something to us in those days.

Grief and sadness tear things down; hope keeps those same things together.

It became part of our routine, the centre point of our focus each day, and when my father put the handset to his ear my mother and I had often shared a glance that shone and sparkled for a brief, magical moment. There seems to me to be some kind of inbuilt human condition that gives hope, even with the most unlikely of outcomes, a feeling that is pure *good*.

Over time that shine and sparkle had begun to fade. My mother's eyes had become deeper and darker, their light somehow lost in her sadness. Her focus had not been as sharp, and when her eyes caught mine at that moment they had begun to lie. Her face would muster a smile, her cheeks rising automatically, but her eyes would tell the truth. Despair and frustration. The sparkle was fading, and whatever I had had that resembled a sparkle was fading too.

After dinner, that evening my mother and I had gone into the conservatory as usual, the routine driving us in there. We had sat on the sofa, waiting for my father to make the call. My father had been staring out of the window into the garden.

It was a beautiful garden, although I hadn't realised that for many years. Seeing that garden every day, playing football in it, climbing the apple trees and rolling down the grassy banks on my bike had made me take it for granted.

It was only when I had left the garden that I began to fully appreciate it; the simple absence of something so common had created an affection for it that had never been there before.

My father's eyes had been lost in the garden that night. They had been somewhere else, sinking into the earth, buried in the black soil, suffocating, smothered by its heavy apathy.

I remember him turning to us, my mother and I, and slowly looking between our faces. I will never forget that look. He had turned into an old man. His face had looked tired and grey, his mouth pursed and thin. His eyes were vacant, distant and the once-fine lines that surrounded them had become deep-set trenches, marked and tired from war.

He had been beaten, physically and emotionally, by the thought that we would never know what had happened to my sister or whether she was even alive. His eyes had told us this in that look; the look of a man who had run out of hope. He hadn't looked like my father then, and hasn't to me ever since. He had turned away from us and looked out into the garden without saying a word. My mother had begun to cry and I had put my arm around her out of instinct. The phone had remained on the table.

My sister had no longer just been missing in that moment. In that act of resignation, she had disappeared.

12

Davi insisted on getting me a drink, even though I said I didn't want one, so I ordered a coffee and sat down with Tee. After quickly serving another customer, Davi came over and joined us, standing beside Tee and listening intently to our conversation.

After the first couple of awkward exchanges, I opened up to Tee in a way that surprised me. I don't think I ranked him above me, which probably helped. It gradually seemed okay to be giving a piece of myself away. What I found strange was that, as I began to tell him Charlotte's story, my mind didn't actively select a mode. I didn't look for one. I simply started talking and it all came out. I wasn't sure what to call that unexpected state, but I didn't have enough time to consider it. My sister was the only other person who had made me feel like that before. Maybe it was a mode of its own.

In between my rapid explanations, Tee asked me countless questions. His English was impressive and I had to remind myself to pay attention to his questions at one point because I was so surprised by how good it was. He seemed interested in London and my life there, but only became involved to the level of excitement when I told him why I was in Cambodia.

It spilled out of me, every last detail on my sister and her disappearance. I told him and Davi everything I knew about the case and how I was hoping she would still be alive and that I would find her and take her back to the UK and that everything would go back to the way it had been. Davi ignored several customers while I was telling the story. Several times I glanced over and saw them waiting impatiently at the stand before sighing and walking away.

Davi had a real *presence* as she stood and listened to me. She was the kind of person others around seemed aware of, although I'm not sure she was aware of that herself. Her black hair was glossy and thick. It hung around her shoulders, tucked behind her ears. She looked to be in what I guessed would be her mid-twenties, young enough for her face to still be made up of soft features. Rounded cheeks and wide eyes framed a small button nose and large, full-bodied lips. Her skin was smooth and clear, and she had a small mole on her right cheek.

When she smiled you could see that, as with so many other Cambodian people I had seen, she had poorly treated teeth, which were jumbled and stained in places. It was a lovely smile, though. It told me a lot. When I spoke of my sister, Davi's gaze and attention were unbreakable. It made me feel at ease. She hung on to my every word, which, if I'm honest, I loved. That hardly ever happened to me.

'So where was poster about the volunteering, Mr Ethan?' Tee asked. He had taken to calling me Mr Ethan, in spite of me telling him not to.

'Well, that's the problem. I don't know. It was in a cafe somewhere in Phnom Penh. That's all I have to go on.'

'I must tell you, Mr Ethan, and you will not find this easy to hear. There are many, many cafes in Phnom Penh, my friend. Many, many!'

'I know, I know. I thought if I started somewhere I would eventually find it. I have to… try.'

My voice faded out at the end of the sentence and there was a short silence before Davi spoke for the first time since she had said hello. 'You will find her.'

She spoke with such clarity and reassurance that I looked straight into her eyes. I never normally did that; my social mode wasn't that capable. But I wasn't in social mode. I was still in a temporary, modeless state. What startled me, however, was that I had never heard anyone say those words before. I simply wasn't expecting to hear them. I wanted to write an aphorism right then and there, but that part of my brain wasn't working.

There was no way she could know that. It was bizarre that she would say it. But I couldn't look away from her smile. A strange feeling came over me. I thought of the sparkle in my mum's eyes and the days when the telephone had still meant something. Initially, I couldn't work out exactly why Davi's words had made such an impact on me. And then I realised.

I *believed* her.

'Well, Mr Ethan, if you be liking some help to find cafes and the poster then I am at your disposables.' Tee said this with a smile. He seemed to genuinely care, which was another thing I wasn't used to. On hearing those words my plan to find the poster crystallised and set instantaneously.

'If you accept, maybe I can pay you to give me a tour of the cafes in Phnom Penh, Mr Tee? Only if you want to, of course...'

'Oh, that is a most excellent idea, Mr Ethan! Though I must say you will only be paying Cambodian price. This is a tour of necessity, no? Not a fat tourist looking for sights to see! Phew! Never have I been given such an important job!'

Tee smiled again. As he did so, Davi leaned in and knocked the peak of his cap over his face. I laughed with them and my brain started working and an aphorism popped into my head.

People are only as nice as you give them the chance to be.

I thought briefly and was confident that there was some truth in it. I wondered how nice everyone I hadn't dared to speak to might have been and was ashamed that I hadn't been braver in my life.

Davi stood up, collecting our cups and bottles before returning towards her stand.

'Good luck, Mr Ethan. You must come and tell me of how you are doing.' She smiled again as she retreated.

I stared at her as she slowly strode back towards the steaming kettle. How much money had she lost in that space of time because of me?

'Okay, Mr Ethan! We begin now, yes? Come, I will take you to the *farang* cafes outside of the street.'

I stood up and stretched my arms out above my head. Looking out towards the street, the reflection of the sun on the corrugated iron roofs caught my eye. It looked beautiful. Beams of sunlight hanging above the street in strip lights.

Tee also stood up and walked up the street towards the spot where we had first met. He gestured for me to follow and I took one last look at the roofs before drawing my eyes back to the road in front of us. I felt the dust on my feet as I followed Tee towards his moto.

I took a deep breath and let it out slowly. I wanted to give the air enough time to make me feel alive.

13

I spent the rest of the day with Tee. We must have visited around fifteen cafes on our tour of Phnom Penh, each with an owner who ultimately offered a similar shake of the head. The variety of sights and smells we experienced around the city was astonishing. It was difficult to take it all in. Phnom Penh contained more contrasts than I had ever seen before in one place.

Winding our way through small, narrow streets on his moto took up most of our time. Every so often we would come across a wide main road, similar to the one we had driven down on my way from the bus station the day before. At these points, the feeling of the city would change. The thin, mazy side street would be opened up on either side by an intensely busy road. The road would take an age to navigate across before closing in on us again as if nothing had happened.

The volume of traffic in the city was enormous. There were so many motorbikes. Cars were vastly outnumbered on the roads and I could see why. They simply weren't manoeuvrable enough to get through the sea of bikes. Tee wove his way in and out, overtaking and undertaking swiftly, all the while turning around and talking to me about where we were going next. I had my hands wrapped tightly around his waist, my fingers whitening more and more as the journey progressed. I was no longer modeless. My focused-alert mode was working overtime.

The side streets were nearly always full of people chatting, working, standing, sitting, laughing and living out their lives. We briefly appeared in and out of their experiences, providing a cameo role each time we hopped off the bike and walked into the next cafe on Tee's list, as if we were extras in someone else's film or they were extras in ours. I wasn't sure which way round it would be. Each cafe owner was happy to talk to Tee, and they often spoke for five or ten minutes. I would linger awkwardly by the side of the road as they chatted and laughed. Sometimes we would be offered a small, spicy snack to nibble on or a deliciously cold drink. But ultimately, we were given the same response each time.

Eventually, when it reached evening, I suggested to Tee that we head back and try again the next day. I was exhausted and needed to escape. Climbing off the bike when we reached the hostel, I stood next to him, the engine still running, and arched my back, stretching my arms out behind me. There was a brief silence, and momentarily all I could think of was when Tee might have had his bike serviced last.

'I come back tomorrow? Still many more cafes to see, Mr Ethan.'

'Yes, tomorrow. Thank you.' I said, handing him our agreed daily fee. 'What time shall I meet you?'

'Well,' Tee said, looking at his Casio watch. 'When do you like, Mr Ethan? Any time is okay by me.'

I looked at my wrist, although I wasn't wearing a watch.

'Shall we say nine o' clock, here?' I said, plucking a number out of the air.

'Okay, Mr Ethan!' And with that he smiled again, gave me a thumbs up and drove off down the road.

I waited and watched until I could no longer see his bike. The red tail light disappeared around a corner. Should I have asked him to join me for dinner? I could only guess that he struggled for money. I could have bought him a nice dinner to say thank you. I could have asked him if Davi wanted to come along. The money I had given him for the day didn't seem much, but he had looked happy with it. Was I taking advantage of him? I couldn't tell.

I remained standing in the place where I had got off the bike, one hand on my hip and the other rubbing the back of my neck. I stood there in that position for five minutes or so, though I couldn't be sure. I always had trouble telling how much time had passed if I had no way of measuring it. A slight breeze brushed the hair on my arms and I looked up at the night sky. It was deep blue; a giant ocean around me. The dark feeling again.

I turned and walked back into the hostel.

*

My father had never asked me what I spent my money on. I don't know if he knew what I was planning to do or whether he simply didn't care. He had been so distant before I left that I probably could have done anything and he wouldn't have noticed.

When I had told them where I was going that night I had been surprised by my father's reaction. His words had hurt me. They had hurt as the push might if someone were to push you in front of a train. I had felt sore and shocked and confused, but I also knew that the real pain was yet to come.

14

'Ethan! Ethan! Hey, man! Where you been, brother?'

I was walking past the mirror in the hallway when I heard Jon-Paul's voice calling out from the common area. Stopping in front of my reflection, I paused. I had almost made it back to the bedroom.

'Ethan!' Jon-Paul called my name again.

I hesitated, stuck to the ground. My reflection was looking at me. It looked tired and confused, but it had a voice. This is your choice, it said. You can be *more*. I reluctantly obeyed it and walked into the common room. Jon-Paul was sitting on the cushions at the far end of the open area with the same group from the night before. Jacob was holding a joint above his head and the air around them was thick with the smell of it. The lake outside sat still, the same way it had the previous day.

'Ethan! Good to see you, buddy! Where you been at today? You been on the tourist trail?'

I made a snap decision, though I couldn't fully explain why. It *felt* right.

'Yeah, I picked up a tuk-tuk and took a tour to see some of the sights,' I said.

'Nice, nice. Where did you go? Palace? Markets?'

'Yeah, all of those. The main places really. It's been a pretty draining day.'

'You can't do that stuff and not feel knackered after,' Jacob said, looking into the glowing embers at the end of his joint.

'Yes, yes.' I said.

I was standing near the group, my hands in my pockets. My weight was shifting slowly from foot to foot, in a mode of its own. There was a silence and I wasn't sure where to rest my eyes. I caught Jon-Paul's gaze by accident. His eyes were bloodshot and his eyelids looked heavy and strained.

Leah was sitting just to the side of the main group talking to some guy wearing a sickly yellow T-shirt. She smiled and her teeth glistened as a shark's might before it devours its prey. Gesticulating hard as she spoke, she was obviously giving one of her talks again. The guy was leaning in close to her and his thigh was touching hers. She looked up and I moved my eyes as quickly as I could, though she must have seen me looking.

'What have you been up to today, Jon-Paul?'

On impulse, I turned my attention back to Jon-Paul. He stood up as I asked him. He did a stretch as big as a cat that had woken up after a long nap at the zoo.

'Felt like raw shit when I woke up, man, I can tell you! Didn't surface 'til gone three and I've been here chilling out with these guys since then. We're heading out soon for food and drinks if you're up for it? Should be a good one.'

'Well, I'm pretty tired to be honest. It's been a long day.'

'C'mon man, I can *promise* you some good times! We're going to this super cool bar, you're gonna love it.'

'Well...' My mind was unhappy. I wasn't used to being invited out. I was used to staying in. It was a well-established routine of mine. But I was also used to hating myself, and not all familiar feelings were good ones. It was one of those routines that existed because of a lack of passion to try something new. Because of *fear*.

'Dude, you're coming! End of. It'll be awesome.'

'Okay... sure.' I gave in and my thumb tensed against my forefinger. 'I could do with a shower first, though. What time are you heading off?'

'Whenever, man. No worries, I'll make sure everyone waits for you. Be quick, though. I'm hungry!' He flashed me another grin and sat down again.

The bedroom was even warmer than usual once I was back inside it. I had a quick shower before spending ten minutes trying to decide what to wear from my small collection of clothes. Packing had happened in a hurry and I hadn't brought anything for a night out. I didn't know what was appropriate for an evening at a strange bar in the capital of Cambodia. I threw most of my clothes back in the bag as soon as I had taken them out, wondering why I had packed them at all. Eventually I settled on my favourite jeans and a yellow and blue T-shirt.

I quickly tried to style my hair, taking a couple of goes to get it right, before returning to the common area. My sister used to tease me whenever she came into the bathroom and saw me fixing my hair. I used to spend longer on it than I do now. I liked to have it a particular way. It had to be neat.

Charlotte never spent long in the bathroom or standing in front of a mirror. She was lucky as her hair was thick and wavy. She could let it fall and it would look interesting and individual, in a *cool* way. I remember Mum talking about how lovely Charlotte's hair was when we were younger. She used to say it was a shame she didn't do anything with it. My hair, on the other hand, had always been straight and boring. A little too mousy brown, as Mum would say. I've always had to work at making myself look interesting.

When I reappeared in the common room, only Jon-Paul and Elodie were left on the cushions. Everybody else had gone.

'Here he is! I thought you were never coming out, buddy!'

'Sorry, sorry. I didn't think I took that long. Did I? Sorry. Where's everybody gone?'

'Leah got real hungry so everyone went to eat. I said I'd wait here for you and we'd meet them there. So, ready to go?'

'Yeah. Sorry for making you wait.'

'Don't worry about it, man. Okay, let's go! Mustn't waste valuable drinking time!'

Jon-Paul and Elodie stood up and headed towards me and the corridor. Elodie smiled at me as she walked past, but looked away quickly. She was short and petite with light brown hair tied back in a tight ponytail. I couldn't remember her saying a single word since I arrived. I smiled back and followed them down the dark corridor. The sky had turned black.

A bottomless hole waiting for me to fall into it.

Jon-Paul beckoned over the first tuk-tuk driver he saw and we climbed in.

15

After a short journey, which wouldn't have taken long to walk, we got out and headed into a strange place for dinner.

It had been a noisy ride on the tuk-tuk with Jon-Paul talking feverishly. He was sure there wasn't anywhere like the place we were going to in the UK and that I was going to love it so much I wouldn't believe it. Elodie had stayed quiet, looking out at the road for the most part.

She had glanced in once and I had caught her looking up at the sky after Jon-Paul had claimed it was the best pizza place outside of Italy. She had seen me glancing at her as she did this and had hunched her shoulders and shaken her head. I had looked at the sky as she had done and she had smiled at me. It had made me feel good. I had taken the chance, employing my social mode as best as I could, and asked her what she thought of the restaurant.

'Do you want the truth?' she had asked.

I had nodded and leaned in so I could hear her as we raced along. 'It's called Lucio's. Lucio's is a fake Italian restaurant that's just up the road, and within easy walking distance, but everyone always takes a tuk-tuk to get there.

It serves an assortment of poorly replicated Italian food in a brightly lit room with faded pictures of pasta on the walls. The furniture is made of worn-down bamboo and reeds, and in the centre of each table is an ancient, melted candle inside a small, dirty glass bulb.'

She had cupped an imaginary glass bulb in her hands as she continued to shout to make herself heard over the roar of the engine.

'The restaurant is way overpriced for what it is, especially given the quality of the food, but it's always full because it's the only place that serves a Western menu on the street. Many of the other restaurants on the street serve such good local food, but nobody wants to go there because it isn't pizza.'

'Don't listen to her!' Jon-Paul had shouted. 'No pissing on the parade, Frenchie! It's fucking great, you'll love it! Hey, can you believe that guy back at the hostel? Only took his hand off Leah's thigh long enough to stand up! She needs to chuck him and come see me, if you know what I mean!' He had laughed and leaned out of the tuk-tuk shaking his head in the breeze, his mouth hanging open and his tongue sticking out.

I had grimaced and turned back to Elodie. 'I take it you don't like pizza, then?' I had said, pushing myself to keep up the conversation.

'Don't get me wrong, I like the taste of real pizza....' she had replied. 'I don't like the taste of fake pizza because, well, it makes me think about things. I'm halfway across the world and could eat anywhere I like and have some real, delicious, Cambodian food.'

'Why don't you?' I had asked.

'I… don't know,' she had said, frowning. 'I… really don't know. I eat the same practically tasteless, bland food most nights, with the same people. You're right,' she had said, nodding. 'I should eat somewhere else.'

We had soon arrived and Lucio's was exactly as Elodie had described it. The large doorway was made from cold glass and steel; the opposite in every way to the one at our hostel. When we walked inside we were hit by warm, stuffy air and the faint smells of baking and sweat. It was incredibly noisy; the sounds of clinking cutlery and conversation filling the large space. We waited momentarily before Jon-Paul spotted the rest of the group and we joined them around a long table. On our way over to them I noticed that every table was full of tourists.

The further in we got, the more impressed I was by how right Elodie had been. It was the perfect Italian restaurant for people who knew nothing of Italy. Not that I knew much of Italy, but I knew it wasn't that. There were funny old pictures on the walls of pizza and pasta dishes. The pasta in the pictures was faded grey, cardboard, and the pizza dull, used hubcaps.

Soggy breadsticks sat limply on every table in plastic beakers. The food was cheap, but at least it looked better than it did in the pictures. However, nothing tasted of anything. The cheese didn't taste of cheese. The tomatoes were not tomatoes. The pizza dough was a strange sort of sweet bread that should have been part of an iced bun. It wasn't what I had imagined I would eat in Cambodia.

The meal went by quickly. The conversation was loud and often impenetrable. Leah talked about a volunteering thing she wanted to pursue, something she had been planning for a while. It reminded me of the email from my sister. I wondered if she had taught at this orphanage Leah wanted to go to. I thought I could ask but found no satisfactory way to do so.

I concentrated on my pizza for most of the meal, looking up whenever Jon-Paul shouted out in my direction, but otherwise slowly digesting the conversation around me. I noticed Elodie did the same. She was sitting across the table from me and barely looked up as she was eating. Her fork movements were deliberate and slow. It seemed to me that she had problems with her social mode, as I did. I was getting to know her a bit more as the meal went on.

When all the food had gone and the bill came there was a complicated operation to ensure that everyone had paid for their share. Lots of coins and notes exchanged hands several times. The calculations weren't all accurate and this frustrated me.

When it was finally over I got up out of my chair and was glad to leave. The cool night air outside was a welcome change from the thick-baked, sweaty smell of Lucio's. I was ready to go back to the hostel but everyone else was going for a drink, and once again Jon-Paul refused to take no for an answer. His speech had begun to slur by this point and he kept telling me how great his happy pizza had been. I didn't know what he was talking about, but after some application of pressure I agreed to join him for one drink. He high-fived me before running up behind Jacob and pulling his trousers down.

The bar we went to could be heard from the far end of the street. Some kind of dance music was pulsating out of it in invisible ripples from a stone dropped in water. The entrance sucked in all those around. The sound of bass-heavy trance split our atoms as we walked through the doorway.

Once inside, I could hardly hear anyone. Unsure of what to do, I stood at the bar for a while holding my beer. I saw people all around me smiling, laughing and dancing. People drinking and talking. Moving to the music. People enjoying themselves and having fun.

It made me think.

It had been a long day and, against my will, I regressed into my self-preservation mode. I began to get stuck on the questions that popped into my head. What was I doing here? Why did I think anyone else wanted me to be here? Why was I wasting my money going out to places like this?

I didn't have a never-ending supply of money; only what I had worked hard to save up. If I wanted to save my sister I needed to spend as little as possible on myself. What was it Charlotte had said?

I feel so selfish for my travelling. It appals me that I lived just for myself for so long.

I closed my eyes briefly and let the music become my experience; let it take me away. I wanted to feel something different. To not imagine what my sister would have thought of me at that moment. To not think what my parents would say. To not worry that the others might find out what kind of person I really was.

To not let the darkness take me again.

The ripples of sound flowed through me. I tried not to think of the stone that was making them. The stone that ruined the perfect calm of the water. The stone that had been dropped on me and was still falling.

I needed to change my focus, so I added up the bill for dinner, correctly, in my head a few times. Maths is maths. Maths is right. Maths is true; at least, I thought it was. After breathing out I opened my eyes and tried to concentrate on the room. I had already bought a drink and didn't want to waste any more than I already had, so I decided to stay just long enough to finish it.

Through the fake smoke, I could make out Leah and Jacob sitting at a table with a few others. I employed stealth mode and walked over to join them. It seemed to work. No one paid me any attention as I sat down at the edge of the group. Christina, Manuel's girlfriend, was talking loudly. They both tended to speak a lot, Christina and Manuel, but rarely to each other.

'Have you ever considered the notion that the world is all just ideas in the mind of God?' Christina asked.

I knew straight away that I had not considered that notion and wondered how many people sitting around the table had. How many people *anywhere* had? I leaned in closer to try and hear her voice above the music. It was a distraction from the stone, at least.

'I mean,' she carried on, 'if you look at objects in the world, stuff that we perceive, like… this glass.' She picked up her drink and held it in the air, raising her eyebrows. 'How do you know that it exists? *Really* exists? Sure, we can say that it exists *now*, because we're experiencing it. But if you think about it, the only time you know it's there is when you *are* experiencing it. How do you know that anything exists when you aren't looking at it, or hearing it or touching it?'

There was a pause, during which no one said or did anything. 'There's no way of *knowing* for certain. But we all seem pretty sure that this glass does exist when we aren't experiencing it. Right?'

This time as Christina paused there were a few nods around the table. I noticed Jon-Paul was looking over at some girls by the bar.

'So if objects, stuff in the world, can only be certain to exist when they're being perceived in our *minds*, we have to ask what it really means for something to *exist*. It must mean that for something to exist it is being perceived in a mind, otherwise we can't talk about an object's existence.'

I realised I was frowning, but I didn't know why.

Christina carried on. 'So how can we explain things existing when no human mind is perceiving them? Well, if they're going to exist in those situations, which we would all assume they do – stuff doesn't seem to vanish when no one's looking at it – they require another mind to do the perceiving. A non-human mind. We have to ask: what kind of mind could perceive everything, at all times, everywhere? God's mind.'

She put the glass back down on the table. 'Nature, the universe, all the physical laws – think about how *predictable* natural laws are – and all the stuff within all this relies on the permanent will of God's mind. Otherwise they wouldn't exist. Everything we experience is an idea in the mind of God. That's why everything is so ordered and structured and exists even when we can't experience it. Only a *great* mind could conceive of that.'

I put my drink to my lips and tried to imagine God perceiving me doing so. The sound of a glass smashing somewhere nearby brought a cheer from others in the bar. Jon-Paul had disappeared by this point. It made me smile as I pictured God with his collection of ideas and Jon-Paul drunkenly stumbling around inside them, messing them all up. Would God's ideas be different from mine? Am I nothing more than an idea in the mind of God? What if he were to stop thinking about me?

As I was wondering what was wrong with stuff being stuff, I looked around and saw Elodie standing by the bar. She was clasping her glass, or God's idea of a glass, tightly. She smiled at me, and for a moment I almost forgot the ideas and God and existence and darkness and the stone that was still sending ripples of guilt through my insides.

Elodie moved in my direction and as I tried to come up with something to say that would make me sound clever and Carstairs-like, Jon-Paul appeared out of nowhere and crashed into her. She fell uncomfortably and Jon-Paul's momentum carried him over and he landed heavily on top of her. The beer she was clasping spilled all over both of them as they hit the floor. I saw her wrist turn and she cried out.

Jon-Paul was laughing and some of the others joined in. He didn't even look at Elodie as he tried to get up, rolling around on the floorboards and slipping once before pulling himself up with the help of a chair and eventually sitting down. I leaned over to try and help Elodie but she shrugged off my arm and picked herself up before quickly disappearing in the direction of the toilets. Why wouldn't she let me help her?

Jon-Paul leaned in next to me and was still laughing as he held his glass to the sky.

'To good times!' he roared.

Everyone clinked their drinks and took a swig. I put my bottle to my lips and kept it there. The cold bubbles went up my nose and started to make me choke, but I still held it there. Some had spilled onto my chin and began rolling down my neck. By the time it had dripped onto my shirt I had finished. I slammed the bottle down onto the table.

Jon-Paul slapped me on the back. 'Nice one, bro! I knew you were a good guy, Ethan! Yeah!'

What kind of God would have these ideas?

Jon-Paul turned back to Jacob and Leah, and I picked my moment to stand up and walk away. The shouted conversations continued behind me and the ripples still flowed, gradually getting further apart as I walked out the front door and down the street. I spoke to the first moto driver I saw and got a lift back to the hostel. I said nothing as I paid him.

Walking back through the dark corridors of the hostel, I passed the mirror. Why did they have to put a mirror in the middle of the corridor so that everyone had to look at themselves every time they passed it? I fumbled for the keys in my pocket before opening the door to my room and lying straight down on the bed.

*

I burst out of the backdoor and ran straight for my bike, pushing the stand up carefully and, using both hands, wheeled it as quickly as I could to the starting line. I counted them, three paving slabs back from the edge of the patio, and stopped, manoeuvring my bike into position. Climbing on and lining myself up, I waited until I had the angle just right before lowering my head. My chin was touching the handlebars and my elbows were raised. I took a deep breath. I was ready.

I pushed off with my foot and began pedalling as fast as I could. Soon I was off the patio with a bump and landing on the grass. The vibrations of the earth were shooting up the front wheel, through the handlebars and into my arms. Heading for the apple tree I made a left turn, putting my foot down as I did so. I tucked my head in and began the best bit, building up speed as I hurtled down the hill of our garden, aiming straight for the honeysuckle at the bottom. The hot air streamed past me. I gripped the handlebars tightly and kept as low as I could.

Charlotte was at the bottom of the hill by the honeysuckle.

'Lottie, Lottie! Look at me!'

She didn't turn round. She was kneeling down, facing in the opposite direction, and was right in the middle of my racing line. My path round to the washing pole was blocked. That was my favourite route. My race course.

'Lottie! Hey, look! I'm coming through!'

I was fast approaching the bottom, aiming right at the spot where Charlotte was kneeling.

'Lottie! Out the way!'

She still didn't turn around. I was too close to stay on course. I pressed the brakes hard and skidded down the last section of the hill. Wobbling under the strain of the brakes I felt my balance go. The bike fell from under me and I rolled off. By that point I was going slowly enough that it didn't hurt. I could smell the cut grass around my face as I tumbled through it. Out of breath, I came to a stop on my back right next to Charlotte.

'Hey, why didn't you move?'

I leaned over and nudged her in the ribs. No response. Sitting up and brushing the grass out of my hair, I frowned and twisted around to look at her face. She was crying. I looked down to see a hedgehog by her knees, uncurled and stationary. Charlotte had her hands in her lap. Her tears were heavy and her nose was running into her mouth.

'What is it?' I leaned in to look closer.

'It's a hedgehog. It's dead,' she said, without looking at me.

'Where did you find it?'

'Here. It was just lying here.'

A pause followed as we both looked at the hedgehog. It had a tiny nose and feet.

'We should tell Mum and Dad. I'll go get them.' I made for the house but Charlotte turned and grabbed me.

'No! They'll tell us to leave it or put it in the bin or something. We need to give it a proper burial. Go and get a tablecloth from the dining room.'

'What for?'

'So we can cover it, stupid.' Charlotte was talking forcefully, amid continual sniffs and wipes of her eyes.

'We'll wrap it up and bury it here under the honeysuckle. Quick, hurry up or it won't get to heaven.'

I left my bike on the grass and ran back up the hill. My heart was beating faster and faster. I clambered to the top and jumped back onto the patio before reaching for the handle of the back door and pushing it open. I threw my shoes off and hurried into the dining room. Mum was in the conservatory and Dad was upstairs in his office. I knew they wouldn't see me. Opening up the oak drawers of the dresser one by one, I rummaged until I saw a tablecloth. I grabbed it and closed the door as gently as I could before taking off again. Stuffing my feet into my shoes, I ran back towards the honeysuckle.

'Here!' I handed Charlotte the tablecloth and stayed next to her, gulping in as much of the warm air as I could with each breath.

Charlotte took the tablecloth and unfolded it. She laid it out on the grass, picked up the hedgehog and delicately placed it in the centre of the spread next to an embroidered red rose. The hedgehog was still and silent. I caught one last glimpse of its soft, soil-brown tummy before it was covered in white polyester.

I helped Charlotte dig a small hole under the honeysuckle with my hands and we placed the bundle inside. We brushed the soil back over the hole and sat there in silence for a moment. I could hear the sounds of lawnmowers and traffic in the distance. The smell of a nearby barbecue sizzled faintly in the air.

'Do we need to say something?' I looked to Charlotte for guidance.

She waited a long time before answering.

'No. The hedgehog's gone now. We helped him, Ethan. We've done our part.'

I looked at my sister and was happy that the hedgehog would get to heaven. Charlotte stared at the sky and wiped a tear from her cheek.

'Let's go inside, Ethan. I can't bear it any more.'

At dinnertime my parents asked Charlotte why they couldn't find the tablecloth that matched the napkins and place mats. I hadn't ever noticed the white mats that sat beneath my parents' plates, their blood-red roses embossed in each corner.

My sister said nothing. My mother asked a few times gently before my father grew cross and began to shout. He said that she didn't deserve dinner if she was prepared to lie. He told Charlotte to leave the table. Charlotte sat still and continued to stare at the space in front of her. She was twirling her ponytail between her fingers. My father pulled the chair out from behind her. Charlotte half fell but just kept her balance. Without saying a word she began walking towards the door.

Something was heavy on top of me. I couldn't sit still under the weight of it; I couldn't stay silent with it there. I didn't know what to do. Charlotte was almost out of the room. Why didn't she tell them? Surely they would understand; we couldn't get in trouble for helping out. We had done the right thing.

Charlotte was at the door by the time the weight became too much. I burst and told the room it was okay because we had needed the tablecloth so that the hedgehog could go to heaven. My mother clinked her cutlery down and stopped eating.

'I beg your pardon?'

'We found a hedgehog and it had died. We had to bury it so I found a tablecloth to cover it so it could be buried properly. It's down by the honeysuckle. We covered it up and now we have done our part.'

I held my fork in the air, suspended by the silence.

My father threw his napkin down on the table and stood up. 'You used one of our best tablecloths to wrap up a dead hedgehog? Are you that stupid?'

He turned to Charlotte, who was crumbling by the door. 'I suppose this was your idea! Why do you do these things, Charlotte? Have you no sense of property or value? What were you thinking?'

Charlotte said nothing.

Raising his voice further, my father continued. 'Is this strange behaviour ever going to stop? There's a real world out there, Charlotte. One where people respect other people's possessions and answer when they are damn well spoken to!'

Father was roaring. He was angry and on edge. Charlotte still said nothing.

'Go to your rooms, both of you! I can't believe how thoughtless you are. I thought you would have known better, Ethan. You are *not* to take important things from these drawers, do I make myself clear? Get out of my sight!'

We ran upstairs and Charlotte slammed her bedroom door. I climbed onto my bed and wrapped the covers over me. Before long, the back door slammed and I looked out of the window to see my father marching down the hill in the garden. He headed straight for the honeysuckle and bent over. He pulled the bundle from the ground and walked back up the hill. It wasn't so white any more; it was dirty and grey. I thought of the hedgehog's tiny, soft tummy. It was so strange that it was surrounded by so many prickles.

I heard my parents shouting downstairs and the front door open. The bins were out the front of the house.

I began to cry as I looked at the hole sitting there. A wound in our garden. What about the hedgehog? I buried my head in the pillows and shut my eyes to try and stop the tears. What would happen to the hedgehog now? What if it didn't get to heaven? Where would it go then?

I heard a noise outside my bedroom door. I dug my head out of the covers and turned to see a piece of paper slide under the door. I climbed out of bed slowly and picked it up. The note was written on purple paper, torn out of a spiral-bound notebook. I unfolded it and read it slowly, the paper soft in my hands.

Don't worry, Ethan. You're not stupid. It's the world that's stupid. We did the right thing. I know the hedgehog would think so XXX

I rubbed my eyes and sat down. I didn't entirely know what she meant, but I was glad she had said it. I folded up the piece of paper and held it tight in my hand.

I know the hedgehog would think so.

I loosened my grip. My palm opened and I watched the piece of paper unfurl, crease by crease.

16

Over the following three days my life was split into two distinct entities. It was as if my mind was acting as two different people. The days were spent with Tee, driving around on the motorbike and searching cafes for the poster. The evenings were spent with the people at the hostel, though I was spending less and less time with the group as a whole and more time by myself. Or with Elodie.

The morning after the night at Lucio's, I had bumped into Elodie on my way out of the hostel. She had been surfacing from her room as I was leaving to see Tee. When our eyes met in the gloom of the corridor there had been a brief pause and she had looked away. She had tucked her hair behind her ears.

'Morning,' I had said, breathing after I spoke. My social mode *had* to work this time.

'Morning.'

There was nothing but silence.

'Are you okay? You had a pretty nasty fall last night.'

Rubbing her wrist, she had looked at me. 'I'm okay. My wrist's a bit sore, but it's nothing serious.'

'Jon-Paul can be a bit full-on sometimes, can't he?'

'Yeah. He's... he's not sure when to stop, I guess.'

I had looked outside and seen Tee waiting on his bike.

'Sorry I couldn't help you up. I tried but I, er... I was too late'

'Help me up?' Her eyebrows had been raised.

'In the bar, I mean. When you were on the floor...'

'Oh, then. Oh, no. Don't worry about it. Really, it was a silly thing. I wish it had never happened.' She had looked down at her feet and curled her toes. 'So where are you going today?'

'Oh, er, just more sight-seeing. I've got another day booked with my moto driver. He's a nice guy so I'm sticking with him.'

'Oh, that's great. Well, I guess I'll see you later then.' Elodie had leaned back against the door frame.

'Yeah, see you later.'

Elodie had gone back into her room and shut the door as I walked past and out into the sunlight. I had squinted hard as my eyes adjusted. Tee had been sitting there on his bike chewing his nails. He had looked up and seen me, starting the engine and waving.

That morning, in between cafes, Tee had pulled the bike up outside what had looked like an old school. It was a small collection of grey, cube-shaped, concrete buildings. They were dark and miserable and surrounded by wire fencing. A Cambodian flag was flying in a courtyard at the front and a number of tourists were walking in and out of the main gate. A large collection of seated beggars lined up along the pavement outside, many with limbs missing and all with palms held out in the air.

'This S-21,' he said. 'You want to look?'

'Okay,' I replied, not sure what S-21 was. I had heard of it, but I didn't know what had happened there.

Tee climbed off the bike as he carried on speaking. 'Important you see this, Mr Ethan. If your sister lost in Cambodia then you must understand Cambodia. So you must understand S-21, yes?'

17

An old Cambodian woman was crying next to me. She was weeping quietly and I only noticed because I looked at her by accident. Her eyes and forehead were tight. She held a tissue to her nose with one hand and had the other wrapped around her waist. We were standing in front of a wall of black-and-white photographs. People's faces, one after the other. Old, young, male and female. Some wore glasses. Some had moustaches. None were smiling.

All of them were dead.

They had all been killed in the building we were both standing in. I found this hard to understand. There was so much *depth* it wasn't sinking in.

There were pictures of the rooms captured in the state they had been left in at the end of the war. There were paintings created by survivors of what had happened there, because no pictures of things taking place had survived. The paintings were childlike in their style, which somehow made me feel uncomfortable as I looked at them.

But there were so many. There was red blood in thick splatters, spraying from a pipe out of someone's outsized, angular head. Matchstick people being stretched in chains between posts. Other disproportionate people were smiling, too large as they watched in the background, all out of perspective. There were matt grey blades held by hands that were painted with too few fingers. Eyes crying azure blue tears that ran in mazy lines down yellow faces.

In another room, information panels explained how many people had been killed and why. Next to these panels was a guest book, in which tourists had written messages. How *terrible* the whole thing was. How they were so *appalled* by it. How we should *give peace a chance*. They had signed off their notes with smiley faces or kisses or hearts. Or *xoxo*.

As I stood there, an American couple took a picture behind me of the crying lady and the photo wall. The room was quiet and because of this the synthesised click of the digital camera sounded louder than usual. One for the album.

It was too much. The dark place crept out from where I had hidden it, and everything felt wrong.

After another minute or so the woman turned and we briefly caught each other's gaze. Her dark brown eyes looked straight into mine. They were all wet, her eyelashes tangled together in triangles by her tears.

I clenched my teeth.

'I'm...' I said for some reason. I didn't know what to say. What *could* I say? *Give peace a chance*? That sentence stirred the darkness in me; it's so *fake*.

She reached out and touched me on the arm before saying something I didn't understand. With one gentle nod, she walked away and I looked out of the grilled window once again.

As I came out, I stopped and handed some money to one of the beggars. He didn't say anything.

I approached Tee and he climbed back onto the bike.

He looked at me in a way I hadn't seen before and said, 'This is Cambodia. This a new country now, but not so new that we forget. You understand, yes?'

'Did you lose someone, Tee?' I asked tentatively as I wrapped my arms around his waist. I had to ask.

'Yes. My mother and father,' was all he said before twisting his hand on the throttle and pulling us out into the city's bloodstream once more.

We rode the rest of the way home as if we were God's flawed ideas in silence.

18

Jacob had been flat on his back for a while, smoking weed on the patterned cloth. He hadn't spoken for some time, but when he heard me explain to Jon-Paul where I had been that day he sat up and began to speak of Cambodia and the war. For ten minutes or so he spoke, uninterrupted, on the history of Cambodia and the death camps that surrounded Phnom Penh.

In those ten minutes I heard many things that reflected exactly what I had read on the information panels earlier in the day. How Pol Pot had wanted to *begin again* and how that had meant setting up a perfect new socialist state. The paranoia and confusion that had set in once emotions, expression and intelligence had become things people could be killed for. The millions of people involved.

It all seemed so matter of fact. So *textbook*. But all I could think of was the crying woman and Tee. The way she had touched me on the arm and how he had said nothing.

Jacob was in full flow by the time he got to S-21 itself.

'S-21 was presented as a prison,' he said. 'A prison for people who went against the regime. But in prisons people generally do their time and get released. You get a sentence, you serve it, you get out. That's how prisons usually work. But in S-21 if you went there, you died. There was no release, no trial, no rehab. That was it. And it wasn't just a few people who went there, either. Thousands and thousands went there, man. And only a handful of those people survived. It's fucking insane.'

I wished he would stop talking, but he carried on. 'And the leaders of the Khmer Rouge claim they knew nothing about it. Nothing! They stand up now – on TV and in the papers and shit – and straight-faced deny they knew it even existed.'

'Really?' I said. The world had to be better than that. 'Surely they can't get away with that. There must be some kind of evidence against them.'

'You'd think so, wouldn't you? Well, they're on trial now – the ones that are still alive, that is – but to be honest there's real doubt about whether these trials will ever even happen.'

'Why?'

'I couldn't say exactly. I guess perhaps the Khmer Rouge still holds too much power in a weird way.'

Jacob paused for a moment, deep in thought, his eyes looking up at the ceiling. 'And trials for war crimes are an incredibly public affair, you know? Which would dredge up the past and wouldn't do Cambodia's current image – in the tourist scene, where all the money is – a whole lot of good.'

He took a drag from a joint that had been passed to him, held the smoke in and continued as he breathed out. 'And that's not the only place where that kind of thing happened. At Choeung Ek – another death camp set up by the Khmer Rouge – they've only dug up eighty-odd of the hundred and twenty-five or so mass graves so far, and they've found eight thousand, nine hundred and eighty-five bodies. *Eight thousand, nine hundred and eighty-five.* Most of those bodies had no clothes, no heads and battered bones. A large number of the ones with heads had skull fractures from short, blunt instruments. Most of the victims were either beaten to death, stabbed to death or had their throats slit. Bullets were too expensive, apparently, so bamboo poles, sharp palm tree leaves or truncheons were used instead.

'Walking around the killing fields, man… When you go you'll see. The signs are so matter-of-fact it's surreal. "This tree was used to beat children to death against".' Jacob painted the words across the air with his hand as he said them. '"Here is a mass grave of a hundred and forty-four headless bodies." It blows your mind. The sheer inhumanity of it. It's scary, man.'

He paused again and ran his fingers through his matted hair. 'The thing is, in some weird way I'm sure Pol Pot thought that he was doing the *right* thing for the people of his country, and that in the long run this was the best thing to do. I can't comprehend how that's possible. Weird.'

He held his breath briefly and exhaled. 'Some fucked-up shit, huh?'

Jacob stopped and stared at the lake that lay out in front of him. He was silent and I thought I ought to say something. I was working hard to maintain my social mode. The practice of the last few days had improved it somewhat, but it still wasn't reliable.

'It was strange walking around those rooms at S-21,' my mind decided to say, 'knowing what had happened there. And so recently. This woman was there today, looking at one of the photos, and she said something to me, but I couldn't work out what it was. She looked so sad. I wish I knew what she had said. You're right, though. The weirdest thing was that it seemed as though Pol Pot had thought that by setting it up he was acting for good. As though he was somehow acting in a noble way. I can't understand that. The stories and pictures on the walls. And this woman crying next to me... It was awful.'

For a minute it was as if the world did nothing.

'Why? Why was it awful?' I turned my head to see Manuel looking straight at me, his eyebrows raised. He had obviously been listening in and was waiting for a response in the way people do when they want to say something else.

Jacob sighed.

'I guess it doesn't seem like a noble thing to do,' I said hesitantly.

I couldn't read Manuel. He wasn't easy to know like Jon-Paul or Jacob.

'Okay, well what is noble, then?' The world had reacted. 'You ever asked yourself that question?'

I shook my head.

'What does it *mean* to be a noble person?' he asked.

'Well... you know.' I wasn't sure how to say what I was thinking. My brain wasn't in my focused/alert mode.

I said something in an attempt to ease the pressure. 'I suppose I would say that if Pol Pot were a noble person he wouldn't have tortured and killed so many innocent people.'

'Why not? How do you think your Great British Empire got to be so *noble*? You say Pol Pot wasn't noble, but you haven't answered my question. What does it mean to be noble? What is it that we should strive towards in life in order to be a noble race of human beings?'

The pressure hadn't eased at all. I had nothing left to offer. I only had one view of the statue; the one my sister had described. 'I don't know.'

'Well, I'll tell you if you don't know.'

Jacob shook his head, but Manuel ignored him and carried on.

'These days people think nobility means being well brought up, helping those in need, sacrificing something for someone less fortunate or being some kind of hero who rescues damsels in distress. We've lost the *historical* meaning of the word. If you look back at all the major societies in history that have been successful and shaped our current world, they have all had aristocratic or noble classes. But the values of these classes, and the behaviour and qualities of those within them, go strongly against what we now value in our society. Most great human achievements have come from the noble classes; doing things that are noble in the true sense of the word, but not how people would see it now. Do you get it?'

Posing the question meant I had to answer.

'I'm sorry, I don't understand you.' Which was *the* truth.

He leaned in closer. 'A true noble person is independent. He interacts with others, like this conversation you and I are having now, but only as a means to an end; a means of expanding his understanding and position of power. He is

119

driven by work and a will to succeed. Not work as in nine-to-five, behind a desk bullshit, but work as in striving to unify his personality and wills and drives and instincts to focus on a *project*.'

He meshed his fingers together. 'Something new. Something valuable. He creates his own values and seeks responsibility to employ them.

'To be noble is to recognise that this life has no goal or purpose other than what we create. It's to recognise that all our social and moral rules are a game we play and that they are absurd. They also understand the *past* and *history*'s influence on the *now*.'

He kept going and I began to wonder how many times he had said these words.

'To be noble involves creative work, which requires an obsessive nature. You need to be indifferent to others' opinions, and certain about yourself and your work. The noble person takes responsibility for the whole human race through his actions of sacrificing others for his own development. That's a big responsibility.

'He doesn't look up to anyone or anything. It is unlikely, therefore, that he will believe in God. A belief in a Christian God belongs to the slaves – the people who are too weak to create their own rules, narrative and truth – not the nobility.'

'Are you saying Christians are slaves?!' Jacob asked in a mocking fashion. 'Because I know plenty who aren't!'

'No, I'm saying Christians suffer from a slave *mentality*. A system of values dreamt up by slaves because they resented their masters. Humble, meek, mild, generous, sharing, sympathetic. Strong people don't have these qualities because they don't need them; *weak* ones do. Truly noble people recognise that the suffering of others is to be used in order for *them* to become greater still. Not everyone is capable of being great; in fact, most people aren't. Most people are only capable of following others and living by their imposed rules rather than creating their own. The noble man's acts are in line with his *project* for personal development as an expression of his will.'

'Manuel, I'm going to stop you there.' Jacob held out his arm to interrupt. 'I agree on the whole projects for personal development shit, but what exactly has any of this bollocks got to do with Pol Pot and what happened in Cambodia?'

Manuel glared at Jacob. 'If you let me finish,' he said curtly, 'you'll understand.'

He angled himself back towards me and Jacob sighed again.

'You see, in the true sense of the word, Pol Pot was noble in *many* ways.' Manuel clearly enjoyed accentuating his language. 'He wasn't afraid to sacrifice individuals for the benefit of the human race as a whole. He could see the bigger picture and he had a project. That project was *socialism.* He unified all his efforts towards that goal and showed such strength in doing so. How could you not be strong if you were doing the things he did? He had an incredibly strong will and imposed it on others, creating new rules and values to live by in the process.

'The only reason he didn't succeed is because he didn't have the resources to do so in a global environment. It wasn't in other countries' *interests* for him to succeed. Not because he was wrong to attempt his vision or because he wasn't a *noble* man. Maybe the world would have been better off under a socialist regime. We'll never know.'

He looked at me and noticed my confusion. I remembered how easy I am to know sometimes.

'Look, I don't expect you to understand.'

His eyes flicked across at Jacob, who was looking away.

'Think about where your lovely life came from, and why it might be that human beings are shitting up this planet now, and have been doing so and going backwards in every way that matters for the last eighty years. How democracy and capitalism won't and *can't* last forever. Then think about how noble our way of life *really is* in the twenty-first century and how someone who tried to change things and invent a new way of life, even at considerable cost, might not be as terrible as you think.

'Ask any Cambodian on the street outside.' He pointed towards the doorway and held his arm in the air. 'They've got nothing and they have to watch you stuff your face, get pissed and take drugs every night, and then clean up after your shit so they can get by. How noble do you think *they* think you are?'

He sighed. 'No great achievement ever came about without sacrifice. Every fucking civilisation on earth was built on sacrifice! Why doesn't anyone ever see that?' Throwing a cushion out of the way, he stood up and stormed out of the shared area, shouting 'For fuck's sake!' as he left.

As I watched him leave I wished I had told him the noblest people I had met in a long time were Tee and Davi. And that it had nothing to do with them having *projects* or *shouldering the burden of humanity*. It was because they loved each other and would help out a stranger, even after the terrible things they must have been through. I tried to write an aphorism, but I was too confused. Maybe the world *was* going backwards. I wondered if I needed a project and whether having one might make me feel *whole*. Another question emerged.

Did I have a slave mentality?

I went to bed that night feeling lost. It took me a while to get to sleep, but when it did arrive sleep took me away to my dark place, where I dreamed of death and torture. The dream was a series of hyper-real, shimmering images, different from anything I could see with my eyes when I was awake. Bodies beaten until I could hear the skulls crack. Music, distorted and painful, filled my ears. I was in the presence of many other people at what seemed to be a Cambodian prison camp.

I was dispensing death to faceless victims.

I wielded a palm leaf, power and violence rushing through my veins. I felt so alive. Bodies were dropping at my will and I could feel the throats cut as I opened them one by one. As I helped slit the throat of one girl I leered with glee, feeling the warm blood on my hands and anger in my heart. But as the body fell to the ground I saw her face. I stopped breathing as my anger turned to desperate remorse and earth-shattering sadness. It was my sister, expressionless and cold. Blood-soaked and lifeless.

An inanimate object. One more result of my bloodlust.

I crumpled to my knees under the weight of what I had done and began to cry, holding her in my arms.

I awoke in the dark humidity of the box-like room, frightened, alone and crying for the loss of the only thing I truly cared for.

*

'There are only perspectives in life, you know? My perspective. Your perspective. Anyone else, no matter who, it's still a perspective. No one's got some kind of special ticket for this. Truth, I mean the kind that doesn't depend on me, or you, or anyone. Truth that floats above all the fake, broken pieces of the people on this planet. Truth that makes any kind of sense of this giant mess. Truth that's just *true*, no matter what, because it's *true*. The way I see it, that kind of truth is a myth.'

As Charlotte announced this, she drew a cigarette from her mouth as actors do in the movies. No matter how much I knew they were terribly bad for her, and how awful they smelt, and how they tarred up and smudged her lungs charcoal black, she still managed to look so *cool*. So effortless. She breathed out the smoke and I watched it disappear into the air.

The sun was oozing down through the patchy cloud in thick, dull beams. The sand on the beach was pebbly and grubby, with the grainy texture of grit. There was a tetchy wind coming off the waves that made each of the hairs on my arms tingle. A fat, bald man was applying cream to himself on a sunbed to my right. He kept missing bits and it sat in sickly, sticky globs on his pink pasty skin amid the furry clusters of hair on his shoulders and back.

Mum and Dad were on a wine-tasting tour and had left us to ourselves for the day. Why people had to tour to taste wine made no sense to me. I don't think it mattered to them. Whatever they drank, they always came home

124

pissed. Chardonnay and Riesling. Sauvignon and Merlot. To us, it was just rich people and bullshit.

The holiday resort offered little for anyone to do other than sit on the beach.

So that was exactly what we did.

As Charlotte exhaled, my mind travelled back to the first time I had seen her smoke. It had been after school one day, in the park. We had been sitting down by the swings as usual, delaying our return home, when she had pulled out a pack of matt red Marlboro, put one to her lips and cupped her hand around a purple plastic lighter.

Looking around the nearby car park to check no one had seen, I had asked Charlotte, in a whisper, why she was smoking. She had blinked, looked up to the trees as though I wasn't even there, and announced that it was because she only slightly preferred the idea of being alive to that of being dead.

I hadn't understood this at all. And I couldn't believe those words had come out of my sister's mouth. My fingers had gripped the bench tightly. She had flicked the wavy hair out of her eyes and taken another draw, her eyes tightening as she exhaled.

My face must have looked confused or shocked or worried or something, because she had sighed and begun to explain herself. And she hardly *ever* explained herself, I mean *ever*. And certainly not without being asked.

Schopenhauer, she had said, claimed that the best thing for a person was to never have been born at all. Life, he had said, was inescapable suffering and only art and music could pull us out of it for brief moments of beauty.

'So if all life is suffering anyway, then why not smoke?

125

What difference does it make? If it gives you relief from the torment of living, then it must be a good thing,' Charlotte had said.

She had added that all the greatest thinkers in history had smoked: Nietzsche, Freud, Sartre, Heidegger and Hume. Tobacco and genius had gone hand in hand for centuries, she had claimed. Self-destruction was a natural tendency for those inflicted with intelligence. A creative mind needs a vice.

On the beach, the wind blew in again and I pulled my knees up to my chin. My mind began to think of her previous announcement. It didn't agree.

'But there *are* truths,' I replied. '*True* truths. There are loads of them.'

'Such as?'

'Well, I don't know.' I had to concentrate for a moment before an answer came to me. Sometimes the most obvious things are the hardest to explain.

A thought arrived and made me smile. 'Two plus two equals four. That's true isn't it?'

'In one way it's true, yes,' she said, nodding. 'But that sentence alone doesn't contain the whole truth. Truth is more complicated than that.'

'Well what's missing then?'

'*Well*, lots,' she said, mimicking me. 'Why do you *want* two plus two to equal four?'

'I don't want it to, it just does!'

'Are you sure about that? Why did you tell it to me? Why did you want to tell me something true?'

She sat up straight and turned to face me.

'To prove my point.'

'Right, so you *want* two and two to equal four because it puts you in a superior position to me by being right and proving me wrong. It puts you in a position of strength. Of power, even. It *improves* your situation.'

'Yes, I guess so, in a way. So?'

She spread her palms into the air. "Don't you think it shows that we create truths to use them to our advantage? Truths don't exist on their own, like trees or planets, or you or I. People *made* them. In which case, truths are invented by people for a purpose. In response to your example, maths wasn't discovered, it's not penicillin or fossils. It was invented because its truths are *useful*. We prefer these truths to things that aren't true because they have so much more *use*. You can do so much with a truth; it can get you places.

'So, if we've invented them for a purpose they have human origins. And anything that has come from people must have come from a perspective, because you can't be a person without having your own perspective.'

Her hands were gesturing quickly, pointing and turning on her wrists.

'And you can't ever escape your own perspective. You're only ever going to be *you*. You can look at the truth from *your* angle, and you can change that angle as much as you want, but you'll never get the whole thing. It's like looking at a statue. You can only ever get your own little view through your eyes. It's frustrating as hell."

The statue. The one she always tried to explain.

She took another drag from her cigarette, holding it in and turning her head before exhaling slowly, as if she wanted to give the smoke as much time as possible to ruin her lungs. As if she were saying, 'Do it. *I dare you.*'

'If you ask me, people are asking the wrong questions,' she continued. 'The whole human race is asking the wrong questions. It shouldn't be "What is true?", but "Why do you want it to be true?" If you look at the world in this way, you can see that truth really comes from what *you* want, and what *you* want is just one viewpoint.'

She looked out at the sea. The waves carried on rolling in as they always did. Water on water on water.

'God, it's annoying,' she said. 'I know I can't, but I really want to see the whole fucking statue. You know what I mean?'

19

As each morning went by I became less and less enthusiastic when I saw Tee outside the hostel. He always smiled and waved, but those actions had begun to feel different somehow. I wanted to ask him about his parents.

However, that wasn't the only issue. I was becoming fed up with the bike. It was uncomfortable and noisy. I had to be careful not to burn my calves on the hot engine as I rode pillion, but I didn't always manage to avoid doing so. The scars from it marked my legs and became itchy at night. I couldn't sleep in that hot box of a room.

The cafes were running out.

At the end of the fourth long day of searching I climbed off the bike, exhausted. Tee kicked up the stand and turned the engine off.

'Still some cafes to see, Mr Ethan. Remember, Phnom Penh big place.' He smiled and his wonky teeth looked muddled and confused.

'I know, Tee. I know. I'm… I'm tired and I don't know whether this was all…' I looked at the floor and shook my head. 'I'm sorry.'

'Tomorrow it will happen, Mr Ethan, I can feel it! Davi

says she knows some places I haven't taken you and that they are plenty popular with *farang*.'

'Really?'

'Oh yes. And Davi very smart. She know things. So, lots of winks tonight and I will see you tomorrow, Mr Ethan. Yes?'

'Yes Tee. Same time tomorrow.' I paused. 'I hope you're right.'

'Davi always right. She a woman after all!'

I looked down at my hands but I had to say it. 'Listen, Tee. About your parents. I'm sorry I asked about them. It wasn't right for me to do that.'

Tee looked at me and smiled. 'It okay, Mr Ethan. You needed to see what happen in my country. My parents were good persons, I don't forget. Me and Davi have difficult life, not easiness for us. But I go towards tomorrow. Always chance of better day one day. You will see.' He kicked up the stand and drove off.

I meandered back into the hostel and had a quick look around the common room. Jon-Paul, Jacob and Leah were there, along with some of the others. Always the same. They were playing cards and bottles of BeerLao were sitting, business-like, beside them. I turned and walked back towards my room.

Since the first couple of evenings I had gradually distanced myself from the group. I usually went to dinner with them but spent little time with them before or after that. I had come back to the hostel after dinner on my own and sat by the lake for the past few evenings. The quiet of the common room while the others were out was incredible. I had the time to think. The quiet. I could order my thoughts, even if it meant thinking how little I had achieved since I had arrived in Phnom Penh.

Jon-Paul had started asking me to come out with him less and less. My lack of enthusiasm at first had seemed to confuse him, but he soon seemed to forget. He had turned his attention to a new pair of guys who had arrived at the hostel two days after me. They were Dutch, I think. They had fitted right in and instantly become part of the group. Theirs were the loudest voices heard at the hostel when they all got back each night.

After dinner the previous night, Elodie had seen me leaving and had asked if I minded her coming back to the hostel with me. I had been surprised but had said that she was welcome to, even though I had been underprepared for it. The evening had still been warm so we had decided to walk back, and surprisingly she had led the conversation the whole way. This had made the whole thing much easier for me to handle.

I enjoyed listening to the curving, rounded sound of Elodie's voice. She spoke with a mild hint of a French accent which I found comforting, soothing almost. When I asked her why she had the accent, she told me she had been born in the south of France. She had spent her early childhood on the south coast as an only child. At the age of seven, her family had followed her father's work and moved to England.

She had initially hated the move; she had hated everything in England. The climate and the London scenery, in particular. It had been too much of a change for her, it seemed. She had found the language complicated and had struggled at school.

When we had arrived back at the hostel we had gone to sit out by the lake. The sun had been setting a deep red. It was the colour of the warm, glowing embers that burn in the last moments of a fire. In this little bit of glowing quiet I had tried to write an aphorism and was getting close to one on beauty when Elodie had decided to speak again.

'So how long do you think you'll travel for, Ethan?'

I had refocused. 'I'm not sure. There are a few things I still want to do. How about you?'

'I've got to go home at the end of July, so I've got four or five months left.'

'Why have you got to go home?'

'My parents have organised a job for me. I'm going to be working for my dad's company.'

'Wow,' I said, raising my eyebrows. 'What kind of job is it?'

'My dad owns a marketing company and I've got a job lined up in the design department.'

'Sounds exciting.'

'Mmm, I don't know. It's such a cliché. It's not what I want to do. I kind of don't have a choice in the matter. My coming away for six months or so was the compromise. They bought me with this trip.'

'They *bought* you? What do you mean?'

'They paid for me to go travelling, to get it out of my system so I'd be ready to settle down and start a real job when I got back.'

'So they're paying for this entire trip?'

'Yep. Everything's going on the credit card. My dad thinks six months is enough to see the world; enough time to be young and free from responsibility.'

She had looked down at her hands, which were resting on her lap. 'I feel no guilt about spending their money, though. I know I'll have to pay it back in another way once I start this shitty job.'

Elodie had looked up and out over the lake. I had seen the final embers of the sun stuttering out of life in her eyes.

I had decided to change the subject. 'So where have you been so far on your trip?'

'Well, I arrived in Bangkok approximately three weeks ago, but instantly disliked it there. Too many people and there was no kind of soul to the place.'

I had nodded, feeling as though I agreed with her even though I had never been.

'So I left quickly and decided, on a whim, to go to Angkor Wat. I'm so glad I did. That place was amazing. I stayed there for nearly a week, looking around all the different temples. Have you been?'

'No.'

'Oh, you should. It's beautiful there. It's made from this stone that's all a mixture of earthy browns, darks and greys, with these faded patterns of white and green edging their way in.'

She edged in the colours with her hands in the air. 'It's not made from cold colours like European castles, but warm, almost live colours. As if the structures were carved naturally out of living earth and sun-baked in a giant kiln.

'I spent a week there but could easily have spent another day or two exploring other temples that were too far out to reach on my bike. Being there made me try to imagine what life would have been like back when it was built. Imagine being a spectator in a living, breathing temple full of Khmer people going about their lives. I would have loved to have seen it, in its original state.'

'It sounds impressive.'

'It really was. I loved it. I didn't know what to do after that. I thought of where to go, examined the guidebooks and here seemed the best option. So I got the bus here and that was roughly a week ago. To be honest, I'm not sure why I'm still here. I haven't decided where to go next, I suppose.'

'Don't you like it here very much?'

'No, not particularly. I feel like I'm filling time… not really *living*. I need to go somewhere new. I don't know…' Elodie had tapered off and sighed.

We had talked until the bluey red of the sky had turned to an inky black. The sun's fire had well and truly gone out by the time we had decided it was time to go to bed. Though it hadn't gone out, of course, it was warming someone else on the other side of the world. Maybe there was someone else in my position staring at the sun somewhere, watching it come up and wondering what the hell they were going to do with their lives.

Before we headed to bed, we had sat in silence looking out towards the lake. I had thought of my sister again and how she would have loved the view. Had she sat staring at this lake too? Or maybe, she was the other person staring at the sun on the other side of the world at that moment. I had really hoped she was.

Elodie had glanced at me for a moment and looked confused. At least, her eyebrows had been crumpled enough to suggest she was. I was still trying to get to know her. She had said good night and slowly climbed out of her chair.

I had stayed out there alone for a few more minutes and had finally come up with an aphorism before going to bed myself.

Maybe our lives aren't anywhere near as important as we think they are.

The following day had been another long one with Tee and I couldn't face the group in the common room when I got back. I fetched my keys from my rucksack as quickly as I could. As I opened the door to my room I heard Elodie's voice from down the corridor.

'Ethan?'

I turned to see her head and ponytail poking out of her bedroom door. 'Hi Elodie. Er... How's it going?'

She had a smile on her face and her cheeks had filled out as a result.

'I've got an idea.'

'Okay...' I said hesitantly.

'If you want, instead of going out with the others tonight for more godawful pizza, why don't I take you up on your suggestion and show you this really nice place I found a couple of days ago? It does great Cambodian food and there isn't a fake pizza in sight!' Elodie held her hands open as she asked.

I thought for a moment. I definitely had a mode that would cope with that situation. In fact, my social mode was strangely easy to employ around Elodie.

'Yeah, sure. That sounds nice.'

'Oh great! It's no fun eating on your own. Okay, er... What time do you want to go?'

'If you can give me quarter of an hour or so for a quick shower I'll be ready.'

'Okay, see you out the front in fifteen then.'

Elodie turned and nipped back into her room. I entered mine and hurried into the shower. I got dressed as quickly as I could and settled on the third T-shirt I tried on. I picked up my little rucksack with my guidebook in, left the room and closed the door behind me.

The air smelt good as I entered the street and saw Elodie waiting by the side of the road. She was playing with the dust in the road with her toe, her arms crossed around her middle.

20

I followed Elodie a short way up the road from our hostel. I had both hands in my pockets and walked almost beside her but a step behind as I tried to keep up. She walked quickly, with deliberate steps; the sort that belonged to a person who never simply walked anywhere without a goal in mind.

Back at home, I had enjoyed taking walks with nowhere in particular to go. Charlotte had sometimes come along in the old days. She had called it *zen walking*. The whole point of the walk, she would say, was that you had no particular place to go. How could you ever get more out of a walk than you expected unless you had no idea where you were going to end up? I wondered whether to tell Elodie about *zen walking* and whether she would think it was silly or not. I wasn't sure, so I decided to keep it for another time.

During our purposeful walk we moved up past the place I had met Tee for the first time. I kept an eye out for him but couldn't see him. We turned left soon after, sneaking up a narrow side road that was only just wide enough to walk through. After twenty metres Elodie turned and stopped in front of me.

'Here it is,' she announced, her eyebrows raised.

She ushered me towards her. The brick wall to my left had a chunk taken out of it and in that space, in the absence of wall, where the corridor widened, sat a restaurant. It was a fairly open place. Tarpaulin covered the ceiling but there was no front wall, which gave it an outdoor kind of feel. It was busy compared with the bricks that sat next to it, more bustling and complicated, and yet in a strange way it was also simpler. I thought of the number of bricks and the amount of effort that must have gone into building these walls, and of how these were just two walls in a world full of them. Thinking about it, this restaurant with the missing wall seemed to make the world a simpler place. It almost took away a little of the *depth*.

The place itself consisted of a collection of small wooden tables and chairs standing on the dusty floor. There were a number of *farangs* sitting around these tables, but I could also see several Cambodians.

'How did you find this place?' I asked.

'A girl who was staying at the hostel recommended it to me. It's pretty cool, huh?'

'Yeah, pretty cool,' I said, nodding.

My eyes wandered the tables and took in the food people were eating. A delicious sweet garlic and chilli smell filled the small space around us. Big bowls of steaming noodle soup and scented fried rice were being lifted into people's mouths with wooden chopsticks. The sizzle and hiss of steamers and woks bubbled beneath the sound of the various conversations taking place.

A waiter appeared from behind a dusty curtain at the

rear of the restaurant with plates of food. He saw us and gestured towards a table in the far corner.

We took our seats and looked together at the handwritten menu on the table. A list of dishes had been written in Cambodian on one side and English on the other. The handwriting was difficult to read; some of its curls and scrawls appeared to be in neither language. With a bit of guess work we soon picked up on the meaning of the odd translations. We talked about what looked good and what she had already tried before making our decisions. Elodie picked up the paper and pencil that had been placed on the table and wrote down our order.

'You order your own food and hand it in to the waiter. No mistakes that way. It's a great idea, isn't it? I think all restaurants should do it.'

The waiter walked in and out through the curtain continuously, but he saw our order and took it into the kitchen with him.

'They cook everything to order, so I hope you're not in too much of a hurry!'

Elodie smiled as she said this. Looking around her, she tucked her hands under her thighs. 'So, what do you think?'

'It's great, Elodie. Really. So different from the other places.'

'Yeah, I hate those other places. Lucio's especially.' Elodie sighed. 'Oh, I'm hungry now after all that talk of food. I hope it's not too long!'

Our bottles of Coke arrived and we both put our straws to our mouths and took long sips. I held my ice cold bottle and, as the sweet bubbles fizzed up my nose, I turned my head to have a look around the restaurant. The people eating here were much quieter than any others I had seen so far in Phnom Penh. The lighting was low and there was no music. The sounds from the busy road could only be heard faintly in the background. I almost forgot that it was there.

The walls were crumbling brick and had the occasional strange, framed picture of Elvis or the Beatles hanging at crooked angles. I was looking at one such picture – a black-and-white print of Paul McCartney wearing a sugary smile – when I saw it out the corner of my eye. I stared at it hard. The lighting was dim, so I squinted just to be sure that I wasn't mistaken. I leaned over in my chair.

'You okay, Ethan?'

'Yeah, I just need to go check on...' I stood up and walked over to the other side of the room. I excused myself and squeezed past the couple sitting next to the wall and stood as close as I could to it. I wasn't wrong. It did bear the words I had been searching for.

Everything rushed around my body at the same time. I was fizzing, bursting, peaking. And yet I was perfectly still. Time dropped away around me; an iceberg breaking from a melting glacier. I stood calm and serene as it floated off into the distance. This was it. It had to be.

I read the words again.

Volunteer English Teachers Wanted.

I scanned the small print beneath this and took in some of the details, although most of them washed over me. This was *the* poster. I had found it. Four days of searching and here it was. But this wasn't a cafe. Why was it here? Did that mean it wasn't the same one? What if other schools were advertising for volunteers? I stood still, staring through the poster, my mind running too fast.

I remembered Elodie and turned to see her looking at me and biting on her straw. She looked worried. I knew I had to tell her. I had thought that I might tell her before that night, but at this point there was no choice. I carefully peeled the poster off the wall and took it back to the table with me.

'Are you okay? What's going on?' She looked down at her Coke bottle. 'If you don't want to eat with me just say so.'

'Oh no, it's not that. I'm sorry. I saw this poster and had to look at it. There's something I have to tell you about why I'm here in Cambodia. It's not for a holiday… I have a… reason why I'm here.'

I told Elodie the whole story. Our food arrived as I spoke and we both ate slowly between my explanations and her questions. The salty spice of my noodles tasted better with every mouthful. When I had finished explaining, Elodie reached over and gently brushed her hand over mine.

'Ethan, I'm so happy you've found the poster. I can't imagine how you must have felt the last few months.'

'I'm happy too. I am. I'm worried this might not be the real thing. This isn't a cafe, after all. It's a restaurant. In her email she said she saw the poster in a cafe. What if this isn't the place?'

'Well, this place is called Sweet House Cafe. Maybe that's what she meant when she said she said she had seen it in a cafe.'

'Really? Is that what it's called?'

'Yes, really! At least, that's what the girl at the hostel told me.'

'Oh, that's great!' I puffed some air out of my cheeks. 'Well, it looks like I'm going to be getting out of Phnom Penh. It's funny. It feels like I've only just arrived. I guess… I guess I know where I'm going tomorrow.'

I looked at the poster as I held it in my hands. There was a black-and-white picture of a young *farang* couple crouching down in front of a classful of Cambodian school children. The couple had their arms around each other. It looked as though the sun was shining in their faces. The children were holding exercise books. Everyone was smiling.

'Where is it?' asked Elodie.

'It says it's near a place called Angk Ta Saom. Do you know it?'

'No'

'Me neither. Well it's got directions for how to get there on the poster. Apparently I need to head to the main bus terminal and go from there. Once I get there I have to find a moto driver and ask for the place.'

'Sounds complicated.'

'Yeah, I've got no idea how long it'll take.' I stopped for a moment as I became aware of what I was saying. 'I hope I can get there.'

Elodie picked up her Coke bottle and examined it. 'You know, if you'd like some help finding it and you wouldn't mind the company I'd love to go with you. I've been looking to go somewhere else for a while now. Of course, if you want to do this on your own I'd understand.'

She raised her eyes and they caught mine for a moment. They were as green as a lost leaf in a forest.

This kind of thing never happened to me.

'No, I'd love the company,' I said, grabbing hold of her words. 'That would be great, Elodie. Thanks!'

We both smiled – big, bold, open smiles – and for a brief moment I thought of the couple in the picture.

That night we headed back to the hostel and agreed to go to bed early so we would be ready to leave as soon as possible the next day. The hostel was deserted when we got in and we were mice in the corridor as we said our goodnights. I walked past the mirror on the way to my room and leaned in to take a look.

I couldn't sleep that night. My mind was full of possibilities. As I lay awake I could hear the hustle and bustle of the city outside; the dull, conflicting beats of nearby sound systems; the scattered voices, joking and laughing in nearby rooms; the clinking of metal and china; the jingle jangle of cutlery and glass; the tempered roar of tuk-tuks and taxis; and the buzz of unlimited fans and partisan air con. There was the hum; the indistinguishable hum that rises like smoke out of the city. A noise, a continuous heartbeat, pulsing and flowing; giving the life to the place. Attempting meditation was hopeless. To keep my mind occupied, I tried to imagine what would happen if the hum were to stop.

I got up at six the next morning having hardly closed my eyes. When I opened my door the hostel was still empty, as it had been the night before. I crept out of my room and turned to see that Elodie was already waiting for me in the corridor.

'Morning!' she said, only just containing the words in a whisper.

'Morning,' I whispered back. 'Ready to go?'

'Yeah, let's get out of here!'

As we picked up our bags, a figure came crashing through the front door and into the corridor. He fell over and lay on the floor for a moment.

'Shit! Fuck me!' he yelled.

'Jon-Paul?' I said, tilting my head to get a better look. 'Who's that?'

Jon-Paul picked himself up off the floor and stared at me. 'Ethan! Christ, buddy! How you doing? How was your night?'

'I'm just off, actually...'

'Had a crazy one tonight, I can tell you! Had a Lucio's happy special, which was fucking awesome by the way, and we went out... where after that? To be honest, buddy, I can't remember much after that. Fuck, how did I get home? Shit, man! Must have been a good night, eh?'

'Yeah, sure. Listen, thanks for all your help Jon-Paul, It's been great. I'm heading off...'

'Listen. Listen.' He held his hand on my shoulder and stumbled into me. 'You know, don't you? None of this,' his arm pointed around the room as he wobbled, 'none of this fucking... shit. None of this shit matters.'

'I...'

'She doesn't love me, you know. She told me. Before I left. Over fucking dinner, she tells me. She says it isn't going to work. It wasn't right. Drinking, you see? *Drinking*. People don't change, she says. What the fuck! What does that even *mean*? What can I do? Tell me, what can I *do*?" He pointed his finger at me. 'She didn't have a fucking answer. Well, fuck her. You know?'

'I'm not sure...'

'Okay, okay...' He pulled away again. 'Fucking life, right? *Life*. Shit! Am I right or am I right? No problem, buddy. See you in the morning. I gotta hydrate, seriously!'

Jon-Paul stumbled past Elodie and half-tripped over my bag before continuing on towards the common room. There was a loud crash inside.

'Fuck!' he shouted.

Elodie and I waited for a moment, both looking in the direction from which the noise had come.

After a silence, I turned back to face her. 'Do you think he'll be okay?'

'He has been every other night, hasn't he?'

'Yeah, I'm sure you're right. Shall we go?'

'Definitely.'

We walked out into the cool early morning air of Phnom Penh. I asked Elodie to wait with the bags for a moment and had a quick look to see if I could find Tee, even though I knew he probably wasn't there. After looking up and down the street I wandered back towards Elodie.

'Is everything okay?' she asked.

'Yeah, I was hoping to say goodbye to the guy who's been driving me around for the last few days, but I can't find him. I wanted to tell him about the poster.'

'I'm sorry he's not there, Ethan.'

Elodie was fiddling with something on her rucksack.

'It's nice that you want to tell him about the poster though. You were lucky to find such a nice moto driver. Most of them are out to rip you off. I remember the first guy who tried to give me a tour tried to charge me fifteen dollars a day! What a joke!'

I was confused by Elodie's words. 'That's not much, surely? That's only approximately eight pounds or something for a day's work. That's nothing.'

'It's a *lot* of money for here, Ethan. He knew what he was doing. Don't forget that the cost of living is much cheaper. If you haggle it'll cost you six or seven dollars for a day's ride at most.'

I frowned as my feelings from the last few days fell down around me. 'Tee was charging me twenty dollars a day. He said that was a local's rate. A special rate because I wasn't just another fat tourist. Because he wanted to help me.'

'Twenty! Phew!' She puffed out her cheeks. 'None of the locals would pay anything near that!' Elodie smiled, but her face changed when she saw my expression.

'Oh...' was all I managed to say. I hated myself a tiny bit more.

'I think we'll have to get going if we want to get the bus,' she said.

Elodie was still looking at me and trying to change the subject, but I could only look at the ground and think of Tee's smiling persistence. Of course he wanted to take on my job. It meant endless days getting paid to travel between cafes talking to his mates. I had thought that he was easy to read.

'I thought he was my friend,' I said.

'Oh...' was all Elodie managed to say this time.

There was a pause. 'I'm sorry, Ethan. Maybe he was your friend. Maybe he needed the money.'

'Maybe.' I chewed off some of the dead skin from my lip and thought about Davi. Had she had meant anything she had said to me? She probably hadn't. How could she? Why would she? She had seemed so honest. So *sure.*

Maybe it was *a* truth that they cared, but *another* that they needed the money. But that didn't help me feel any better.

After a minute of us both standing at the side of the road without saying anything, Elodie put her hand on my arm.

'Forget it, Ethan. It's not your fault. Come on. We need to go get this bus, yes? We've got a sister to find!'

She smiled at me and the image of the couple in the poster appeared in my head again.

'Okay,' I said, sighing.

I took one last look down the street before putting my bag on my back. As we began the walk to the bus station I worried briefly that I had forgotten something in my room. I rearranged the bag by shuffling my shoulders so that the straps were more comfortable and took a slow, deep breath. Another aphorism popped into my head, but it came straight from the dark place so I tried to ignore it. The trouble is, I've never been good at keeping my dark place in check.

People will ruin you any chance they get.

I hoped that wasn't *the* truth. I had only just met Elodie.

Part 2

'Hello. Four-three-seven-one.'

'Ethan, is that you?'

'Yes.'

'Thank God! I thought you might have been Dad for a minute.'

'Really?'

'Yeah, you sound a lot like him on the phone.'

'Really?'

'Yes, really! Unfortunate, I know. Anyway, how's my little brother?'

'I'm okay. Where are you? Mum and Dad are going mental. They've been shouting at each other all week since you've been gone.'

'No change there then. You should be used to it by now.'

'Yeah, but this is different. Where are you?'

'If I tell you where I am you've got to promise me you're not going to tell them.'

'Why not? They're worried, Lottie. I've never seen them like this before.'

'Well they'll get used to it, I'm sure. I'm serious though, Ethan. If I tell you where I am you can't go running to Mum and Dad with this. I don't want them to know yet. You've got to be strong, pretend you don't know. I'll tell them when I'm ready.'

'Okay.'

'Promise?'

'Yeah, I promise. Where are you?'

'I'm in Thailand.'

'Thailand? Jesus, Charlotte! They think you've gone to stay with a friend or something!'

'Good, that'll give me a bit more time.'

'Time for what? Why are you in Thailand? When are you coming home? You know uni starts in a week. Dad's flipping out.'

'I know. That's part of the reason I went away. I can't face uni. I can't face that life any more.'

'What do you mean?'

'Everything, anything. I can't face it. I just had to leave.'

'Why?'

'I had to get out. Dad sat me down and gave me one of his lectures.'

'Oh God!'

'He was talking about university and the importance of study and hard work, and what I should do if I wanted to make something of my life. And the whole time he was talking I couldn't help but stare out of the window at the garden. It was weird. It looked so intricate, so delicate. Like an undiscovered forest. It had never looked like that before. All the green leaves were brushing the sky and they were surrounded by this warm blue colour that floated in the background. It was as if a thousand lights from the sun broke through the moving trees with every word Dad said, sparkling and illuminating the French windows. Wind-up birds were chirping as if powered by clockwork in the background.

'Dad carried on evangelising and I pictured the insects on every branch of the trees, tiny and small, free to crawl, to climb and to explore. As I looked out the window, life filled that one square of the room. You couldn't imagine it, Ethan. The windows glowed and shone. It was as if my insides had been painted onto the world right there. It was such a warm and powerful sight I had this feeling like I wanted to cry. But all that warmth, all that power couldn't penetrate inside that house. Do you understand me, Ethan?'

'I don't know. I'm not really sure.'

'The coldness of that room and all of Dad's words soaked up the trees, the leaves, the warmth. It mopped up the parts of me that nearly made it through – the sun, the branches, the birds – 'til there was nothing left. It was all stuck outside and I was cold and alone in the dark. Dad kept on talking and all I could look at was the window. And then I saw it. You wouldn't believe it, Ethan, you really wouldn't. A blue tit landed on the windowsill.'

'A blue tit?'

'Yes. This beautiful, perfect little bird. Its head and wings were so blue, honestly. Blue like the ocean. Blue like the sky. And it had this patch of yellow on its breast that shone like the sun. I don't think I'd ever looked at one before. And I couldn't believe what it did.'

'What?'

'It turned its head and looked in.'

'Really?'

'Yeah. This little dot of colour in the dark just sitting there, staring at me through the window. Looking right at me, it began to sing.'

'Wow!'

'And my heart, Ethan, it just, I don't know. It was like my heart could hear it singing. Loud, clear and purposeful. It was calling to me. And everything grew louder. I could hear the birds and the branches in the breeze. I could hear the insects and the leaves. I could hear the clouds collide and merge. I could hear every sunray break as it hit the trees. And the light that was stuck in the windows sprinted and flooded into the room. Before the cold could steal it and take it away from me I leapt up to catch it. As the bird flew off I felt like, standing there, I was somehow holding on to the world. It was amazing. And I just knew.'

'Knew what?'

'That life was so much bigger than this. That I couldn't go to university and study for three more years to get something I didn't want. That the world was something to be loved and not just lived through. So I stood up and left the room. I can't explain it any better than that.'

'You stood up and left?'

'Yes.'

'What did Dad say?'

'I don't know, I wasn't listening. He was shouting something, but he couldn't stop me, Ethan. He can't take the world from me any more. It's inside me and I've got to be out and among it. I've got to *live* it. That evening when we were out in the park I had already bought my tickets for the next day.'

'Oh, I thought you were a bit funny that night. Why didn't you tell me? How did you afford the ticket to Thailand, anyway?'

'Well I've been saving for a while from the cafe job and now I'm eighteen that money from Great-Aunt Wendy came through. It was more than enough to get me a flight to Bangkok.'

'So what are you going to do now?'

'I don't know for sure yet. This first week has gone so fast. I've met a really nice Swedish couple and I'm going down to one of the islands with them tomorrow. It's so beautiful here, Ethan. You'd love it.'

'It all sounds so exciting. England is so boring. Maybe I could come and visit you.'

'Maybe one day, but not yet. I need to be on my own for a while. I hope you understand.'

'I guess so.'

'Look, I've got to go. My money's running out.'

'Oh.'

'I wanted to explain to you, Ethan. I needed you to understand why I went. I hope you can be happy for me and that you'll be okay without me.'

'I wish you hadn't gone. It's horrible at home at the moment.'

'I'm sorry. Understand that this is something I've got to do. Remember that question I mentioned?'

'About the stars?'

'Yeah, don't forget it. I'm serious. It'll keep you going 'til you can come visit me someday.'

'Yeah.'

'Bye. I'll contact Mum and Dad soon and let them know where I am. Gotta go.'

'Bye. Just tell me quick, what do you mean holding on to the world? Charlotte? Charlotte?'

21

Seija leant over in her hammock and passed me the joint. She tipped her perfect neck back and looked up at the ceiling above her. Placing her hands behind her head, she exhaled slowly.

'Charlotte's little brother. Christ.' She gently shook her head, 'I still can't believe it.' Smiling to herself, she crossed her legs. Her smooth skin caught the moonlight. 'Unbelievable.'

That day had gone by in a haze; so fast it had only just begun. And yet there I was, lying in a hammock underneath Mr Kim's house next to Seija, the girl from my sister's email.

The journey from Phnom Penh had been easier than I had thought it would be, though perhaps I had unfairly imagined it to be something of an impossible trip.

Elodie and I had said little to each other after we had taken our seats on the bus. I had fought hard not to slip into my self-preservation mode and tried to focus properly on the scenery that was passing by the window. Travelling out of the capital, the concrete blocks and busy roads had soon given way to farming huts and rural countryside.

Everything was dry and dusty. The orange dust an ultra-fine blanket or a filtered lens through which we had to view the world.

The first leg of our journey had ended at a place called Kampot. This was where the relative luxury of a full-sized coach had left us. We had pulled up in line with several other colourful coaches and everyone on board had begun to pour out.

When we had eventually stepped off the bus we had been pounced upon by the local minibus drivers, all of whom had tried to shepherd us in their direction. There had been a moment of confusion as neither Elodie nor I could understand where these bus drivers were going. Thinking of my arrival in Phnom Penh, I had tried to remember Jon-Paul's advice, but was so unsure of myself that any confidence I may have had got lost among the loud voices and the clamour. I had begun to use the exchange rate to calculate the price of the bus in my head.

Fortunately, Elodie had managed to explain, through pointing and the use of a map in my guide book, that we wanted to go to Angk Ta Saom. Once the drivers heard this they had all seemed quite surprised. They hadn't believed Elodie initially and I had been no help when it came to convincing them otherwise. It had taken a little while, but Elodie was strong-willed and soon enough we had been bundled into a nearby minibus that already seemed to be full. I had been impressed by her. She was so small and yet she had a big *presence*. It was a different kind of presence from Davi's. More intense. More fragile. More honest, perhaps. I hoped so. We had waited ten more minutes before the minibus moved off.

Several stops, many new passengers and an hour and a half later, the minibus had pulled over. The driver had got out and shouted 'Angk Ta Saom!' to us before sliding open the door.

We had mountaineered our way out of the bus, over all the people and their bags, and had been left by the side of the road. As the bus had driven off, it had covered us in a layer of the orange dust that already covered everything else. It was omnipresent, clinging to my sweat and coating every part of me.

Standing by the side of a road in an unknown part of a foreign country, I had started to try doing calculations again. Elodie, looking around her, had spotted some men with motos on the other side of the road. Soon enough, a couple of them had looked up, seen us and crossed over.

Elodie had given them the name of the school – ETP – and one of the men had smiled, signalling with a nod that he knew the way. We had climbed onto a couple of motos and ridden off into the dust.

The landscape was dry, barren and alien in its sparseness. Rice fields were all churned up with dry soil. Solitary trees dotted the fields and shot out of the ground almost vertically, as if they were planted wooden poles. Their leaves unfurled in a ball of green feathers at the top and they stood proud, hovering above the brown earth beneath them. The trees sprouted, sporadic and sparse.

It had been a strange scene to look at as we sped along the baked-mud, single-track roads, and I hadn't been able to take my eyes off it. It had been beautiful to me, though I didn't know why.

I had imagined what it would be like during the rainy season. Full of life and as bright as a green colour from a cheap child's paint palette. Stunning in its rejuvenation and growth.

The world as it should be.

After half an hour we had slowed down and turned right onto a narrow, windy path that cut between a group of shrubs. We had soon driven through a gate and stopped in an open patch of land outside a house. A cow had been standing in the dust in front of us. It was angular and bony, its skin drawn over it like a drum. It had looked at me for a moment, its eyes all black and sort of dead. I had blinked and the cow looked away, turning back to the small pile of dried grass in front of it. The moto driver had kicked up the stand and ushered me off the bike.

I hadn't been sure what to expect of ETP. I hadn't known whether it would be a school similar to those in the UK or some kind of shelter for children. Or whether it would be another backpacker central like in Phnom Penh. Or simply a deserted hole. In fact, we had arrived at somebody's home.

The house was raised on stilts, as seemed to be the custom in the area, and had the familiar, box-like shape and design I had seen throughout the bike journey. However, the front of the house had been adapted. It contained a small classroom area with a chalkboard, a world map, a wooden table and some tiny plastic chairs.

We walked towards this area and saw that there were a couple of hammocks swinging beneath the building, between the stilts. As we looked over we had seen a table and chairs next to them, occupied by six *farangs* and a few local kids. Their shouts and cheers had revealed that they were playing snap.

We had walked over and introduced ourselves to the *farangs*, who had stared up at us from their game with a look of surprise. They had put their cards down and stood up to say hello. There was a Finnish couple, Mimi and Filip; three English lads, Liam, Craig and James; and a Swedish girl, Seija.

Sieja had carried the conversation, which was initially a little stunted, and had continued to talk after everyone had made their introductions. She had explained that Mr Kim, the man whose house it was, and who ran the school, was out at a cock fight, but that he would be back later on for dinner. She had told us to dump our bags and follow her around for a quick tour.

Mr Kim's house, it seemed, was fairly self-sufficient. He owned three pigs, five or six chickens, and the cow that had stared at us on arrival. They all roamed freely around the small grounds of the house. Two noisy dogs had been employed to keep the other animals in check, but they weren't doing much good as they tussled around the front yard. The hammocks were ideal for keeping cool in the hot days, Seija had explained.

Around the back of the house there was a half-built toilet and washing area. Within a waist-height wall was a bricked-in, tiny square pool of water for washing, which was refreshed every day from the lake up the road. There was also a donated porcelain squat toilet. This, apparently, was the envy of the village, where holes in the ground were the norm. A cooking area sat nearby. It was a simple brick pit with a metal grill.

To the side of the house were the beginnings of what we were told was to become an orphanage. It was the outer walls of a small brick building, which Mr Kim intended to use to house local orphans and give them an education. It didn't yet have a door or even a roof because apparently the money had run out. It looked sad sitting there without a purpose, derelict and as dusty as everything else.

The house itself was reached via a short, steep set of wooden steps at the front. Climbing in through the front door, a dark space suspended from the world by stilts had opened up in front of me. I had been surprised to find that it contained one large room. There was a small walkway down the middle, with a collection of sheets hanging from thin lines either side to create 'private' spaces. Within these hanging cubicles I had seen small collections of belongings, roll mats, backpacks and books, all of which were half-disguised through the thin sheets. It was a small space and had been stuffy in the afternoon sun.

I had carried our bags into the house and laid them out in the only spare cubicle. It was small, but big enough for two people to sleep side by side. This meant I would be sleeping next to Elodie. I had hoped she would be okay with the arrangement. She would have to be, I had concluded, because there was nowhere else to sleep. If anyone else had arrived they would have had to sleep outside.

Talking to Seija, I had soon realised she played the role of mother hen to everyone else there. She was well respected and helped the others out. Having been there for some time she seemed to know everything that was going on and I could tell she had a position of responsibility at ETP. Not an appointed one, but one that was recognised by those who met her there, myself included. The others had been there for varying amounts of time, but none for more than ten days apart from Seija. It seemed there was a high turnover of volunteers because the lifestyle was difficult to adjust to.

'A lot of people come here expecting electricity, running water and a bar around the corner,' Seija had explained, 'but they're pretty surprised by what they get. A hard wooden floor, squat toilet and no shower aren't everyone's idea of a good time.'

The English lads had begun talking to Elodie and Seija had turned to me and asked me where I had been and how long I was intending to stay. I had struggled to believe that she was talking to me and had been doing my best to keep up my social mode. Elodie had looked over every now and again, darting her eyes over at Seija before returning them to the conversation in front of her.

Seija shone out from the world as a 3-D image on a 2-D landscape. She was beautiful. It was *the* truth. It had to be, because it was impossible not to notice. As we talked, her long, untidy blonde hair had hung loosely over her shoulders. She had drawn some of it back from her forehead with a clip so that it lay smooth among the long waves around it. She had freckles from the sun and they decorated her cheeks and nose as if they were dots in an impressionist painting. Her blue eyes were framed by her blonde eyebrows and long lashes. Her Scandinavian features were unmistakable, and yet she had something unique. Something different. Even though she wore no makeup and had tangled, unwashed hair, it had been difficult for me not to secretly delight in the way she looked.

Hearing her talk I had been listening to sunshine. She had talked of the world as though she was in love with it. It was instantly infectious being around her. In those first moments my world was a better place when she was near. It was odd, but I couldn't explain it any better than that. She had an instant effect on me and I had loved talking to her.

'You must like it here if you've been here for so long?' I had said at the beginning of our conversation, once I had mustered the courage to speak.

'Yes, it's so satisfying doing this every day. It's like charity, but with instant results you can see with your own eyes. I love it. I love the lifestyle, the people, the kids. The whole thing. It's made me a better person being here, I'm sure of it.'

'How long are you intending to stay?' Once I had asked one question and felt that it had been a success, others gurgled embarrassingly out of me. 'Don't you get lonely? Don't you miss home? How did you adjust?'

'I don't know. I tend to take every day as it comes. I don't miss home so much. I don't miss places. I miss people sometimes. My sister, my parents, my friends. But then I miss friends I've made out here too. The only sad thing about being here is that everyone moves on.'

'You must have seen lots of people come and go in your time here, I suppose.'

'Yes, loads. I've made some very good friends out here. I miss them a lot.'

I had wanted to ask and had found no mode to hold me back. Even if she didn't know Charlotte, she might find my reason for being there *heroic* in some way. Brave. Impressive. Tee and Elodie had seemed to think so.

163

But Tee was a liar.

I had caught another glimpse of her freckles, so beautiful on her skin, and decided that nothing so perfect could have any reason to ruin anything.

'I don't suppose you met someone called Charlotte out here, did you? She would have been here a while ago now.'

'Charlotte? Yes, I came here with a girl called Charlotte.'

'You did?' I had forgotten the freckles. 'Was she English? Was she here recently? Do you know her surname by any chance?'

'Yes, she was English. It was… what was it? Willis, I think.'

'Charlotte Willis?'

'Yes, that's her. Why? Do you know her?'

I had been amazed. 'She's my sister!'

'No way! Really?' She had looked at me from a different angle. 'Really?'

'Yes!'

Everything had fallen into place. My memory had kicked in. The email. Seija, the friend who had taught Charlotte about the world and taken her to the teaching place. The beautiful one. How right Charlotte had been. This was *her*. I was talking to the girl who had left Phnom Penh with my sister.

The next few hours had galloped past in a fever of my own excitement. Seija and I had talked about Charlotte: what she was like, what they had done together, when she had left, whether she had spoken of me. The words she had used to describe her time with Charlotte drifted from her mouth and I had breathed them in deeply, every one.

As if I had needed any more of a reason to want to be near her.

The sun had begun to settle behind the house and the red sky had rose-tinted the scene around us. I was sitting in a postcard. I hadn't smiled or laughed like that for a long time.

I don't know how long we had been talking for when the noise of an engine had made me look up. A moto, piled up with boxes, had pulled into the front yard.

'Supplies,' Seija had said as she stood up to help unload food from the moto. I had turned and looked around for Elodie. She hadn't been there. Worried for a moment, I had asked Liam where Elodie had gone.

'She went inside, mate. She said she was tired from the journey. Think she's going to have a lie down.'

Liam had a thick northern accent. I had liked the way it sounded.

'Oh okay, thanks. I might go and check she's okay.'

'All right, mate. See you in a bit. We'll be eating in a bit, as soon as Mr Kim's back, just so you know.'

'All right, I'll be back in a minute. Thanks.'

I had stood and climbed the steps up to the house. Elodie had been lying on her roll mat in our cubicle. Through the sheet I had seen that her eyes were open, but when she saw me she closed them and turned away.

'Hey, is everything okay?' I had pushed the sheet to one side and sat down next to her.

'Yes. I'm fine. I'm just tired. I'd like to get some rest if that's okay.'

'Okay. Sure. You'll never guess what. Seija knows my sister! Can you believe it?'

165

'That's great,' she had said, still facing away from me.

'Yeah. I still can't believe it. It means I'm making progress, real progress, for the first time in so long. And Seija's great. She's been telling me all sorts of stuff about Charlotte. I think they were close.'

'That's good, Ethan.'

'Yeah, it's unbelievable. I've got so much to find out. Hopefully Seija might know where Charlotte was planning to go next. I should've asked that. I'll do it at dinner. Dinner's going to be soon, apparently.'

'I'm not hungry.' Elodie's eyes had remained focused on the clouded, glassy sheet that was hanging still in front of her.

'Oh. Well, shall I call you when Mr Kim arrives?'

'No, I'll be fine.'

'Wouldn't you like to meet him? It sounds as if he is a pretty amazing guy. We could both talk to him at dinner.'

'Ethan, you've obviously got enough friends to talk to tonight. Go have dinner with them. I'm sure Seija will be more than happy to talk to you more. You don't need me there.'

'Okay. I thought you might be hungry, that's all. Are you sure you're okay?'

'I'm fine.'

'Okay, see you later on.'

I had climbed down the steps and looked back to see Elodie curl her legs up and wrap her arms around her waist. As I lingered on the stairs, a man had arrived on the back of a moto. He had looked over at the house and I had walked down the last few steps towards him. It was Mr Kim.

Mr Kim had an angular face. His eyes were small and dark and sat either side of a wide, flat nose. His mouth was small and was oddly outsized by a square jawline that protruded like scaffolding from his neck. He had thick, greasy black hair. As he had walked towards the house he was wearing a plain, dark-collared shirt and a pair of navy blue shorts. The shorts had revealed a wooden leg, beginning at the knee, on his left side. A large wooden foot, with toes carved into it, had walked in the dust alongside a solitary leather shoe.

'Mr Kim, we have some new volunteers,' Seija had said as he approached us by the steps.

'Good, good. I hope you're making yourselves at home.' He had kept walking around to the rear of the house as he said this.

'Oh yes we are, thank you.' I had said, unsure of what else to say.

'I will come to you and say hello in a moment. I believe my wife should have dinner ready for us now.' He had continued walking round the side of the house until I couldn't see him.

'Come, sit. Natakan will bring the food out in a moment now that Mr Kim is back.' Seija had ushered me to the table. 'Is Elodie coming down for some food?'

'No, I think she's tired and wants to rest at the moment.'

'Okay, well we have a few biscuits for later if she gets hungry.'

We had been joined by the other volunteers as we sat down at the table. As soon as we were all seated, Natakan, Mr Kim's wife, had arrived with the food. She was a small, quiet lady who kept her eyes down as she laid out our plates. Her short, dark hair hung behind her ears. She had deep-set brown eyes that looked tired. Everyone thanked her, but she had offered no reply.

We had each had a plate with an omelette in the centre and unidentified greens on the side. A large pot of rice had sat in the middle of the table, which we had shared.

Mr Kim had soon joined us. He had asked my name and where I was from. He had said little after this and eaten his food with speed and intent. The atmosphere around the table had been a jovial one. As I ate my omelette, which contained a delicious combination of onions, chilli, garlic and peanuts, I had laughed and smiled at the conversation around me without having to worry how to employ any modes. Liam, Craig and James were funny guys and had competed with each other to be the centre of attention, which suited me fine.

Mr Kim had disappeared soon after he had finished eating and had briefly mentioned money. I hadn't thought it would cost anything to stay there, but it did. Five dollars a day, plus any donation I was willing to make towards the orphanage. I had explained that I would pass on the information to Elodie and that we would pay him at breakfast the next morning.

He had left the table and, as we all ate our last mouthfuls, Natakan had come to clear away the plates. The one and only light bulb, powered by a car battery, had been switched on by the entrance to the house. Mimi and Filip had said their goodnights and climbed the steps into their makeshift bedroom. I had silently retired to a hammock as Liam, Craig and James continued their conversation together at the table. Loud laughter had punctuated their words.

Seija had walked over and climbed into the hammock next to me. She had lit a joint and started swaying herself gently from side to side. My hammock had moved a little from the vibrations of hers.

'Unbelievable,' she had said.

That was the beginning of the end of a long day.

We talked for a little longer, but after taking a few drags of the joint she had passed me my eyes were beginning to close. I wanted to stay up. I had so many questions to ask and her undivided attention, but I couldn't keep my concentration.

I also knew that I could have written an encyclopaedia of aphorisms about Seija, but I didn't have the focus to do it. I made my excuses and went up to the house.

As I slid into my sleeping bag and lay on my back on the wooden floor, Elodie turned towards me. I hadn't realised she was still awake. Without looking at me, she lightly rested her hand on my stomach. I turned my head to look at her.

'I'm happy you've found something out about your sister, Ethan, I really am,' she whispered quietly. 'It's wonderful news. I'm sorry I was a bit grumpy earlier. I was tired, that's all.'

'That's okay, don't worry about it. I'll fill you in on everything tomorrow.'

'Okay, night night.'

'Night night.'

As I lay there with Elodie's warm hand resting on my stomach, I thought of everything that had happened over the previous five days. How far I had come. How much closer I felt to Charlotte. It *was* unbelievable.

The sheets hung, womb-like, around me and I soon fell into a deep sleep.

22

I awoke too early the next morning to the sound of crowing. Loud, incessant crowing from Mr Kim's cockerels, who were right underneath me. As I opened my eyes it was light in the house, but still cool. I stretched out my arms and felt a sharp pain down my back. The wooden floor was hard and uncomfortable. Twice in the night I had woken up as I had tried to turn over. The roll mat I was lying on had done little to help. No better than cushioning a punch with a glove, it still bloody hurt. I looked over and saw that Elodie was still asleep. I thought of the hand she had put on my stomach.

Outside, I could hear Seija and the others' voices. I sat up and rubbed my eyes. It was time to get up. I climbed down the steps with my washbag and saw the other volunteers sitting at the table eating breakfast. Noodle soup. It smelt good. I didn't know whether I should stop and talk to them or head straight for the bathroom. Fortunately, as I stood there, James looked up and made the decision for me.

'Morning!' he said. 'How did you sleep?'

'Okay. Not great. That floor's pretty hard, isn't it?'

'Aye, it sure is, fella! You get used to it after a few nights, don't worry. It's probably good for you in the long run! Things that make you feel like shit usually are! At least, that's what I'm telling myself. You want some breakfast?'

'Yeah, I'm...' I was consciously unaware of how I looked. 'I'm going to have a wash first, I think. I need to wake up. Is that okay?'

'Sure, your noodles might be a bit cold but it won't make much difference, they'll still taste the same. Plain and watery, just how I like them! Is Elodie awake yet?'

'No, not yet.'

'Well she'll need to get up soon if she wants something to eat, I'm afraid. Classes start in an hour and Natakan cleans everything up before school starts. That includes the food, whether it's been eaten or not!'

'Okay, I'll wake her and let her know. Thanks.'

I climbed back up the steps and woke Elodie. She sat up and looked a little confused as I spoke to her.

'Okay, I'll be down in a minute,' she said, ruffling her hair. 'What are we doing today, do you know?'

'Not really. School starts in an hour, so I guess we'll find out. I'm going for a wash, so I'll see you downstairs in a bit.'

'Okay,' she yawned. 'Thanks Ethan.'

'Sure.'

Washing with cool, stagnant water the dust dripped off me and, drying my face with my towel, I was new. I had shed an old skin. I brushed my teeth using bottled water and wandered back to join the others.

Elodie was eating a bowl of noodles hungrily. Craig was performing a card trick with her, giving her his full attention. She watched and smiled when he revealed the card she had chosen. As I approached the table she looked up at me and grinned.

'You should see Craig's trick,' she said with a mouthful of noodles. 'It's really good!'

I pulled out a chair and sat down.

'Here, have some cold instant noodles,' Craig said. 'Unfortunately, they're not quite as awesome as they sound!'

Elodie laughed and Craig handed me a bowl.

'Are you teaching today, Craig?' Elodie asked.

I grabbed a spoon and started eating. The noodles reminded me of lunches I had eaten during the summer holidays back home.

'Yep. Same time as usual. We normally teach two lessons in the morning and one in the afternoon. Not a lot gets done in the time between morning and late afternoon, it's too hot. The first lesson starts at seven thirty and lasts about an hour. That's with the intermediates and teenagers who aren't at school any more. Then we go to the school in the village and spend an hour teaching the teachers there at eleven, when the kids are having their midday break. The next lesson is at three thirty in the village. That one's for any schoolkids who want extra English after they've finished for the day.'

'So it's just three lessons a day?'

'Yep. Three lessons a day. You teach whoever turns up.'

'What do you teach them?' asked Elodie with a splash of noodle juice on her chin.

'Whatever you like. Anything English.'

'Such as?'

'Well, we've just finished doing colours with them and we're going on to do days of the week next. The people who left a couple of days ago had done numbers and letters. There's no real system to what you teach, you just do what you want. I think they get stuff repeated a lot, but they never lose their enthusiasm. It's remarkable. You should see them. They *love* it, whatever you do.'

'What should we do today?'

'People usually start by observing the others teach and later in the day you get going yourself. You can watch me and Liam this morning if you like. We'll be here with the intermediates.'

'Great, thanks.'

'No worries.' Craig stood up. 'I'm going for a piss. I'll let you know when we're starting.' He walked off towards the steps.

'How you feeling?' I asked Elodie, putting my spoon down.

'Good. Tired, but good.' She looked around her and leaned in. 'Have you told anyone about Charlotte's disappearance yet? Why we came?'

'Not properly yet, no.'

'Not even Seija?'

'No, I'm waiting for the right time. Maybe today. I don't want to tell everyone, just Seija. She might be able to help. Have you seen her today?'

'No.'

'Me neither,' I said looking around me. 'I wonder where she is.'

'I'll go clean up and we can watch the two northern wonders teach a lesson together, okay?'

'Sure, I'm gonna wait here and finish my noodles.'

Roughly ten minutes later the pupils started to arrive. Natakan had whirled around the breakfast table and taken everything away as the first pupils approached the driveway. They each said 'Hello teacher!' as they walked past and found a seat in front of the chalkboard.

Their eyes examined me closely and as they smiled and nodded they might have been a bit in awe of me. I wasn't sure whether that was the case or not because no one had ever been in awe of me before, but it seemed as if they might be. I had to adjust myself in my seat because I had no mode or protocol to follow in such a situation.

They chatted and laughed with each other in Cambodian while they waited for the others to arrive. Once the attention was off me, I relaxed a little. I listened hard, trying to make out any of the words they were saying, anything recognisable, but there was nothing.

I had always enjoyed languages at school, because understanding new words was like piecing together a puzzle. An unencountered word could be linked to encountered words that shared the same Latin stem, or be understood based on the context in which they were being used. The puzzle could be solved and offer a tiny piece of *certainty*. But here I had no other pieces to go on; no context or previous connected encounters.

When Craig and Liam arrived they all said 'Hello teacher Craig! Hello teacher Liam!' in volunteered unison.

Craig and Liam smiled as they said good morning in return.

I turned to see Elodie take up her place next to me at the table.

She grabbed my arm. 'What did I miss?'

'Oh, nothing yet. They've just arrived.'

'Oh good!'

Craig began to ask the students how they were. There were nine of them altogether: five girls and four boys. I couldn't tell how old they were, but they looked to be in their teens. Liam picked up a piece of chalk and began to write carefully and neatly on the board.

Teacher Liam and Teacher Craig.

Today is Tuesday the 19th of January

Today we will be learning about – Days of the Week

The students proceeded to copy down what Liam had written. I was amazed. I could see their writing. It was meticulous; every word crafted onto the page that was treated as a work of art. This habit continued for the entire lesson. The effort they put into copying things from the board was only matched by the enthusiasm with which they repeated any piece of vocabulary Liam or Craig introduced.

'Monday.'

'MORNDAY!'

'Tuesday.'

'CHOOSDAY!'

'*Today* is Tuesday.'

'*TOODAY* is CHOOSDAY!'

The lesson went by quickly in this format: Liam and Craig introducing a new piece of vocabulary, the class saying it aloud and writing it down carefully in their books. When they were asked questions individually they rarely knew what to say, or even understood what they were being asked, but their effort and enthusiasm never waned.

One girl was an exception to the norm. She spoke excellent English and stood out from the others in terms of her understanding and pronunciation. She was better-presented than the other children, her hair neatly brushed as she sat upright in her chair. Every so often she would look over to where Elodie and I were sitting when she answered a question.

Liam and Craig were patient with the others, giving them clues and hints whenever they asked questions. The English words they taught were repeated back to them in their broad northern accents. This made me and Elodie laugh, which caused the pupils to giggle too.

Halfway through the lesson, Seija appeared in the front yard on the back of a moto. She was carrying a box of fruit. It was a giant, globe-like, green fruit with nobbles all over it. The moto driver kicked up the stand and held the box for Seija as she stepped off the bike.

I looked up and waved hello. She strode over to where Elodie and I were sitting.

'Hey guys,' she whispered. 'How's it going?'

'Good thanks,' I hurriedly whispered back. 'Have you been anywhere exciting this morning?'

'Not really. I was in town for a meeting with the local town council. We're trying to get funding for the orphanage and Mr Kim reckons that having a *farang* at the meetings might give the project more sway.'

'You were in a town council meeting? Wasn't that a bit weird?'

'I'm fairly used to them now. They mostly stare at me and talk around me. Nobody actually talks *to* me. I don't know how much difference I've made, but it's worth a try.'

'Yeah, I guess it is.'

She nodded over to the front of the classroom. 'How are Liam and Craig getting on?'

'Good. The kids are amazing. They're so enthusiastic!'

'That's how they are. It's wonderful.'

'Yeah.'

'Oh, listen, I have something for you. I forgot I had it yesterday, but I'm sure you'd be interested in seeing it.'

'Really? What is it?'

'Follow me and I'll show you.'

I looked across at Elodie, who was still sitting silently beside me.

'Come on!' Seija beckoned me towards the house and started to walk off.

Elodie looked at me.

'I'll be back in a minute,' I said, jumping up to follow Seija.

Elodie's eyes were fixed on the lesson as I walked past her.

Seija had gone into the house, and when I climbed the steps I saw her outline sitting cross-legged in her sheet-bound cubicle.

'In here!' she called.

I walked towards her and sat down. Our knees brushed as I folded my legs.

'Here,' she said, handing me something. 'I've kept it with my personal stuff for such a long time I forgot I had it.'

It was a tatty, brown, leather-bound book. I turned it over in my hands. It felt worn and textured. Its smell reminded me of an old pair of gloves my father used to wear in the winter. The book was heavy, thick and had a nice weight to it. There was a piece of old string tied around it several times from the spine to the middle, finishing in a simple knot. The threads of the string were coming apart at the ends. The corners of the book were turned up and dog-eared, but someone had cared for it.

'What is it?' I asked.

'It's Charlotte's journal. I found it by her bed the day she left. She must have forgotten it. I never opened it. She's your sister, so it only seems right that you should have it. It's up to you whether or not you want to read it.'

I held it in both hands and stared at it. Charlotte's journal. Was I really holding it? This moment meant so much I didn't know what to do. Surely I should open it. I knew my sister had always been intensely private, but this wasn't the time to be polite. I had to know more: where she had been and where she might have been planning to go. I was sure Charlotte would think I was doing it for the right reasons.

I untied the knot and slowly unwound the string from around the journal. It fell open at the first page.

Charlotte's Journal
A beautiful world means nothing if you don't partake in it

THE TRAVELLING MOMENT
Something you want to do and has worth (you may not know this until you do it)

+

Something you couldn't do anywhere else

+

Something that isn't spoilt by anything

=

The Perfect Travelling Experience

It could be over a period of time or a single moment, as
long as it affects you deeply enough.

Beauty that serves <u>no other purpose</u> rules my existence
and should rule everyone else's.

The front and back covers were stuffed with torn sheets
of coloured paper, tickets, bits of money from various
countries, stickers, handwritten notes and cards. There
was a list written along the inside of the front cover, which
was entitled *Perfect Travelling Moments*. Around seventeen
items were written underneath it; all place names with
little detail added. For example, *Lunch on Intibula Island,
El Nido, Philippines*, or *Swimming with turtles, Sipadan,
Mabul, Malaysia*.

I didn't recognise most of the place names but I
had heard of the countries she had been to: Malaysia,
the Philippines, Laos, Thailand, Indonesia, Vietnam,
Cambodia and Singapore. I hadn't realised she had
travelled so much. I only knew where she had been from
her emails and I thought that had been it. I was resentful
that she hadn't emailed more. Why had she left out so
much?

'Shall I leave you to have a look at it?'

Seija had sensed my slipping away.

'Sure, thanks.'

'I hope she doesn't tell you off for looking when she
sees you! Where is she now, anyway? I'd love to see her
again at some point.'

I owed her an explanation; she had helped me more
than she could know.

'I don't know where she is at the moment. She's been missing for more than six months.'

'What?'

'The police have given up looking for her.'

'Oh my God!'

'The last time anyone knew where she was, she was in Phnom Penh. She emailed me and told me she was going to volunteer somewhere she'd seen with you on a poster. And after that nobody knows. That's the reason I came here. When you told me you knew her that was the first piece of news I'd heard that meant she had been alive beyond Phnom Penh. And now I've got her journal. I can't thank you enough, Seija.'

'Hey, don't thank me. Just make sure you find her, okay? She was too strong to disappear Ethan. She's not that kind of person.'

'I know. I want to believe that. I can't imagine her not finding a way through whatever she got herself into.'

'Have a good look at the journal. She may have written where she was planning on going next. I remember her writing in it at least a few times while she was here.'

'Thanks Seija.'

'I'll let you have a read. I'll be downstairs if you need me.'

Seija leant on my knee as she stood up. She winked at me and left. I watched the sheet flutter in her wake before returning my eyes to the leather-bound book in front of me. I turned the first page.

Charlotte's Journal: Day 1

Have just bought this from the market on Khao San Road

below my hostel. I saw it on a stall as I walked past and it chose me. I think it knew that I needed someone to talk to.

I've been in Bangkok for a couple of days now and I think I'm going to move on soon. Bangkok is a vibrant, bubbly city. It's like an overexcited kid who's been given too much sugar. It's agitated, it can't sit still, it wants attention. It wants to do things. It wants you to do things. Like ride a tuk-tuk, or buy a suit, or drink some fresh orange juice, or take a taxi, or see a ping-pong show, or 'just have a look'. Everyone's trying to get my attention and take my money. And yet I feel more comfortable than I can ever remember being.

I spent today and yesterday walking around the city. I went to one tourist spot (the Temple of the Emerald Buddha) and although it was beautiful I knew I couldn't face going to any more. Too many people. Too many reminders. The city itself is what interests me. It has so much character to it and mingles the old with the new with dexterity. It's becoming strangely normal to walk past a digital camera shop with flat-screen TVs in the window and stumble into a mobile restaurant made from a bike and a wok. They sit together well, side by side.

The food-on-wheels carts are everywhere. Pad Thai, fried rice, fresh fruit, coconuts, Thai curries, pancakes. Each cart has its own speciality and they're all delicious. I've never eaten such fresh, tasty food. It's amazing. Eating dinner last night I met a Swedish couple – Sven and Malin – and we ended up going for some drinks together afterwards. It turns out they're going to an island called Ko Chang tomorrow and they asked if I wanted to go with them. They are lovely people and I said yes. I needed a place to go. Bangkok is *great, but I feel as if that impression will fade the longer I stay. Besides, I need some beautiful scenery. It might help me find some answers.*

I called Ethan today. It made me sad to speak to him. I wish he could escape too, but I don't think he's ready yet. He needs to find his own way through and maybe me not being there will make life easier for him in the long run. Maybe Mum and Dad will love him more as a result of my absence. I hope so. Maybe one day they'll work it out.

I turned the page and carried on, engrossed in the book, as if it were a story. As I read, the world disappeared and all that was left was me and the journal, floating, suspended in time and space inside a sheet-bound cubicle. It was magical; I could see into my sister's mind. It was the key that could unlock the door I had never been able to open. I had always seen her life as extraordinary and now I had an inside view into what that meant. More than that, though, I had found a tiny part of my sister. A small piece of my search was complete. I read and I read and I read.

The next thing I was aware of was a voice. Elodie was calling to me from the top of the steps.

'Ethan! Lunch is ready!'

23

Lunch smelt delicious. I could taste it before I even sat down. The sun was shining and the sky sat, clear blue, over the fields as I pulled out a chair next to Elodie. I wanted to tell her about the journal, but Mr Kim was speaking. I waited impatiently for him to stop but soon began to listen to what he was saying.

He was telling the story of his life during the time of the Khmer Rouge. He told it with emotion, and in a questioning manner – that of a child – when he spoke of things he still didn't understand. His voice was passionate and strong and held the attention of everyone around the table.

Samnang Kim had grown up as one of two brothers on a farm in Angk Ta Saom. His father had worked the farm and grown a mixture of crops while his mother had run the house and looked after the boys. It had mainly been subsistence farming, but they had earned a little extra, affording them a few comforts, such as the occasional fish for dinner from the market.

Mr Kim had had a typical childhood for a boy in his village. He had worked with his father and learnt the skills and methods used for farming. He had been happy as a young boy, and had been close to his brother and the other young children in the village.

Mr Kim had been an eleven-year-old boy when he saw his father dragged away from the arms of his mother and shot in the head by the AK-47 of a Khmer Rouge soldier. His father had protested that he wasn't an intellectual – that he was just a farmer and he only needed his glasses in order to harvest his crops – but all this had been to no avail. He had been shot in the head, hauled onto the back of a jeep and driven away.

Young Samnang Kim had stood there and cried, unable to move. With tears flowing, he had watched through blurry eyes as his fourteen-year-old brother had chased after the jeep raging, yelling at the soldiers to give his father's body back. The voice his brother had used was one he hadn't heard before. It had been stinging and cracked, with a sadness that had boiled over into unbounded anger.

Samnang had slowly raised himself to his feet and stared as the captain had stood up in the back of the jeep and aimed his gun. He had shot Samnang's brother as he ran just paces behind the truck. Eight bullets, one short burst to the chest and he had fallen, dead. The soldier had fired shots into the air in celebration and the jeep had driven off in a cloud of dust, a family destroyed behind them.

Life had been forced to continue after this; his mother had had no other choice. Samnang had been sent to school like all the other children in the village. He had studied during the day and worked on what was left of his father's farm in the afternoons and evenings. His mother had worked hard to keep the crops growing, but she hadn't had

185

the strength or the knowhow to produce anything close to what they had needed. She had begun to sell off parts of the farm that she had been unable to maintain. This had continued for several years. Mr Kim and his mother had just managed to survive in their makeshift family.

At the age of fifteen, on what had seemed to be a normal day at school, Mr Kim and his friends had been pulled out of their lessons by a group of soldiers. As they left the building Samnang had no idea what was happening and had been offered no explanation. The men's guns had made him silent and afraid. He had been put into a jeep and taken to Western Cambodia in order to fight with the government army. He hadn't been given the chance to say goodbye to his mother and the only people who knew where he had gone were his classmates, who had all been taken with him. On that day, Mr Kim had been enlisted for the army, which was engaged in a vicious war with the Khmer Rouge.

For four years he had fought in the army. Many of his classmates had died. The conditions were harsh and the soldiers were offered little food and water. Disease was rife and life was a commodity that held trivial value. At one point Mr Kim and his fellow soldiers had been fighting in the same region without moving for months. Their minimal water supplies were beginning to run out, but they had no access to any water sources because the Khmer Rouge soldiers had blocked their exits. The situation had become desperate. Mr Kim and three other soldiers had been sent out into the jungle to look for water.

They had moved slowly, trying to avoid detection from the Khmer Rouge and travelling only at night. After more than a week of barely sleeping and an ever-growing thirst, they had found a waterfall. Excited, they had run down towards it, anticipating its fresh, clean drinking water. There had been a loud explosion and Mr Kim had thrown himself to the floor.

He had looked over to try and locate his fellow soldiers, but had only been able to make out one of them: his friend, who was lying, blood-soaked, on the ground. A mine had gone off beneath one of his friend's legs. There was a cry of agony. Mr Kim had listened to the cry, his heart thumping, his breathing loud and fast. But his thirst had drowned everything out. In the week leading up to that day, he had had nothing but puddle water to drink. He had got up and continued moving towards the waterfall, his mind dripped dry of concern.

The explosion had turned him upside down. The noise and the light had been all he could see for a brief moment as he flew into the air. He had landed on the ground and had been filled with intense pain. His left leg had been blown off at the knee. He had lain there screaming, as his friend had done only moments earlier, before passing out from the blood loss and dreaming of his own death.

When Samnang was rescued a day later the whole area by the waterfall had been bordered off. It had been littered with mines. Luckily for him, another group of government soldiers had come from a different direction and heard his and his friend's screams. Mr Kim had been carried out of the jungle and taken to a medic. He had been fortunate; he had managed to keep the use of his left leg from the knee upwards. His friend hadn't been so lucky.

Samnang had been sent home on crutches, no longer

any use to the army. When he had eventually arrived back at his childhood home his hair had been long and he was unshaven. He had turned from a boy into a man. When he had entered his home his mother hadn't recognised him. She had believed that Samnang was dead. She had been cross and confused; she hadn't known who the man standing in front of her was. She had already held a funeral for him and burnt incense in his honour. She had mourned his death; the death of her second son.

It had taken five tearful hours to finally convince his mother that he was who he had said he was. Even the neighbours had become involved as this supposed stranger had begun to break down in Mrs Kim's front yard. But she had eventually believed him and had taken his head into her hands as they both wept once the realisation had flooded home.

Mr Kim had worked on his mother's farm for a while, but had found that he wasn't much use with only one leg. He was less useful than he had been as a young boy. He had been redundant, without a purpose. He had begun to have trouble sleeping at night and would wake up feeling pains in the part of his leg that was no longer there. He knew he needed something else, something meaningful to do, but he had no idea what that could be. He had begun to learn English from a textbook he had found, late at night and in secret, for fear of being arrested.

After a few weeks back at home he had decided that he needed to find another way to earn money and had come up with a plan. He had moved to Phnom Penh and become a cyclo driver. For six years and using a wooden leg, Mr Kim had driven the pedal-powered taxi, living off one meal a day and sleeping on his bike by the side of the road. He had had to fight off thieves, hunger and illness on many occasions during that time. But he had saved all that he had earned and returned home with three hundred and fifty dollars.

This time when he walked back through the door of his childhood home he had had no problems with his mother recognising him. However, she had been furious with him for staying away for so long. She had hit him and shouted at him as he tried to explain. When she had calmed down and he had explained to her how much he had saved, and how much a dollar was worth, she had been overjoyed. She had broken down and cried. Three hundred and fifty dollars had been a huge sum of money for them.

Mr Kim had devised a plan during those long hours as he took tourists around the streets of Phnom Penh. He had explained to his mother that he wanted to use this money to set up a school that taught English so children in the area could get an education, escape the fields and make better lives for themselves. He had begun to travel to many local offices, fighting to get a permit to set up the school. Although the Khmer Rouge was no longer in power at this time, many of the local officials had been installed under their regime. Education had still been considered suspicious and anyone asking to set up a school was treated with great caution.

It had taken six long months, but at the end of this period he had gained a permit to teach and had enough money to extend the family home and turn it into a school. That had been the beginning of ETP – Educational Training Provider – and since then he had lived off the donations of volunteer teachers who visited the school and taught English to the children from the village.

When Mr Kim finished speaking there was silence. What could anyone say to follow that? Mr Kim turned his attention to the bowl in front of him and bit into his food with force, chewing loudly, his mouth open. Seija was staring out at the cows, her focus in the middle distance. Elodie had her chopsticks gripped tightly in her hand over a plate of untouched food.

'It's a terrible story, isn't it?' said Seija, turning to look around the group.

'Yes,' I answered.

'Now you can understand why I must ask you for money,' said Mr Kim.

He looked at me with his deep-set eyes. I could gauge no emotion from them. They reminded me of the staring cow. His voice had been angry and passionate as he had related his story, but his eyes had shown nothing. I got the sense he wasn't so easy to know.

'Yes, of course. How much do we owe you?'

'Five dollars a day for food and sleep. And anything else you can give for the orphanage. My wife will collect the money after lunch. Thank you.'

Having said this, Mr Kim returned to his food and to the state I was used to seeing him in: withdrawn and detached. As if he had switched himself on and off again.

We finished eating quietly and I didn't mention the journal to Elodie until after we left the table. I told her while we were rummaging through our money belts to find the dollars for Natakan, who was waiting outside.

Elodie seemed pleased, but her reaction was contained,

muted. She didn't hug me or grab me by the arm. She didn't lean over and kiss me congratulations. There was no big smile. She was just quiet. I was angry with Mr Kim. He had stolen something from me in that story that I wanted back.

Outside the house, Elodie gave Natakan thirty dollars. I handed over ten and found a hammock so I could return to my sister's journal.

-o-

Charlotte's Journal: Day 19

As I walked down towards the beach today in the blue sky and the yellow sunshine, I could feel my essence glowing. My every step was taking me closer to where I wanted to be. And I felt invincible. How could anything go wrong? The sun shone on me and I was radiating. I pulsed, I flowed. I was breathing out through the cracks in the pavement.

I was revolving the earth, turning it under my feet. My body was connected to the world, while my mind floated among the clouds. And I could see everything from up there. I was complete and unafraid. I was nothing.

My physical presence began to dissolve and pure emotion arrived. I was simply a bundle of experiences and nothing more. I could hear beautiful birdsong and wondered where this was in my head. I was separation. I had been completely undone. I moved on, unattached, as though I had evolved again.

In that moment I knew. In reality, everything is sunlight.

-o-

24

That afternoon I taught my first lesson with Elodie. We borrowed two of the local children's pushbikes and cycled into the village. I had been so glued to my sister's journal. It was captivating, fascinating. I had read and reread passages, trying to absorb their meanings, hoping their wisdom would somehow feed into me through the pages. It was full of not only tales of her travels, but poetry and aphorisms. I was trying hard to understand them, but Elodie had told me she wanted to teach and had asked me to do it with her. So I did.

The classroom in the village was more of a shelter than a building. It had no walls, only four pillars that held up a prism-shaped roof. A tiled floor had been laid beneath the roof in the shade but it had cracked and started to come apart. A large piece of wooden panelling had been painted black and erected at one end of the floor. This makeshift chalk board was all the room had to offer and the only thing that made it recognisable as a classroom.

When we arrived, a few children were milling around under the shade of the roof. They were younger than the children we had seen Liam and Craig teach earlier that day and there was a considerable age gap between them. There were tiny children there with matted black hair and smudged faces who couldn't have been more than four or five. Their huge eyes opened as wide as they could when they looked at us. We were a different species.

And there were wiry, taller children who had grown up a bit and begun to thin out in the beginnings of their teenage years. Their ragged, dirty clothes looked small on them; they had clearly grown out of them several years earlier. They all looked over when we arrived and rushed to meet us, grabbing our hands and shouting 'Hello teacher!'

After five or ten minutes of hellos, the number of children had increased dramatically. Around fifty children were surrounding us, smiling and reaching out their hands to hold ours. There was a lot of pushing and shoving to get near us, and Elodie and I looked at each other with concerned smiles.

In the midst of this scrum, the realisation that we had no idea how to settle these children down and get the lesson started became highly apparent. I searched for an appropriate mode to deal with the situation but realised I didn't have one. The only one that kept trying to force its way in was my self-preservation mode, and as much as I wanted to slip into it, I knew it wasn't right.

The pushing was becoming quite rough and some of the younger kids were getting elbowed or lifted out of the way. Their tiny faces looked disgruntled, and yet in spite of their expressions they were accepting of this deposition. There were no tears, no tantrums. Simply resignation.

The moment we began telling the kids, with a complete lack of success, that we should start the lesson, we heard a loud, high-pitched yell from behind us. I turned around and saw the well-presented girl from the earlier lesson. She looked different from the happy, giggly, confident girl I had seen before.

She was striding towards the children with a stick in her hand and she had a look of pure ferocity on her face. The children immediately pulled away from us and started to sit on the floor in rows. The girl carried on yelling and, as she got nearer and nearer, more of the kids began to sit down. She raised her stick during her final approaching steps and that was enough for the remaining children to join the rows.

'Hello teacher,' she said. 'My name is Sunita. How are you?'

I was one of the students as she spoke to me, stick in hand.

'Hello Sunita. My name is Ethan. This is Elodie. I am fine, thank you.'

Sunita smiled and nodded, and no one said anything.

'So, are you here to help us teach the lesson?' I asked.

'Em, yes, that is correct. My job is to help the teachers at the school in the village.'

'Oh, so you work at the school as well?' asked Elodie.

'Em, yes. I wish to be a teacher of English. Like you!' She smiled.

'Oh, that's wonderful,' Elodie said.

The fifty or so children were sitting in silence, cross-legged and gazing up at Elodie as she carried on the conversation. I preferred not to look at them at that moment and concentrated on Elodie and Sunita.

'Should we begin the lesson now?' Elodie asked.

'Yes, yes. Now is the lesson time,' replied Sunita.

'Do you have anything we can use to scribble on the board with, or present with?' I gestured in the air with my hands as I asked.

'Sorry? My English.' Sunita's face crumpled up.

'Sorry. Do you have anything we can write with? Like chalk?'

'Chalk? Oh yes.'

She turned and yelled at the children, who were sitting in silence watching our discussion take place. A girl who had been sitting on the floor in the front row, not three feet from Sunita, stood up and walked purposefully towards us. She reached into her pocket and produced a small piece of chalk. She held it in her open hands and presented it to me. It was a gift. It was the most important thing in the world at that moment.

I took it and said thank you. The girl smiled and shied away.

I started to write on the board and Elodie spoke to the class.

Teacher Ethan and Teacher Elodie
Today is Tuesday the 19th of January
Today we will be studying - The Kitchen

Elodie and I had discussed what we would teach while we were cycling to the village. We didn't want to teach something they had learned before, but were struggling for ideas for a new topic. I had suggested the kitchen, and after a brief discussion about how we might teach it we had settled on that.

I began to draw pictures of different kitchen utensils and implements on the board: pans, forks, knives and jugs.

As I drew, the chalk scratched along the blackened wood and left staccato lines of white dust. I'm not a great artist and the pictures were poor, but they were recognisable.

Charlotte used to say that art was *the highest form of human expression*. It helps us *bend* the world to our point of view, she would say. It allows us to put a little piece of ourselves and our perspective into the outside world. This meant, she said, that with each thing she placed within it, the external world became a tinier bit more the way she saw it.

I had enjoyed art at school, but had been frustrated by my clear lack of ability. My attempts to paint the world or sketch it or model it or sculpt it had never turned out as I had envisaged. I could see what I wanted to create in my head, but couldn't *do* it. This annoyed me because I couldn't understand why that was. Art became one more thing I wasn't as good at as I would have liked to be.

As far as I could tell, the world did not resemble my way of seeing it at all.

While I was attempting to draw, Elodie was using Sunita's stick to point to the different items on the board and was calling out their names. As the lesson went on the children in the class soon became more comfortable and revealed their personalities to us.

As I continued to draw, it struck me how similar the characters in this class were to my old classes at school. How it was that I had travelled halfway around the world and yet the children I had met showed the same characteristics as those back home?

Sunita watched us as we taught, if it could be called that. She stood with her hands on her hips for most of the lesson. Her eyes surveyed the children with a concentrated stare. She moved closer to us at the front when we asked certain members of the class to come to the board and use the stick to point out certain items, which we would name in English.

She put her hand to her cheek as this activity went on and would unleash her yell if any of the volunteers did something slightly irregular while up at the front. The pride and excitement of the volunteers were embodied by their full strides and beaming faces each time they stepped up to the front.

At the end of the lesson, Sunita led the whole class through a rendition of 'If you're happy and you know it' with eight verses and many different moves. After that, the class sang a song for us. It was called 'the Sunday song' and was sung in English. I didn't recognise it, but the children all knew it word for word.

The song was a sad one. There was a love that had been lost. They sang it happily, apparently oblivious to the meaning of the words. I fought to keep a smile on my face as they looked at us intently. My focused-alert mode, which I had chosen as the best one for teaching, was tiring by that point and I felt myself losing concentration as the song drew to a close.

After this, the children waved goodbye and every single one came up to us and shook our hands. Some wanted high-fives, while others presented us with flowers as gifts. The way they gave these gifts, presenting them with both hands like the chalk earlier, as though we were deserving of some kind of medal, meant I wasn't sure how to accept them.

When the children finally started making their way home, Sunita came over to join us.

'Thank you very much, teachers,' she said quietly. 'Have you eaten?'

I looked over to Elodie, who had just high-fived a skinny, round-headed boy for the fourth time.

'Well we ate at lunchtime,' she said, finally waving him goodbye.

'Em. Now is later. Please, come with me. You can see my house.'

'Oh, should we? We don't want to intrude.' Elodie glanced across at me.

'Come, come.' Sunita began walking and waved her arm for us to follow.

'We walk now and take bikes.'

Sunita led Elodie and I in a little peloton of children's bikes back to her house. It was only a ten-minute cycle through the village, and yet we heard 'Hello teacher! How are you?' shouted in our direction at least six times. Children would run out of their houses as we cycled past and shout and wave, jumping around and hugging each other in delight. Elodie and I smiled and waved back each time, trying to match their level of enthusiasm but not managing it.

Sunita rode side by side with us, her head held high. She never waved to the children and ignored their shouts, riding elegantly along with us like the swan to our excited signets.

Elodie and I looked at each other as we waved. She was changing at ETP. She no longer always looked at the ground, avoided attention and simply listened. She was opening up her real self as the sun reappears from behind a passing cloud. I was glad she had convinced me to teach the lesson that day.

When we arrived, Sunita's house looked the same as Mr Kim's from the outside, only without the school extension at the front. She laid her bike on the ground and beckoned us towards the front steps that led inside.

'Come. Please, come.'

We put down our bikes and followed her inside. As we walked up the steps I smelt the stale smell of week-old washing up. The house opened up in front of me and, instead of being enclosed and cluttered like Mr Kim's, it was open and sparse. Inside was one big room. There were piles of grubby sheets in the two far corners, which appeared to be sleeping areas, and plain wooden flooring in between.

A woman was washing dishes to the left of us as we walked in. She was bent over the solid pans, scrubbing them in a tiny, dark-coloured bowl of water. Her hair was tied behind her head, but straggles of black and grey fell down over her face. She looked up at us and instantly stopped scrubbing.

For the tiniest of moments she stared at us as I imagined a baby might look at somebody's face for the first time, all amazed and confused. She looked at Sunita and began to yell. Her yell was the same as Sunita's had been earlier, high-pitched and angry, and yet it had a depth to it; a resonance that Sunita's did not have. It was a short outburst, to which Sunita replied quietly and briefly before turning to us.

'I am sorry. We cannot eat today. My mother has no

food to offer you. I am sorry.' She looked away from us as she spoke, her posture different from the one she had held on the cycle ride.

'Oh, that's okay,' said Elodie softly, 'please don't worry. It was very nice of you to show us your home.'

'This is my mother.' Sunita opened her palm towards the woman in the corner, who was standing up tall and straightening her dark dress. It looked old and was covered in a patchwork of stains. Elodie and I said hello and she bowed to us in a simple, delicate movement.

'Please, sit, sit,' said Sunita pointing towards the middle of the room.

We sat down and Sunita's mother came to join us. It seemed everyone was unsure of what to do, so a difficult piece of silence began to sit between us. We tried to talk to the mother, but she simply smiled and nodded at every question.

Sunita was tense and sat upright, like the back of a chair.

In the silence, my eyes were drawn around the room and I noticed how little Sunita's family had in comparison with Mr Kim. I had seen Mr Kim's sleeping area and he had a large mattress with clean sheets and comfortable cushions. I wondered how much of the volunteers' money had been spent on those things.

After a few minutes, Elodie decided that the silence had sat for long enough and said that we ought to be getting back to ETP. I hurriedly agreed and, although Sunita didn't smile at this, the chair-back posture gave way to something more natural. Her mother bowed to us again as we walked towards the door and I bowed back.

We thanked Sunita and she simply thanked us in return. She walked us to our bikes and held her head high once again as we waved goodbye.

During the cycle ride home, Elodie and I talked and talked about the lesson and our strange insight into Sunita's life. As we pedalled, we turned the events of the previous couple of hours over and over on the wheels on our bikes, laughing and smiling with each push of our legs. When we turned into the driveway at ETP and saw the other volunteers we were arriving home.

'Ethan! Ethan! Come here!'

I looked up from my Lego. I was halfway through building a castle when I heard Charlotte's voice from across the hall. The front and the left-hand side were finished. They were the right height and I had even managed to leave the proper thin spaces for the archers to fire their arrows through. However, after a loud, lengthy rummage through my cardboard box, I had realised I had run out of grey, six-block pieces. And that I didn't have enough grey four-block pieces to finish the rest of the castle.

That was no good at all.

It meant that I would have to use blue and red blocks to complete the back and right-hand side. The castle would look all wrong. Castles aren't supposed to be different colours. They're supposed to be grey with black or white ramparts and bright flags. They're supposed to look as if they're made of solid, inches-thick English stone. As if they could fight off any army or outlast a giant siege. Of course, they would have a brown gateway. And even maybe a darker grey turret or two. But they never had blue or red in them.

'Ethan! Come on! I've got a surprise for you!' Charlotte called out to me again.

I put down the blue, eight-block piece I held in my hand. I was glad to stop. I needed to rethink my whole plan for the castle. It was all going wrong.

'Coming!' I shouted back, crawling up off my knees and out of my bedroom door.

My knuckles knocked quietly on Charlotte's door. It was ever so slightly ajar, but I couldn't see anything inside.

I waited while I heard her shuffling around inside her room. Perhaps I could make a smaller castle, I thought as I waited. Maybe more like a watchtower. Taller but narrower. That might work.

'Okay. You can come in now.'

I waited a moment. 'Come in?' I asked.

'Yes! Come in, before I change my mind!' Her voice sounded excited. I had heard it many times like that before, but not since the birthday party.

I raised my hand and waivered slightly before pushing the white-painted wooden door that led in to Charlotte's room. It swung open slowly and what had been a sliver of light gradually filled the darkness of the corridor around me. I stood in the doorway and looked in.

It was completely different to my room. Her desk was overflowing with crumpled and uncrumpled pieces of paper. Clothes hung messily over the back of her chair. There were knitting needles and bundles of red and brown wool on the floor. Little straggles of it ran over the green rug in funny, complicated patterns. Her long windowsill had four dolls on it sitting next to each other. They looked all worn and tattered as they sat there in wonky positions, half-leaning off the edge.

Posters covered almost all of her walls. There were pictures of flowers, waterfalls, mountains and animals everywhere. Fluffy white seals, diving dolphins and hugging penguins were sellotaped at different angles, overlapping each other. There was a picture of a rainbow over some big, snowy mountains.

Standing there in the doorway, looking around, one poster caught my eye. It was a picture of the sun setting somewhere over the sea. The sun was red and the sea was still. It was hard not to look at it, but I didn't know why. Why would someone take a picture of the sea and the sun? I supposed it was because most people can't see them on usual days.

Charlotte was standing in the middle of her room, pointing at something in the way one of those women on game shows do. The prize she was presenting was something she had built, which was sitting in between her and the bed. It looked to be made of a mixture of cardboard boxes and garden poles and sheets. She was leaning on it with her left arm and smiling.

'Don't think that because I let you in this time it's going to become a habit,' she said sternly. 'Now, do you want to know what I've made you?'

I thought back to the previous thing Charlotte had made me. It had been a time travel machine that could take me anywhere in the future as long as it was in her room. It had been called the *timetravelator*. Each time I had got out of it I had to ask her how the world was and she would look out the window and tell me. I remember travelling to lots of different dates, far into the future, but outside had usually been sunny and bright, with the odd flying car or nuclear explosion taking place.

The time before that it had been the *infinitireader*, an infinite library. Charlotte had told me that each time I went in to take a book out it didn't make any difference to the number of books that were still in there. I had gone in and taken several books out and told her she was wrong, waving them in front of her, but she hadn't listened to me.

'What is it?' I asked as I spied her latest contraption, bouncing on my toes and smiling.

'Well,' she said. 'It's what I like to call a *transformatron*.'

'Wow!' I shouted by accident. 'What's that?'

'If you go inside, it'll change you into anything you want. You just have to tell me what it is you want to be and I'll set the dial.'

She pointed to a piece of corrugated cardboard with buttons and knobs drawn on it.

'Once you're inside I'll set the parameters and then *alakazam*! You are whatever you want to be!'

'I can be anything I want?'

'Yep, anything you want. But only I can see you. That's the nature of the *transformatron*. Only those who know how it works can see its effects.'

'Okay,' I said, nodding. It made sense. Charlotte's inventions always made sense.

'So, what do you want to be?'

I scratched the back of my head. It was a difficult decision. I loved Charlotte's presents, but they were always hard work.

'Come on, come on!' she said, twiddling her fingers in the air in front of me.

'I don't know! This is hard!'

Thinking some more, I looked up again at the poster of the sea and the sun. I picked something and clenched my fists. 'I want to be an eagle. A big, giant eagle with big, giant feathers and wings.'

'Good choice!'

Charlotte danced around quickly and pointed to the *transformatron*.

'Quick, get inside, so we can transform you. The machine wasn't built to last forever!'

I pushed aside the sheet that covered the entrance to the machine and crawled inside. It was hot and stuffy in there and everything was a dark orange colour. I took a big breath in and out.

Charlotte's voice called out from the normal world. 'Okay, here we go!'

I could feel her pushing the cardboard and the poles around me as they started to shake. She made a buzzing sound and then stopped.

I waited a moment.

'Is it done?' I asked, gripping my knees in my curled-up position. I was running out of orange air inside the machine.

'Yep, come out and I'll tell you how you look.'

The cool outside whisked into me as I pushed aside the sheet and stepped out of the *transformatron*.

'Wow!' Charlotte clapped her hands together and looked at me. 'You look great! You've got such a big beak!'

She laughed and I felt my nose.

'Come on, let's see those wings!' she shouted.

I opened out my arms and spread them into the air.

'They're beautiful,' she said. 'Just beautiful! Get ready for take-off!'

I waved and felt the air under my wings take hold and float me up off the floor. I flew around her room, flapping and gliding, as Charlotte ran around me, laughing and cheering me on. Each time I did a lap of the room I looked at the poster with the sun and the sea as I passed it.

I imagined flying out into the red, sparkly sea, gliding on a cool breeze and travelling as far as my giant feathers would take me.

25

That afternoon I had spent so much time retelling the events of our lesson to the others with Elodie that I had almost forgotten my sister's journal. Everyone except Seija, who was once again somewhere else, sat around and listened to our recounting of the lesson and subsequent invitation back to Sunita's house. Apparently, Sunita had invited some of the others back to her house after lessons. Elodie had been told she was lucky because it was usually only men that got the invite.

Later, when I did get a moment to myself to open Charlotte's journal once more, I flicked straight to the last page she had written. I wanted to see if she had given any clues for where she was planning to go next. As I began to read I realised I was in luck.

Charlotte's Journal: Day 700 and something

Have just finished packing. I'll be sad to leave ETP. This place that has given me so much and rewarded me in ways that are pure good. In my last class today I got given a coconut, three mangoes, some flowers, some waterlilies, two sweet potatoes, some vegetables I don't recognise, a drawing and several sticks. They are such good-hearted children. Their eagerness and love for me as their teacher has almost become too much; I don't deserve that much adoration. It has been a selfish pleasure in many ways teaching here; instant hits of satisfaction that don't warrant praise.

This has been such a good, wholesome experience. Not thrilling or full of pleasure, but a kind of deep, lower-level satisfaction that I'm not sure I've felt before. I've learned so much from the people here and their lives that I feel I can move on now. I'm not sure they have anything more to give. Seija has decided to stay. I guess it's up to her. I think she feels comfortable and settled, but I haven't completely felt that here. It's been so rewarding, and yet still something in me feels a little out of place.

One of the guys here, Alfonso, is taking me up to his friend's guest house in Don Det. I haven't been there yet, but I've heard interesting things about the place so I'm looking forward to it. A new place, a new challenge. He says he can get me a job up there in the guest house. I'm running low on money now. I hate the constraints it makes on my life. Surely the world would be a better place without it.

So, Makkar Guesthouse could contain my foreseeable future. I hope so. The beauty of the world is within me now and it continues to grow bigger and bigger. I don't even like thinking of home now. It all seems so arbitrary there. I don't think I can even relate to it any more. Life as a divided item, different elements in different compartments. I can't understand the point of doing a job you hate so you can buy things you don't need or even genuinely want. It's such a strange concept. I don't know if I'll ever go back. I think that part of me is almost completely lost now.

I read the last sentence several times and wondered what it meant. Did she include me in that? Was I completely lost to her? My happiness at finding Charlotte's next destination was obscured by this sentence. It was as though one of Mr Kim's white sheets was hanging between it and me, not letting me near, keeping it just out of my reach.

I got up and showed this last entry to Elodie. When I had explained what it said she took the journal and read it carefully for herself. After a couple of minutes, she finished and looked up.

'Sometimes I don't understand your sister.'

'Me neither. She's different in this journal, changed somehow. I don't get some of it, her poetry in particular.'

'Well, whatever she's talking about, it looks like we're going to Don Det next, doesn't it?'

She smiled and scratched her elbow as she said this, as if it were no big thing.

I leaned forward quickly. 'Do you want to come? I was going to ask, but I wasn't sure. I mean, it's a bit more of a trip this time I think. I don't know, but it seems further away...'

'If you still want the company I'd love to go.'

'Oh, I want you to come; it'd be great if you came. I just didn't know if you were fed up of looking yet. It's kind of a weird thing that I'm doing.'

She leaned forward in her seat as I had done. 'Fed up? No way! This is an adventure! Something real and exciting. Who else could I get this kind of experience with?'

I laughed. 'Not many people, I guess!'

'Besides, what better way is there to spend my dad's

shitty money than on rescuing Ethan Willis' sister from the evil traps of the world?'

Elodie also laughed and there was such warmth at that moment that I wanted to hug her right there. I wanted to snuggle up into her warm body, for her to keep me safe from the evil traps of the world. Right then, whatever evil or darkness there was, it couldn't touch me.

We spent the next hour asking the others about Don Det. Apparently, it was a popular travellers' destination in Laos and everyone around the table contributed a little information. We soon found out that Mimi and Fillip had been there before. They explained how we could get there. They spoke English with such a strong Finnish accent I was amazed the children could understand them.

'Well, you need to go to Krachie first,' said Fillip, pointing in the air as he did so.

'That's in the north of Cambodia,' added Mimi.

'Yes, so how is the best way to get there?' Fillip stroked his beard. 'I think if you go back to Phnom Penh and then...'

'Yes, yes, then catch a bus up from there.' Mimi finished off Fillip's sentence. 'You can cross the river at Krachie and get to the border with Laos on the other side.'

'When you cross the border, you can get a bus...'

'Or share taxi...' Mimi's finger waved as she interjected.

'Oh yes, or share taxi, from there to the boats and on to the islands at Don Det.'

'Lovely islands at Don Det, so pretty. I am sure that you will love them so.' Mimi placed a hand on Elodie's knee as she said this.

'How long do you think it will take?' asked Elodie.

'How long?' They looked at each other.

'Hmm, I would say it could be done in a day,' Fillip said.

'Yes. Two days might be easier, but I think if you leave early enough you could be able to get across the border in a day,' added Mimi.

'A day, yes,' rounded off Fillip. 'You will need to leave very early, but it could be done.'

'Okay,' I said, turning to Elodie. 'Tomorrow?'

She nodded and tucked her dark hair behind her ear. Our secret was bonding us together.

'Oh, you are leaving tomorrow? So soon!' Mimi's eyebrows were raised.

'Yes, sorry. We have…' Elodie looked at me as she spoke. She already understood. 'We have a friend to meet in Don Det and we have to head up as soon as possible. We've had a lovely time here, though. It's a shame that it's been so short.'

'Such a shame!'

'Yes, such a shame,' said Fillip. 'Still, you must come to the wedding with us tonight.'

'Oh yes, you must!' beamed Mimi.

'What wedding?'

'There is a wedding in the village and they have invited Mr Kim and all of us to attend.'

'Yes, very exciting! The whole village is going!'

'Oh that sounds wonderful,' said Elodie, putting her hands together. 'When do we go?'

'I think someone will come and fetch us when it is time. We are not invited to the ceremony itself, just the party after. But it sounds exciting!'

'Very exciting!' Elodie replied.

26

Our dinner of omelette, rice and greens went by quickly that evening, with everybody talking about the wedding. We could already hear loud music coming from the village and this put us all in a kind of pre-party atmosphere. Even Natakan raised a smile when Liam jumped up and gave her a bow as she came to clear away the plates.

Seija had come back late that afternoon and brought back a few cans of beer from the market in the larger village next to ours. This was a treat and we ate and drank noisily in the comfort of the warm evening air. I remembered my first meal in Cambodia at Lucio's and wondered whether Jon-Paul would ever dare to do anything like this.

As we were finishing dinner a man came up the path and stopped in front of our table. He was middle-aged, tall and had long arms. His chin was unshaven and his soft jawline was outsized by an exceptionally wide mouth. He began to talk to Mr Kim. It was a fast, loud conversation and he wobbled a little as he spoke. His eyes had spindly cobwebs of red around their pupils. I could smell the alcohol on his breath.

After a few moments of animated conversation,

Mr Kim announced that it was time for us to go to the wedding. The man got agitated and excited as we all stood up and bounded down the road with all of us following behind. It was only a little more than a ten-minute walk to the wedding party. The music got progressively louder as we approached and when we reached the other side of a large group of trees it was at a level that couldn't be ignored.

The man led us through the trees and ushered us towards a large group of people on the other side. It appeared we had arrived late in the wedding proceedings. A table that had once had food on it was all but cleared. There was a group of men dancing in a circle under a sheltered area in front of us. A similar-sized group of women sat to our left on a collection of plastic chairs, their collective gaze fixed on the men dancing. The dancing was slow and gentle. There was a system to it, with the men moving round in a circle and all making the same motions with their legs.

Once our presence had been noticed the men smiled, came over and took each of us by the arm. We were led onto the dance area and soon realised we were expected to dance. This concerned me and I froze. The women watched as we stood there, unsure of what to do. As I contemplated joining in with the dancing I was handed a large cup. I looked inside and saw a dark, purple-coloured liquid. It was thick and smelt strangely alcoholic.

Fillip saw my face and leaned over.

'It's rice wine,' he said. 'It doesn't taste too good, but it certainly gets you drunk! Cheers!'

He held up his beaker and bumped it against mine.

We both took a big gulp and I grimaced.

I looked around me. The women were all obviously staring at us. I recognised Sunita in the group along with one or two girls from the intermediate lesson I had watched that morning. I saw giggles spread through the group and turned around to see that Liam, Craig and James had started to dance. They were trying to dance in the same way as the other men, but were causing much hilarity. Some of the men almost fell over laughing, doubling up and clutching their stomachs.

Mimi had led Elodie over to a couple of free chairs to the side of us. They were soon joined by some of the younger women from the group, who huddled around them.

Seija was talking to Mr Kim, her ear close to his mouth as she tried to listen. I saw her down her cup of rice wine and waggle the beaker for a refill. Men had begun to gravitate towards her, poisonous insects around a beautiful flower, sniffing her scent and wanting to be close to it. She didn't give any sort of response when she looked up and saw four or five of them standing around her while she talked to Mr Kim. Her beaker was swiftly topped up by one of the men. He had his eyes all over her. It made my mind think of a horrible stain on a delicate dress.

As I looked on someone put a hand across my shoulder. One of the local men was standing next to me, his body leaning against mine. He was a little shorter than me and much slighter. His oily face was sweaty and hot. The grey shirt that hung off his slender frame had darkened in patches. He smelt of rice wine infused with a long day's worth of body odour. Little sprouts of dark hair grew from his upper lip and chin in patches.

He made eye contact immediately as I turned and began to talk to me in Khmer, waving his free hand in the air as he did so. I couldn't understand a word he said, but he kept on talking and nodding at me. His hand gestures were grand and I got the feeling this was a serious conversation.

Time moved on and I continued to nod whenever he did and smile every so often as he spoke loudly with his arm still around my shoulder. Seija had been topped up again by the time he finally let me go. I moved quickly when he removed his arm from around my neck, finishing my cup and escaping to the seats next to Elodie and Mimi.

Elodie looked up as I sat down.

'Hi.' She had a cheeky smile on her face. I hadn't seen that look before. 'Are your ears burning?'

'No, why? Should they be?'

'Oh, they most definitely should be!' She turned her chair round so that it faced mine.

'Why? Who's talking about me?'

'Well, wouldn't you like to know?! You're the hot topic of conversation right now among those women over there!'

A jumble of faces looked in my direction as Elodie pointed to the large group of women sitting a few yards to my left. I looked away as soon as I saw them.

'Really? Why? What's it about?'

'Well, the woman in the centre, can you see her? I don't know if you recognise her, but that's Sunita's mum.'

I risked a quick glance. It was Sunita's mum, but she looked different. Her hair was tidy and washed. Her clothes were clean. She looked happy.

'Oh yes, I recognise her. What's she got to do with anything?'

'Well, apparently she thinks you would make an excellent husband for Sunita. Having met you today she wants to try and set you two up!'

I flicked my eyes over to Sunita, who was chatting with her friends not two yards away.

'Yeah! They've been chatting about you all evening, apparently! How funny!'

'Oh God! What do you think they're going to do?'

'I don't know. I guess we'll have to wait and see! Oh, by the way, I've booked us a couple of motos into town for early tomorrow morning.'

'Oh, great. Thanks.'

'I'm quite excited about going now. Also, I think Seija may have told Mimi and Fillip about Charlotte over dinner, which I didn't think was very thoughtful of her.'

'Well I guess I didn't tell her not to let anyone else know, so we can't blame her too much. Anyway, it doesn't matter now. We'll be gone tomorrow morning.'

'Yes, but I still don't think it was her place to say anything. And wait, we haven't left yet… Here comes Sunita.'

Sunita had stood up and was walking towards me. 'You might be here for years yet! Don't say you weren't warned!'

Elodie turned away slightly in her chair.

'Hello, Mr Ethan. How are you?' Sunita reached out and shook my hand. At least twenty pairs of eyes followed our hands as they moved.

'Hello, Sunita. I am fine, thank you.'

She sat down on the chair next to mine. Our plastic arm rests were touching.

'Em, you are liking the party?'

'Er… yes. Yes, very much,' I said, nodding again like I was still in conversation with the Cambodian man from earlier.

'That is nice.' She smiled, but it was quick and temporary. 'Em, you are from England?'

'Yes, that's right. I'm from London.'

'Oh, London. I would like to go to London.'

'Well, I'm sure you can one day.'

'I wish, but no. No money, Mr Ethan.' There was a pause. My hands gripped the edge of my plastic chair.

'Em, my mother. Em, she would like to know if you have girlfriend in England.'

I bit my lip and looked over to the dance floor. I wondered briefly how it might be to have a Cambodian girlfriend. To live in the fields as a farmer and teach English in my spare time, hanging under my house in a hammock during the hot hours of midday. Maybe that wouldn't be so bad.

'Oh… Yes I do, I'm afraid.'

Elodie angled her head in my direction.

'She lives in London as well.'

Sunita looked at her hands in her lap.

She said, 'Em, okay', before standing up quickly and walking back over to her mother.

I could see that a big conference was beginning to take place.

'Is that true?' asked Elodie, turning herself back round once Sunita had gone.

'No, but I had to think of something.'

She looked at me for a moment and a big smile spread

across her face. 'You lied to her! That poor girl. Her heart crushed by an English cad! You devil!'

'Oh, thanks very much! I feel bad enough as it is. You're not helping!'

Elodie pushed at my knee. 'I'm only joking. I'm sure she's got someone else lined up. Don't worry! Look, they're already staring at the dance floor. They must be eyeing up their next prey!'

Elodie was right. The women were staring at the dancing area, but as I turned I soon realised they weren't eyeing up the other men. They were all staring at Seija, their eyes burning holes in her perfect back.

Seija was in the middle of the dance floor and was dancing with two empty beakers in her hands. She was surrounded by several local men. Some had their hands on her; others were dancing up close behind, pressing their bodies against hers. Her eyes were closed and her arms were raised above her head. Her blonde hair flew as she twirled. Her top was floating just above her stomach, revealing a band of pale, smooth, creamy skin.

She was dancing as if she were in a nightclub. Her hips were shaking and curling to the beat, her legs twisting and turning in the dust beneath them. Her body was moving in a different way from anyone else's.

The slow, systematic dances of the locals had been forgotten; relics of the evening in which dance had been used for a different purpose. She was casting a spell with the music and her combination of rhythm and movement were being used to bewitch any man who saw her. The men on the dance floor were fighting to get near her. There was some pushing and shoving as they tried to edge each other out of her vicinity. Out of the corner of my eye I could see Elodie shaking her head.

When Mimi turned around and saw what was happening, she leapt up. She walked towards Seija and spoke into her ear for a moment as the men continued to push their way in, touching and feeling anything they could grab hold of. Mimi put her arms around Seija and gently tried to angle her towards the chairs. After an initial refusal and a throwing up of her arms, Seija stumbled from the dance floor with Mimi's help. They were having a conversation as they sat down. Seija waved Mimi's arms away from her until she wrapped them tightly around her and held on. They swayed as they hugged, their bodies seaweed in a drunken tide.

The dancing gradually came to an end after that. The music continued but the men were beginning to sit down. Some were still drinking, many were falling asleep. The women had started to disappear. We waved goodbye as they left and they responded in kind, often smiling as they did so. They did not address the men at all on their way out. Why was that? None of the women had been drinking and I supposed they were simply not interested in talking to their incoherent husbands. I thought of my parents.

Liam, James and Craig danced their way over to where Fillip, Elodie and I were sitting. They suggested it was time to head back to Mr Kim's house and we all agreed. The mood had changed, though I couldn't explain why. We collected Mimi and Seija on our way out and followed Mr Kim back to our ETP home.

During the walk back from the wedding Seija jumped up beside me and put her arm around me. It stayed there for the whole trip, the soft inside of her elbow resting against my neck. She said she wanted to tell me about the travelling she had done before arriving at ETP, and that's exactly what she did.

With the loud music still cluttering my ears, I felt the attraction of a real travelling experience for the first time as I walked with Seija. The way she spoke and what travelling meant to her filled me with a sense of admiration. Through Seija I was beginning to understand my sister a little more. She explained her travels, swaying slightly with another cup of rice wine in her hand, in a way that my sister never had.

'I travel to see different ways of life and to dive into them as deep as I can go. It's not about sightseeing, or drinking, or partying, or holidaymaking, you know? They hold their own places and attractions in their own right, but they're not the bright lights of travelling. They're the jagged rocks, not the smooth pebbles.'

She smoothed out the air with her hand. 'And, yes, often to get to the smooth pebbles on the beach you have to clamber past the jagged rocks and the steep drops of the cliffs on your way. There's the odd shimmering rock pool to hold your attention, but it's the sea you're really aiming at, isn't it? That's the ultimate glow. It's easy to get consumed on the route towards it, playing in the cliffs and the rock pools and forgetting where you were headed.'

She took another sip of her wine. 'But if you tread enough steps and focus on the goal you first aimed at you can navigate the rocks and begin to feel the smooth pebbles and warm wash of the sea under your feet. This is the real experience of travelling, where the gold is hidden,

Ethan. That's where you want to go. To see different lives, different cultures, different hearts and be part of them. To touch them. I've done that; I'm a part of them.'

She waved the hand that held the wine in the direction of the wedding. 'This is the aim and the beautiful reward. This is when your knowledge blossoms and grows; when you bathe in the many differences of the world and let their influences wash over you like lotion; healing your ignorance and imperfections; teaching you the secrets of nature and existence.

'This has nurtured me in a special way, given me an extra level of sensibility and self-awareness that has sculpted confidence and personal modesty out of the putty mould that was my unfinished intellect. You are moulded into a smoother, more beautiful aesthetic shape that matches the world ever so slightly more. The future will improve because of these experiences; simple earthly involvement that can't be provided in any other way.'

She was a preacher evangelising her faith. Even drunk, her words and her beauty were magnetic and drew me towards her. They clung to me and I couldn't peel them off. In all honesty, I didn't want to peel them off. I wanted to be a part of them; I wanted them inside me. I wanted to be inside them, to have them fill my head. I wanted to travel and taste just a little of what she had described. I didn't care if she was right, these experiences might somehow make me *more*. I wanted to see the world as she had done; to live it and feel it. I wanted those experiences so I could talk to her as she did to me.

I told her I was leaving early the next day to try to find Charlotte. She told me how wonderful it was that I was trying to find her and that she thought I was already beginning to mould to the world. She said that when I left I should always remember to try and feel the smooth pebbles.

We all stayed up talking and laughing outside the house until the energy of the evening had gone.

27

I had just fallen asleep when something moved my foot. It didn't wake me properly the first time, but when it happened again I opened my eyes and looked up. At the foot of my sleeping bag, half inside the hanging sheet, was Seija.

She saw my eyes open and instantly put her index finger vertically across her lips when I took in air to speak. With her other hand she beckoned me towards her, silently slipping beyond the sheet.

I glanced across at Elodie. She was fast asleep. I gently moved her hand from around my waist and slid out of my sleeping bag as quietly as I could. I shuffled to the edge of the cubicle and peered out. Seija was kneeling by the doorway. She beckoned me towards her once more before slinking down the steps.

I pulled a T-shirt over my head and crawled out in the direction of the door. The cool air hit me as I put my foot on the first step. A shiver ran up my back and across my shoulders. I could still hear faint music from the wedding across the fields. I descended the steps carefully, trying to avoid their unforgiving creaks and groans.

When I reached the foot of the stairs I turned to see Seija standing in front of me. Her hair was tousled and untidy. She had on a loose-fitting, cream-coloured nightie with lace trimmings around her breasts. One strap had slipped off her shoulder and was sliding down her forearm. The bottom of the nightie hung midway between her hips and her knees. It twitched in a moment of cool breeze. I could see her thighs in the starlight.

She grabbed me by the hand and walked off quickly, pulling me behind her. The dusty ground was cold on my bare feet as we rounded the corner and walked into the orphanage. She sat up on the table inside and brought me towards her. The hum of the insects in the fields around us filled my ears. The blood moved through my veins, my heart beating faster and faster. I started to shake.

'Hey. Hey,' she whispered, the words dripping from her mouth. 'It's okay. It's okay. Come here.'

She took both my hands and drew me in until we were touching. The softness of her legs wrapped around mine. Her feet hooked onto the backs of my knees and fitted as if someone had designed them to be there. She put my hands on her waist and moved hers up my body until they were cupping my cheeks. I looked up. My shoulders were shaking and I couldn't make them stop.

'It's okay,' she said. 'I know you want to. Just try and relax.'

And then she kissed me. She tasted of rice wine, but I didn't care. Her lips were soft and her tongue was warm and moist. She kissed me with my head in her hands and my own sense of separation and self was salt dissolving in water. I wasn't anywhere to be found.

Under the light of the stars, we were uncovered wires brushing against each other and sparking in time. Synapses pulsing and striking, pushing electricity back and forth. Lightning linking the earth to the sky. The sun setting itself home again at the end of a beautiful day. Dots joined in a star system, intrinsically but inexplicably linked. Lives falling out into another and fusing into one. Moonlight kissing the sea at the end of the night. Raw emotion that consumes all; complete and perfect in every way.

We were feeling into each other's souls and touching their essence, where nothing is hidden and everything is revealed. Where there's only vulnerability that can't be seen any other way. I was seeing the world through new eyes, untainted and full of possibilities. It unleashed a pure desire to love and be loved that I didn't understand.

As it happened, it seemed that the world was flowing as one, through me, through her, connected, synchronised. Life was in everything: the table, our bodies, the stars. I was part of it; part of something perfect. It was inside me and I was inside it. It was internal satisfaction that made me modeless. I was alive and part of existence; this living thing that encompasses everything and goes on forever.

When it was over we lay on the table for a while and stared up at the sky. She was lying on her back and I was curled up against her. The fingers on my right hand were intertwined with hers, connected as a chemical bond. Looking at the stars, I thought of my sister's question. It was starting to make more sense now.

After an age, she spoke. 'We should go back inside,' she said, still staring straight up. 'It's getting cold and I'm tired.'

I looked at her face. In the faint light it was coloured pale blue with speckles, as if it were a bird's egg.

'I don't feel too tired. Maybe we can stay out here a little longer.'

'No, I think it's time we went in. You've got an early start tomorrow.'

'Well... I don't have to go tomorrow. I could stay another day. I'm sure one more day wouldn't hurt. If you think that might be a good idea...'

Seija turned to look at me. On its side her face became dark in the shadowed starlight. 'Ethan, you're sweet. You know this wasn't any more than what it was though, right? It's the end of a long night. I'll still get up and teach in the morning and you'll still get up and go look for your sister. This was lovely, but let's not spoil it.'

She softened her voice, as if she were informing a family of a death. 'Tonight was just tonight, okay?'

She leaned her head up and kissed me on the cheek. I hardly felt it.

We stood up and walked back to the house, Seija leading the way. When we reached the steps, she stopped and kissed her fingers before planting them on my forehead. I watched her climb the steps. She moved up them as silently as a black panther. I followed a moment later and quietly shuffled into my sleeping bag.

I turned onto my side, facing away from Elodie, and rested my head on my arm. I chewed the inside of my bottom lip. I wished this stupid wooden floor wasn't so hard.

It was already beginning to feel like a dream.

The near darkness of a London night sky covered the window. Inside, the television stared at me. Even without the sound on I could tell that the man with the glossy hair was explaining to the woman in the flowery dress how she should style her living room. Amid all my nerves and concern I began to feel a sense of anger at all the people involved in the television show. It struck me how many people were probably involved in producing this show. And how many people the idea must have been approved by in order to be turned into what I was seeing. Casting directors, crew, producers, cameramen, presenters, studio bosses and runners.

The person who came up with the idea for the format was probably enjoying a glass of overpriced wine right then, funded by a television studio that believed it knew what I was interested in. Why should anyone be told how to present their own living room? How on earth can there be one accepted way to style a room? Why is the organisation of inanimate objects in any way important?

Perhaps this person was concerned that when she died, her living room would reflect on how she was remembered.

'She always had such a sense of style.' I supposed this was something one could say at a funeral, but I became intensely afraid that someone might say that at mine. There must be something better that could describe a person. I was sure there was.

I wondered what anyone would say at Charlotte's funeral. She had once told me that we are *beings towards death.* Sitting out by the road in the small patch of grass at the front of our house watching the cars, she had announced that our whole lives are essentially a disaster because we all are thrown into them with no choice but to die at some point. Our deaths define our lives, she had said, and this is why our lives can never be *complete.* I hadn't known if I believed her, or if she had meant it, but it had scared me.

Our whole lives are disasters: I wondered if I should say this at her funeral, but realised that I didn't even know if she would ever have one. I didn't know if there would ever be any kind of end to her disappearance, be it recovery or death. I realised that it might never be resolved, that I might never *know.* And that made thinking hard and the dark place slither out, so I stopped.

I had left that night for the airport. It was a cold night and I remember how strange that had made me feel. I tensed my muscles in the evening air and became aware of my skin as a separate entity, attached to the cold rather than myself. I wrapped my scarf around my neck and zipped up my fleecy coat.

Hunching my shoulders and striding down the street, I pictured myself in a film scene and briefly considered what song would fit as the soundtrack to that moment. I often did this, turning my life into a movie. It gave me something to concentrate on when I was uncomfortable or sad. It was another distraction from being faced with too much *depth.*

This time, though, I quickly dismissed the idea. Why would anyone want to watch a film about the minutiae of my life? I supposed to myself that everyone secretly believed their life was important enough to warrant a film, even if it were only one of those pretentious shorts that are supposed to have a profound meaning even though nothing happens.

The world disappeared as I turned the corner onto the main road. I chose to think of something else and the words my father had said to me that day began to run over and over in my mind. I turned them over, repeated them, rephrased them, reinterpreted them. How could such a simple phrase lead to so many ambiguities? I ran through the situation again, trying to view it from different perspectives and through different filters. As if it were a movie. My life as viewed through a warped, coloured lens, performed in front of an audience of none.

Never mind, it was in the past. And what was it Charlotte had said on another occasion out the front of the house? *Only the present exists. It's forever present, never past or future. All that exists is now.*

I had tried to derive comfort from this, but it had confused me more. If what she had said was true, why did it feel as though every part of my life was stuck in the past?

28

I awoke the next morning feeling tired and hot. Elodie was already up and packing.

'Morning, sleepy! Come on, we've go to get a move on! Our motos are already outside waiting.'

I sat up and rubbed my eyes. The dust had begun to make them itchy and I couldn't rub it out. Picking first myself and then my sleeping bag up off the floor, I slowly began to pack my rucksack. The events of the previous night loitered in my mind, as weeds in a flowerbed.

Seija's last words had swallowed anything good that had come from it. How could she have been so cold?

I thought of Elodie. She would never be able to see me in the same way again if she knew. I didn't know how much she would care, but I decided not to tell her.

How could it have been so good, so beautiful, and meant so little?

I stopped packing for a moment and sat on my knees. I looked up at the dark roof. I made another decision. If it didn't mean anything to Seija, it didn't mean anything to me. This was her fault, not mine. I picked up the last of my stuff and forcefully pushed aside the sheet that was keeping me from the world. I could deal with this, I told myself.

Most of the others were still asleep as we quietly washed and grabbed the few belongings we had left outside the house. We said little during this time, busying ourselves with the final checks of our bags and belongings. Once we were ready, with our bags on our backs, Elodie turned and looked at me.

'You okay?' Her eyes were tired, but open and wide.

'Yeah, fine. I didn't sleep very well last night. That floor. Once we get going I'm sure I'll be okay.'

Elodie turned her head and looked around. 'Doesn't look like anyone's about to say goodbye.'

'No, I guess not.'

'Oh well, it's a shame. I'm sure we'll see some of them again.'

'Yeah, you're right.'

'*Allons y*?'

'Yeah, let's go.'

As we drove off down the lane on our motos, I turned to take one last look at the house. I caught a glimpse of a face disappearing behind the door. Seija's blonde hair looked tired and faded as it quickly shut itself away, back inside the suspended building it had been a part of for so long.

As I saw this I somehow felt sorry for her, because for all her passion and beauty I was sure she was missing *something*. She had to be if she behaved that way. And that *something* seemed important. And although I wasn't sure exactly what *it* was, I was sure that *I* had it.

As we joined the road the sun was beginning to rise.

It was a dot of orange dye that was slowly seeping into the soft swirls of the sky around it. We rode fast through vast, open areas of flat land. I spread my arms open on the back of the bike and let the wind blow through me, a wonderfully cool antidote to the already consuming heat of a brand new day.

The previous night was being swept away with the wind, and its actions and complications were left behind in the dust. The sun was rising around me and I was new. I was alive. I was happy to be there.

It hit me: the appreciation I had of being here and seeing something I would never see again. The fact that this moment in my life, this beautiful moment, would only ever happen once. I thought for the first time how this experience, this recovery, this quest, whatever it was, was doing me good.

Part 3

I looked out of the window. She had always told me to look out of the window if I was feeling sad. She said there was always something beautiful to be found in a garden; you just had to look for it. So I did.

Outside in the garden my father was raking leaves. Big, arching strokes of his arms were dragging the metal wires across the grass. His sleeves were rolled up around his elbows, his arms thin and pale. From my perspective the check of his flat cap covered his head and face.

I was glad of that; I didn't want him to see me looking.

On the ground the leaves were somewhere between life and death; fallen from their source, yet not quite passed away. Layers of autumnal yellows and browns, speckled with rusty reds and greying greens, all being raked and tidied into clean, geometrical shapes. Piles of scattered colours, squared at regular intervals, placed in set positions in the garden. The jumble and tumble of rustling dead skins all fixed into neat, organised stacks. The growing patches of grass appeared from beneath the rake as they had when we had shovelled snow from the garden one cold winter years before. I thought of that time and the snowmen we had built together; of a time when we had been a family.

I raised my eyes. At the back of the garden the apple tree appeared naked. Leaning and tired, it slumped down over the grass. The honeysuckle bush next to it had died years earlier. Strangely, my father had never taken the time to get rid of its dead remains.

When had I last been out in the garden? I definitely hadn't been out in it since Charlotte had left. Initially it had become overgrown and unruly after she disappeared, my father not having the time, or seemingly the desire, to tend to it. The grass had grown long and the borders between lawn and flowerbed had smudged and blurred. In bad weather, when it was windy, the garden moved as one, flowing and swooping in different directions as if it were trying to escape. I had enjoyed the garden like that. It had reminded me of Charlotte.

But as time had gone on, and Charlotte's disappearance had begun its journey from denial to acceptance, my father had begun to take an interest in the garden again. I couldn't remember exactly when it started, but I remember what he had done. It had always been the same. He would put on his old jogging trousers, the ones with a hole in the right knee, dig out a rugby shirt, replace his slippers with mouldy walking boots, neatly tying them hook by hook until they were over the ankle, and disappear out the back door. This had gradually become something he did more frequently. He tidied and worked outside on a regular basis; most days, in fact.

He had started going out there for increasingly long periods of time. Often he would stay out until it was dark, and I would look for him from my window, wondering what he was up to. Scanning the darkness, I would make out his silhouette, always hunched over a flowerbed or kneeling at the foot of the tree, only the movement of his arms separating him from the rest of the night.

By this point, the garden had never looked so neat. The flowerbeds had all been trimmed back, tidied and square-edged. The patio had been cleared of weeds, and any sign of mud and mulch had been scraped away. The grass had been mown and strimmed until it was angular in its perfection. The garden table and chairs gleamed, the shiny metal polished and reflective.

This was why the falling leaves annoyed my father.

Sometimes I had heard him talking to himself while he was out there. Every so often from my room I had strained to hear what he was saying, but had never been able to make it out. It had always been a low-level mumble, something not designed to be heard. This was one of those instances. As I watched on, he was talking to himself quietly, shaking his head every now and then to get his point across.

It annoyed me that he spent so much time on the garden. The perfect orderliness of it all made me feel sick to my stomach, causing a churning wrench of my guts. Charlotte had been gone for some time and all he seemed to care about was unnaturally shaping the patch of land out the back of our house.

Our conversations had become increasingly brief whenever I saw him inside. We would pass each other on the stairs or nod hello on the way in or out of this dead living space. Each time I tried to remember the last time I had seen him smile.

Looking out of the window, I had wanted to go out there and kick down all his piles of leaves. To run around the garden, crashing into every geometrical heap and destroying their clean lines. To ruin the perfect tidiness, the synthetic order, the planned terror of it all. To tell him to let the leaves fucking be. To ask him why, in all these years, he had never spent as long on us as he had on the garden.

But I didn't.

And I didn't find any beauty in the garden when I looked out into it that day.

29

The water was as still as glass as we got into the boat. It reflected blue and grey until you looked closer and it became transparent.

When I was little I had thought the sky was blue because it reflected the sea. I had been certain of it until I had spoken to Charlotte one day and she had laughed.

I remember her telling me that the sky wasn't blue because of the sea, but because of something we couldn't see called the atmosphere. I had asked her how come she knew the atmosphere was there if she couldn't see it, and she had said it was because she had some of it in her eyes. She had told me not to tell anyone, though, so I hadn't. I had kept it; a secret that explained the world only she and I knew.

The atmosphere was a brilliant blue that day and warm and clean around me as I sat on the boat. The short, thin, wooden structure was floating on the surface of the water and cutting through the glass. The petrol motor behind me burbled and gurgled and sputtered and hummed. In our wake, feathers of waves were left to flap their way out into the glass, cracking its perfect stillness before disappearing into its depths.

Elodie was sitting in front of me, her eyes fixed on the horizon. She had been talkative throughout our journey that day but had since become as quiet and still as the water. I looked at her hair, which was tied behind her head. A small loose section was a slender kite flying in the breeze, jumping up and down as the air escaped past us. Her small frame fitted the narrow boat perfectly.

We had been meandering our way along the river through various channels and islands for half an hour. It amazed me that the driver knew the way; to me it was one giant maze. A collage of islands, their green spattered into the water as if by the flick of a paintbrush, each one almost identical to the next. And yet as we rounded another muddy beach, a collection of buildings came into view and Don Det revealed itself for the first time.

We could see a busy collection of people scurrying around on the large beaching area. Don Det was just another island, bigger than most of the others, but while the other islands had been largely ignored, this one was the centre of attention. The front of the boat rode up onto the beach and our driver jumped into the water before pushing the last foot onto the sand.

He rounded the sides and reached out a hand to help Elodie disembark. I climbed out, as did the three other men, and felt the warmth of the water on my feet. Our bags were thrown over the front of the boat and the driver quickly pushed off again. In a matter of moments the boat was sputtering off and away, back into the labyrinth.

It had been a long day; the different legs of the journey having been difficult in equal measure. It had been easier than the previous journey, however, with fewer surprises and moments of ineptitude.

It was six in the evening and the sun was beginning to set on another day. The blue atmosphere was just turning, as if my sister's eyes were beginning to close. It feels as if you lose a day when you spend it all travelling. If anyone was *really* in charge of the universe, they should let us start the day again and wind back the clocks. Who would really know?

I picked up my bags and stood on the beach.

'What was the name of the place again?' asked Elodie, her eyes panning the little beach.

'Makkar Guesthouse,' I said, my bags secured on my back.

'Well, let's see if we can find it then.' Elodie began walking up the beach. 'Come on! I don't know about you, but I'm hungry.'

30

I climbed into my hammock and wished it would stop swaying. I was feeling slightly sick and the gentle sideways movements were only worsening my state. I looked at Elodie in the hammock next to me, already still and asleep, her chest rising and falling softly and slowly. I envied how she managed to get to sleep so quickly. I was tired, but my head was still clogged up and packed in. Smoky and unclear. It was making my thoughts difficult to squeeze out. I looked through the glassless window and saw the pale light of the sun hurrying the last remnants of the night away. An aphorism came to me; the first in a long time.

Darkness is only an absence of light.

It's *true*. That's a good one. I closed my eyes and tried to get to sleep.

It had taken us all night to find Makkar. We had spent a couple of hours asking tourists in the little restaurants and bars along the waterfront if they knew the place, flitting our way between lit areas like moths. But we had had no luck. No one had heard of it. We had decided to get something to eat in one of the restaurants and have a think. It was only when we asked the owner as we paid our bill that we had received any sort of promising response.

It turned out that Makkar Guesthouse was a tiny place set inland. It was far away from the crowds on the waterfront and not a place most backpackers knew. Knowing Charlotte, I should have guessed this.

Don Det had been quiet as we wandered between the restaurants and guest houses. All the buildings along the water were fairly similar; basic wooden structures built high over the rivers on thin frameworks of bendy stilts. Woven bamboo walls separated the rooms, the gaps between the bamboo revealing slivers of candlelight; snippets of the secrets of what was going on inside. The only electricity on the island was provided by generators, which hummed loudly as they worked. There weren't many around, so once it got dark there was little light, which had made our search all the more difficult.

The travellers we had met and asked mainly fell into a single category. They were older than the tourists in Phnom Penh, with flowing, faded cotton trousers, loose-fitting linen tops and bandanas holding back their long, greying hair. Their chunky, wooden jewellery clunked rather than jangled as they gesticulated in the direction of the next place we should ask.

The smell of marijuana was everywhere, emanating from the food as well as the ashtrays. I wondered if anyone had ever attempted to categorise and sort the kinds of people who went travelling into groups as an anthropological exercise. Based on what I had seen, it wouldn't have been difficult to do.

Once we had finished eating we noted down the owner's directions, grabbed our stuff and walked the couple of kilometres out of town to Makkar. The night had been solid black by the time we had left the waterfront. We had begun following a path we weren't sure was even leading anywhere, which had been unnerving. We had stayed close to each other, using the moonlight to guide our footing. Fortunately, after walking for half an hour or so, we had seen candlelight coming from a break in the trees. The sound of running water, a waterfall, had also neared as we approached.

We had rounded a corner and the narrow footpath had come to an end. A large, open area had spread out in front of us. We had looked at each other and smiled in the moonlight. On the right-hand side there had been a collection of bamboo huts, four or five small, closed ones, raised up on stumpy stilts. Behind these there had been one large open hut. Lights and music had been shining out from it and I had also heard voices.

To the left there had been a large tree, gnarled and ancient. It had fluorescent streamers of different colours – oranges, yellows and greens – hanging from its branches. Paintings that glowed in the dark had dotted the tree and the area around it. I hadn't been able to make out what they depicted; their shapes were twisted and odd. The edges of wooden sculptures on the grass had just been visible in the half-light from the candles.

We had walked the last few paces through the clearing and Elodie had taken hold of my arm as we approached the candle light. The music had been faint, its beats whisping out into the air. We had peered into the hut.

'Hello?' I had mumbled in the loudest voice I could manage.

Five faces had looked over at us. Three were locals, their dark brown eyes and hair flickering in the candlelight. The other two had been white: a man who looked to be in his early thirties and a woman who looked younger. The white man's skin was drawn and tight. His cheekbones were high and stuck out, leaving dark indents, out of which his eyes peered. His rough, unshaven face had looked at me with a narrowed expression. My mind remembered the cow from ETP.

'Hello,' he had said in a London accent. 'Can I help you?'

'Er, yes, I hope so. It's a long shot, but we're looking for Charlotte Willis. Do you know her by any chance?'

'Charlotte? Oh, she left, what...' he had looked in the direction of one of the local men, 'over a month ago now?'

There was a nod of agreement from one of the men.

'She went north, up into the conservation area near the border with China.'

'She was here just over a month ago?'

'Yeah, that's what I said.'

I had gathered myself together. Sensible questions had needed to be asked.

'Well... How long was she here for?'

The man's tone had changed and he had sat upright. 'Listen, why do you want to know?'

Elodie had still been holding on to my arm.

'Oh, sorry, I should have said. She's my sister. I'm trying to find her.'

'She's your sister?' His tight face had tightened even more.

'Yeah, I haven't heard from her in over six months and I'm trying to find her again.'

'C is your sister? Fuck! I didn't know she had any family. Well! Look, you'd better come in.' He had gestured us towards him. 'Come in, come in. Sit down.'

'Thanks.'

We had stepped up onto the bamboo floor and taken our bags off our backs. The man had stood up and offered me his hand.

'I'm Steven. This is Claudia, and these are Lan, Sok and Chivvy.'

He had panned across the room with his other hand, and Elodie and I had waved faintly as each person was introduced.

'C never told me she had a brother. She was a bit of a lone wolf.'

There had been a pause and one of the candles had flickered out.

'Sit, sit.'

Claudia had given both of us a big hug. The first thing Steven had done when we had sat ourselves down was prepare some locally produced weed for the homemade bamboo bong that had been sitting in the middle of the floor. He had chopped it and mixed it with bark from a collection that was kept in an old, hollowed-out tree stump.

He had lit it expertly, puffing and inhaling in the right measure for the bark to catch light before taking the first hit, exhaling slowly and pointedly. One of the other guys had refilled it, relit it and passed it to me. Its wood smoke had been thick and a forest fire went down into my lungs. I had passed the bong on and my heart had started pumping blood around my system as if it were trying to put the fire out. My eyes had filled from the inside and started to pulse.

The drugs had started climbing over my brain and were running around the adventure playground inside my head. Elodie hadn't taken a hit and had passed it on straightaway. I had admired her for that.

Leaning backwards, I had decided to lay my head on the floor and close my eyes. I had wanted to ask so many questions but hadn't been able to work out how to ask them. The evening had oozed past for a while from that point. Conversation had pedalled past me, working its way uphill but never quite reaching its destination.

When my heart had eventually slowed down a little I had lifted myself up onto my elbows.

'Ah, he's back!' Steven had looked over at me, a beer in one hand. 'Lan's making some magic milkshakes, you want one?'

'What time is it?' I had asked, squinting.

'I don't know. Two... three maybe.'

I had wiped away some saliva that had been stuck to the side of my mouth.

'Magic milkshakes?'

'Mushrooms blended up to taste like strawberry. You know the type. I'm sure you've had a happy pizza before. The *interesting* kind of mushroom. The ones that let you see things you didn't know were there; change your state of consciousness. Peeling the layers off an onion.'

'I think I'll give it a miss this time, thanks,' I had said, laying my head back down.

'You sure? You don't know what the world's really like 'til you've tried this stuff, I'm telling you.'

'No, honestly, I'm fine thanks.'

Elodie had looked over at me.

Steven had frowned. 'Hey, you sure you're Charlotte's little brother? She used to have these for breakfast, man!'

'Yeah, I guess we're a bit different, that's all.'

'No shit. Different I would agree with.'

Lan had come back in with a bright pink-coloured drink and handed it to Steven. He had taken a big gulp, filling his cheeks before swallowing.

'You know, she was completing her own art collection before she left. She did it every day for ages, spending hours on them. Then one day she stopped. It was odd.' He had taken another mouthful. 'Here, come and have a look.'

Steven had stood up, his legs uncrossing in a way that put a picture of a double helix in my mind, walked down the wooden steps and out into the open grass.

'Come and look!' he had shouted to me without turning around.

Standing up, carefully and with concentration, I had stepped over Claudia and around the back of Elodie. I had stumbled down the steps and out into the dark. Everything had looked black and fuzzy.

I hadn't seen Steven for a moment, my eyes slowly adjusting to the lack of light. Ghosts of flickering candles had faded slowly from my retina. Waiting for a moment until they had gone completely, I had panned around and spotted him over to the left of the tree. I had trodden softly over to where he had been standing.

The grass had been cool under my feet and each blade flattened as I stood on it. I had thought of all the life in the grass, the entire world that lived there, dwarfed by my huge, cumbersome presence. I had wondered what I had killed to reach Steven and whether it would be worth it. How many times had I killed things with my careless steps, excited runs, gentle strolls and clamouring cycle rides? There must have been so much death in my past. A path of destruction that had all been my own doing.

This ought to have meant something to me.

Breathing in the cool night air, my mind had moved to thoughts of Seija for some reason. The memories of the previous evening flickering images in my private cinema. It was odd. As I stood there, I could watch it all happen, as if it were on a movie reel in my mind. As if I was observing a character doing those things and it wasn't me.

I had watched her as she led me into the orphanage, its incomplete bricks and cement a prop in our play. I had listened as she placed her lips on mine and they softly stole something from me. The camera angle had changed as she lay on top of me and ran her fingers through my hair, her body moving slowly, seductively, in the starlight.

I had wanted the film to stop. I had looked up at the stars and tried to think of something else, yet all they had done was remind me of lying in her arms, a piece of her puzzle fitted in and completed. At least, that was what I had thought. I had wondered whether a puzzle was still a puzzle if it had been solved. Were they puzzles any more, or did they become normal *stuff* like everything else?

A puzzle can't be a puzzle once it's been solved. It's just another thing that has lost its purpose; one more thing to be discarded.

I looked up at the sky. Right then it had seemed as if I wasn't looking *up* at it, but really looking *down* upon it. I had become worried that if gravity had decided to stop working I might have fallen at any moment into this massive expanse of black space with nothing to stop me drifting forever. Why did gravity work, anyway? What was it *for*? Did everything have to be *for* something? This question had flummoxed me for a minute, until I forgot what I had been thinking about.

And then I had a moment of understanding. As if an airlock had been opened and my mind had been filled with luscious, clean air. I had forgotten the falling and gravity and the grass and remembered the stars. The stars were a puzzle that was never going to be solved. Maybe that was why they were so important. They could never be redundant or discarded. They would always keep their purpose, even though we might never know what it was. I had smiled. Was that what my sister had meant?

My smile had faded and quickly became a frown. My mind had been thinking of Seija again. I hated the fact that the stars reminded me of her. She wasn't going to take those from me. I had become concerned again that perhaps I wasn't in control of my thoughts as much as I had wanted to be. My thoughts had seemed to occur when *they* wanted to, not when *I* wanted them to.

I had lost what sense I had previously had of the word 'I' for a minute and couldn't work out what 'I' meant. Am I just one thing? If I was one thing, I had been unable to locate or identify it at that point. Maybe all I am is a jumble of different thoughts and perceptions at any one time, none of which are a result of *my* will. I had shaken my head to check whether I still had my will and had subsequently lost my train of thought. Turning in the cool grass, I had looked back at Steven.

'Here's the first one she did,' he had said, pointing to a painting that was hanging from the side of the tree. One of his arms had been wrapped around his waist, the other outstretched in front of him. 'It's fucking great, isn't it?'

The way he spoke meant that his previous sentence hadn't really been a question, which was lucky because I hadn't known how to answer. I had stared at it. It was a canvas painting and had been given a natural wooden frame made from twisted branches.

I had only been able to half make out the painting in the dark. She had used some fluorescent paints and those parts stood out clearly from the canvas. They had been used to outline a picture of a fox. It was a bright blue silhouette. It had its nose in something I couldn't see. In blocks of bright yellow paint, a fluorescent moon and beams of glowing light shone down towards the fox's back. In the background I had made out an outline of trees and fields, but they had all been grey and shadowy. I had looked closer. It had looked a bit similar to England. It had looked like where we grew up.

'Come and have a look at this one. This was the last one she did before she left. Ethan? Hey, Ethan! Have a look at this one.'

'Coming,' I had said, walking past the tree and into the far corner of the cleared area. Steven had been standing in front of a large stump of wood. It was clear that it had been carved, but it didn't have any recognisable shape. At least, I hadn't recognised it.

It was waist height from the ground and essentially circular, a kind of tube, with different parts, some smooth and some jagged, that jutted out. Four points had been carved out of different sides of the tree stump. It had a thick base and narrowed in the middle. It still had the bark on in some sections, while in others it was smooth, shining in the moonlight. A hole had been cut out to one side near the top, which had been rounded and curved. I had run my finger through it. It had felt soft and empty.

Steven had been staring at the stump with a look of intense concentration. 'Awesome, isn't it?' he had said.

I had taken a minute to look at the lump of shaped, dead wood in front of me.

'What is it?' I had asked.

'It's for you to work out, man.'

'What do you mean?'

'I mean, it's whatever you make of it. C never said what it was meant to be. She finished it just before she left, so I can't tell you what it is. If you don't know, I guess you don't get it.'

'Huh?'

'Look, don't look at the outside, look at the inside too. Try to understand what the form is saying to you.'

He curved his hands in the air. 'Look at the whole thing. What isn't there as well as what is. That's what you can do when you peel away the layers, man. When you alter your state of reality. It shows the limits of language as a means of expression.'

'I don't understand what you mean.'

'Well, maybe you just don't get it then. Simple as. Not everyone gets metaphor and symbolism. It requires a certain... *level* to your existence.'

He had spoken in the way Charlotte used to.

Steven had walked back towards the hut. 'I'll see you in the morning.'

I had stood staring at the wooden stump. I had walked around it several times, bent over and tilted my head. I had sat down on the floor and touched it with my hands. I had wondered what my sister would have said if she had been next to me; whether she would have explained her artwork to me or whether she would have simply said what Steven had.

Up until that point, I would have been certain that she would have taken the time to talk me through every detail of it, speaking in a way that made me understand it and see its beauty and truth. But I was starting to be less and less sure of who my sister was, and of whether I knew how she would behave any more. Maybe this was her new form of aphorism; one I might never understand.

I had stared at the tree stump, hoping something would jump out at me. After half an hour I had stood up and gone to bed.

31

That night I had another vivid dream. I was at Makkar and it was daytime. The sun was bright and I could see Elodie in the hut next to me. She was talking to herself, saying things I had never heard her say. She was lying in her hammock and talking about how she wanted to feel me inside her. I was annoyed with her and called her a liar, but she ignored me and carried on as if I wasn't there.

This made me cross, so I got up and walked out into the clearing outside. The sun was burning hot on my skin. The tree stood in front of me, filling the clearing. I stared at it, its ancient roots twisting into the ground by my feet. It looked dead. The only things giving it life were the fluorescent paper streamers hanging off its old, weary branches.

The streamers began to move. I thought it was the wind at first, but they moved towards me as tentacles, their fluorescent colours leaving trails of luminous light in the air behind them as they wound their way towards me. The streamers wrapped around my limbs, their paper strangely coarse, and they cut my skin as they tightened. They kept coming and tangling around me, more and more, tighter and tighter until I fell over. I couldn't move. They were squeezing harder and harder, and the more I fought the more difficult it became.

I looked around for help. I could see Jon-Paul sitting with my father in the open hut across the clearing. They were both taking hits from the bamboo bong and Jon-Paul was shrieking with laughter. I screamed out to them, still trying to wrestle my way free, but they ignored me. I struggled to breathe as the bright streamers began to wrap around my face and neck.

I saw my father look over at me. With his eyes fixed on mine, he opened his mouth slowly and exhaled a deep, dark cloud of smoke that kept on coming. He was staring at me, the smoke billowing from his mouth, and he did nothing. When the smoke eventually stopped, he turned away again.

I tried to shout, my head full of anger, but I couldn't move at all. Seija and Charlotte walked casually past in front of me, oblivious to my presence. My lungs had no air left in them. A final streamer covered my eyes. Everything went black, and I found myself sitting up in my hammock, sweaty and out of breath.

Steven hadn't even known she had a brother.

-o-

<u>Charlotte's Journal: Day 398</u>

Lines slice and divide my sight,
A stretch of grass, a pavement, the sea,
Primary colours split like lovers,
Two foreigners never designed to meet.
Liquid and solid, movement and static,
Trails of foaming white and froth,
I'm blazing a path that leads to nowhere,
Perfection's in wait; hidden, untouched

-o-

32

The morning after the dream, I woke up in the bright sunlight. My mouth was dry and sticky. My mind was drawn back to the morning Charlotte had left, when I had woken up on the grass in the park, hot and sun-baked, just as I was now.

How much had my sister changed since she had gone? She had been away a long time. Perhaps I wouldn't even recognise her if I found her. I hoped she would recognise me, though I didn't know how she would react if I ever saw her. One thing I knew was that she wasn't there and that I didn't want to hang around much longer. I didn't like the place. Maybe it was because of my hangover, but it felt wrong somehow.

Looking over, I could see that Elodie was already up. I rolled out of my hammock, pulled on some trousers and a shirt, and shuffled out onto the grass. Nobody was around. The wooden stump stood to my left. I turned away from it and walked into the seating area we had sat in the previous night. As I walked up the steps I saw Claudia inside, lying on her back on a pile of cushions. Her eyes flicked in my direction and away again once she had seen me.

'Hi,' she said in a flat, directionless voice. 'If you're looking for Steven he's gone into the village to pick up some supplies.'

'Hi. Oh, okay. I don't suppose you know where Elodie went, do you?'

'I think she went down to the waterfall.'

'Okay. How do you get there?'

'Turn left out of here and go down the path that's straight ahead of you.'

'Great, thanks. I'll see you later.'

As I turned to walk away, she lifted her head and looked over at me. Her eyes were narrow, her pupils tiny brown beads on a wooden necklace. The whites of them were laced with a reddish tinge, which stood out from her pale complexion.

'You know, C went to do the loop,' she said. 'If you're looking for her you should go up there.'

She returned her head to the pillows and stared straight out in front of her again.

'The loop? What's that?'

'It's a four-day motorbike ride out in the Laos countryside. You start in one place, drive off-road and end up in the same place four days later; a loop. Steven wasn't going to tell you because he didn't think you'd do it. Plus enough people are doing it already and as soon as something becomes popular enough to appear in the fucking *Lonely Planet* it's ruined forever.'

She took a draw from the cigarette that was slowly ending beside her. 'Anyway, I think if she's your sister and she means that much to you, you should know where she went and make your own choice.'

260

My fist was clenched by my side. I didn't know what to say first. 'Why did Steven think I wouldn't do it?'

'Well, it's a pretty big deal. You have to get your own bikes and drive off on your own. There's no safety net, no tour guide, no proper map. There aren't any cosy hotels out where you ride, okay?' She rubbed her nose. 'I guess he thought you weren't the type. Let's be honest, you're not quite Charlotte, are you?'

As she said these last words she smiled at me. It was a smile you might give a child. When she had finished speaking, she started playing with the edges of her fraying linen top, humming something quietly to herself.

I had frozen. For the whole conversation I had been halfway down the steps. The ice shattered. I started moving. I walked as fast as I could, without running, down the last few steps and out towards the waterfall. Adrenalin was pushing through my body. My teeth were biting down hard on each other.

I broke into a run as soon as I hit the small footpath out of the clearing. I ran, faster and faster, catching my arms and legs on the branches and leaves as I sped past them. The hot air was inflating my lungs and I could feel the oxygen being sucked into my bloodstream, forcing its way around my body to my muscles. My bare feet thumped down onto the dry, muddy ground. The jungle ate me up as I tore into it, its canopy dwarfing me and blocking out the sun.

By the time another opening appeared I was sweating and hugely out of breath. I stopped and put my hands on my knees, hunching over and swallowing hard. Drops of salty sweat ran off my eyebrows, the sea washing out of my skin. It was only then that I looked up and saw the waterfall in front of me.

From high above me, a powerful body of water was cascading down into a fizz and a bubble in a turquoise plunge pool beneath it. The fall was wide and thick, white and rough, strong and aggressive. It was one single thing, a wall of nature, solid and alive. And yet as I stared into it I knew it was millions of tiny individual particles, each one falling and passing from my view after the next. As my pulse slowed down the sound of the rushing water grew louder and louder. It was such a clean noise, so simple and uncomplicated. Raising my eyes slowly up to the rocks and trees that surrounded me, I realised it was beautiful.

'Ethan! Over here!' Elodie called out.

I hadn't noticed her. She was sitting on a smooth rock beside the plunge pool waving at me. When I saw her, I could only think that she looked as though she belonged there; a natural piece of the surroundings. Beauty sits with beauty. She was art that made sense, more than any dead tree stump ever would. I walked over.

'Isn't it wonderful here?' she said when I sat next down next to her.

'It's great, really.'

We sat in silence and gazed for a gentle passing of time. I was trying to work out how to say what my mind was thinking.

I tried. 'Listen, Elodie, I want to get out of this hostel. Apart from here, which is lovely, I really don't like this place. To be honest, I don't like Steven much, and I don't think he likes me for some reason.'

'He's an arsehole. You shouldn't worry about what he thinks.'

Elodie's tone was firm as she spoke.

'You're right, Ethan, this place isn't great. Maybe she loved the waterfall, but I don't know why your sister would have stayed here for any length of time, I really don't.'

'I know. I don't know either. It worries me, Elodie.'

'What does?'

'Well, I've been so focused on trying to find Charlotte that I never considered what might happen if I actually did. What if I find her and she's completely changed? What if she doesn't want to know me any more? I guess I shouldn't be surprised. She's just… She's always been so much more than me.'

I breathed out slowly. 'Looking back, she never needed me. It was always me who needed her. No wonder she doesn't talk about me to anyone. I'm nothing, compared with her. I don't even know what I'm doing most of the time.'

Elodie adjusted herself on the rock, turning towards me. She softly put her hand on mine. 'Ethan, what's making you say these things?'

'Nothing. Everything. I don't know. It's just true. I'm weak. I'm confused. I'm boring. I've got nothing that's… different. I have no edge. My life isn't exciting. I'm not adventurous.'

'That's not true.'

'It is true. If it wasn't for you I probably wouldn't have even made it this far. I'm mediocre. I'm… afraid. And I'm sick of it. I'm sick of never being someone, never doing something great. Never doing something worthwhile.'

'But you are, Ethan. You are. Look at where you are. You're out in a jungle, in Laos, searching for your lost sister after everyone else has given up. That's got to be one of the most worthwhile, exciting, brave things I can think of.'

'Listen,' she tilted my head up to face hers. Her eyes were leaves shining green in the sun. 'You're not weak or boring, okay? You're kind and caring. You're thoughtful and gentle and funny and warm. Do you think I would go travelling across Southeast Asia with any old person? I've wanted to tell you this for ages, Ethan. You're the loveliest, sweetest person I know. Don't...'

I did something I had never done before. Impulse took over.

I kissed her.

I lunged in and my feelings gushed out, crashing and flowing until they gradually stilled. I raised my hands and grasped her cheeks, holding them tight and never wanting to let go. As we kissed, with the water falling beside us, I was a natural piece of the surroundings like Elodie. Beautiful.

When the gushing finally slowed she pulled away and looked at me for a moment.

'Let's get out of here,' she said, her eyes tied by an invisible string to mine.

'Yeah, lets.'

I paused for a moment. Who were they to know me?

'There's a motorcycle trip that could lead us to Charlotte. Claudia just told me about it. I'd love to go on it with you if you're still up for carrying on the search.'

'A motorcycle trip?'

'My sister went to do it, apparently. It's out in the

countryside in Laos, further north somewhere. Four days off-road, no hotels, no maps. You up for it?'

'Four days off-road, on motorbikes?' She smiled a perfect smile. 'Sounds exciting! Let's do it!'

-o-

<u>*Charlotte's Journal: Day 243*</u>

> *I'm running now I'm free,*
> *Yes I'm running now I'm free.*
> *But there's nothing worse than freedom*
> *When you have no place to be.*

-o-

33

We had left that afternoon as soon as we had packed and found out from Claudia where the loop began. Steven hadn't returned by the time we left, but I had seen him driving a jeep through the main village as we were getting on one of the boats. He had either ignored us or simply didn't see us. Elodie had opted to choose the former. I genuinely didn't care.

As our boat pulled out from the land and began its journey away from Don Det I looked at the stillness of the water around me. How different it was from the water gushing down the fall; what a different experience I was having of what was, essentially, the same thing.

Staring at the water as it glided past us, I glanced further downstream and saw a group of people floating in our path. There were five people sitting in tractor tyre inner tubes, which were bobbing, hardly moving, on the surface of the river. They were all holding oversized bottles of Beerlao from which they were taking giant swigs at regular intervals. One of them was smoking a joint and fussing over it.

Reggae music blared from a small set of speakers that

had been sealed inside a clear plastic bag and tied to one of the tyres. Looking at them more closely I could see they were all young men, all laughing and talking loudly together. They had short, clipped haircuts and an assortment of tattoos. Their skin looked patchy pink and crisp in the sun.

As our boat approached them, one of the men examined his bottle and threw it into the river. It sploshed into the water and sputtered a little before sinking vertically, like the Titanic. He reached around behind him into the water and produced another bottle from a carrier bag that was dangling, attached to his tube by the valve.

'Who's got the bottle opener?' he shouted out into the air, angling his head towards the sky.

'Here!' shouted one of the men behind him, who threw the opener in the direction of his friend. It was a poor throw and didn't make it anywhere near him, sinking with a splash into the river instead.

'For fuck's sake! You twat!' shouted the man.

The rest of the group was laughing. He rolled over to one side and dropped into the river on his belly as a dying seal might.

'You're going in for that!' he said as he swam, his tube under one arm, towards the man who had thrown the opener.

'Fuck off! Get it yourself!' said the thrower, who started to paddle furiously with his arms in the opposite direction.

All his efforts achieved little, however, and he was soon caught by the man swimming towards him. Tipping him over, the man pulled his friend into a headlock and they thrashed around in the water, all arms and legs. Their friends laughed raucously, coughing and spluttering as they did so.

'If you get this joint wet I'm gonna kill you twats!' shouted their friend, who was trying to hold his spliff out of the way of the splashes. 'We're on holiday. Who gives a fuck about a bottle opener?'

Our boat was right upon the men and the two in the water stopped and looked at us as we slowly motored past.

One of them saw me staring and caught my eye.

'What are you looking at?' he said, his eyes fixed on mine.

I said nothing and immediately shifted my gaze, changing position in my seat as I did so. When our boat had finally drifted past them they all burst into laughter once more.

Elodie leaned in to me and put her head on my shoulder. I was glad she was close to me. It was true, or at least it felt true, that finding something beautiful, something unspoilt, didn't happen to me often. I made a promise to myself that I would hold on to those things once I had found them, keeping them special and safe. I put my arm around Elodie, tightened my grip and stared out into the water ahead of me.

Charlotte's Journal: Day 413

I'm sitting here amid moving patterns of light,
My life's limping past right in front of my eyes,
See the world as fluid motion, as one slight change,
Feel the colours seep through to my mind uncontained.
All this means nothing, there's no storm to calm,
I'm tapped into existence as it drip-feeds my arm,
Is that all you know, what dissolves past your eyes?
But my loves and my feelings appear so alive.
As the meaning is lost among the story unwound,
When it all disappears it's only thoughts that I've found,
And in thoughts I think of you, imagine how it could be,
An atomic connection, flowing through you, through me.

-o-

34

It was another long journey to Thakhek, our starting point for the loop. I was almost used to the bus rides by this point. I was growing to enjoy them, taking time to absorb the goings on around me. They gave me time to think; to see the world at my own pace. I had been slipping back into my self-preservation mode less and less of late, preferring to interact with my surroundings rather than detaching myself from them. This was something new for me. There was so much to see that I worried about what I had missed out on all the times I had switched off.

I had travelled using many different types of transport by this point – boat, bus, taxi, tuk-tuk, moto and minibus – and on the final leg of this journey we travelled in yet another different form. This time we were crammed into the back of a converted truck. Wooden planks running across the insides of the truck provided makeshift seating, though once these were full more people came in and sat on the floor, squashed in around everyone's legs, grabbing any space that was available.

As I sat on my plank, a young girl was leaning against my right leg and an old lady was squeezed in against my left. I was also pinned into an upright position on the bench by a young lady on one side of me and Elodie on the other. It was almost impossible to move.

It was strangely fun being in such close proximity to all these people for a couple of hours. It was lunchtime and I got to see the local families get out their packed lunches. They fed each other handfuls of sculpted sticky rice, boiled eggs that contained the surprise of having baby chicks inside, and pieces of chicken that had been flattened out and grilled on sticks.

An hour before we arrived at our destination the journey became hugely uncomfortable. The fun side had become all twisted up in my stiff back. I was glad when we pulled off the road and finally slowed to a stop.

The matter of getting out of the packed truck was in keeping with the manner with which we had been crammed in. It happened all at once.

Once I was clear I stretched myself out in the cool night air. I was glad we had to walk the last kilometre to the hostel marked in Elodie's guide book. It loosened me up again and cleared my head. As I walked, I thought of the chicks that had been boiled inside their eggs, never having even seen the world. It had repulsed me when I had seen it, but I couldn't work out why. Was it any worse than, or different from, the massive slabs of grilled meat? I couldn't decide, and I ran out of thinking time as we approached the hostel from which we would begin our journey on the loop.

The hostel was small. It had a little garden out the front containing potted plants I didn't recognise. The front of the building was made of wood cladding and it had a simple, functional sign stuck above the door that said 'Thakhek Guesthouse'.

We walked in and rang a bell that was sitting on a table in the front room. There was a sticker on the bell that said 'Ring for assistances.' We took a seat on an old, tatty leather sofa and waited.

After a couple of minutes a man appeared. He had clearly just woken up and was rubbing his belly with one hand while scratching his head with the other. His face and hair were greasy. Both displayed a sickly shine in the low-watt bulb lighting. His thin white vest and spotted boxer shorts revealed a pot belly that stuck out from his tiny frame in a surprising way. He yawned and looked at us.

'Hello, good evenings. You want room?' He spoke English with a strong accent.

He licked his teeth and picked his nose as I replied.

'Yes, do you have one free?'

'Yes, yes, of course,' he said, as if it was a silly question. 'Come. Sign in here.'

He walked through a curtain and briefly into the next-door room before returning with a red guestbook.

'Sign in here. Must have details, thank you.'

He handed me the book and I took it from him. It had a textured, cotton surface, which led me to rub its cover with the palm of my hand.

'You hire bikes tomorrow?' he asked, hacking something out of his throat.

Elodie and I looked at each other.

'Yes, that's right. We hope to,' Elodie said. 'Do you know anything about the loop journey? We don't really know much.'

'Guestbook, guestbook,' he said, coughing and turning to go through the curtain again. 'All in guestbook. You read when you sign.'

He reappeared seconds later with a set of keys. 'Room four is your room. Pay me in morning, okay?'

'Okay, thank you,' I said, taking the keys. I was still holding the guestbook in my other hand.

'Sign in! Guestbook important! Government want to take my hotel, must show them I have guests!' He pointed his finger and waved it at the book in my hands before disappearing through the curtain, snorting loudly as he went.

'Okay, sorry.'

I opened the book hurriedly and flicked through the biro-dimpled leaves until I found the last page to have been written on. Looking down from the top there was a diagram, which resembled a rough map, a passage of prose and the four names of the most recent guests to have signed in. I studied the names carefully. There was no mistaking it. Elodie spotted it the same time as I did and took in a near identical intake of breath.

'Charlotte Willis!' she said, pointing to the page. 'Look! She stayed here, Ethan! Only... a week or so ago! Look!'

I didn't say anything. I put my arm around Elodie.

Charlotte Willis. United Kingdom. Student.

These words had such an effect on me. I looked back up the page and began to read what she had said.

The Loop

This is one of the most amazing things I have ever done! Something seriously not to be missed. However, don't follow the route that Klaus and Harriet drew earlier in this book. There is a beautiful underground river just off the road, which they missed out on entirely. Follow the guidelines and map I've drawn below and you shouldn't go wrong.

The loop – 4 Days, 3 Nights   470 km

Day 1 – Thakhek to Baan Thalang
Day 2 – Baan Thalang to Ban Nahin
Day 3 – Ban Nahin to Ban Kong Lor
Day 4 – Ban Kong Lor to Thakhek

Big, open spaces and lunging, rugged cliffs. Little villages and real lives. What scenery!

I hope my guide is useful – I'll be going to the next Full Moon Party. Meet me there if you used my instructions and you can let me know how it went!

I reread the last sentence.

'What's a Full Moon Party?' I asked Elodie.

'Oh, the guys in Phmon Penh used to talk about them all the time. They happen every month on an island in Thailand. Ko Pha Ngan I think. Every full moon there's a massive party on the beach. The way they were talking about them they're huge.'

'Every full moon?'

'Yeah, I think so.'

'Do you know when the next full moon is?'

'I'm not sure.'

There was a pause before Elodie turned towards her bag. 'I could look in my guidebook. It might say in there.'

I signed us in to the guestbook while Elodie flicked through the pages of her guide, muttering to herself in French as she did so. It took a minute, but she stopped flicking and turned towards me.

'Six days,' she said.

''Til the next full moon?'

'Yep. Six days until the next full moon and the next party on Ko Pha Ngan.'

'Well,' was all I could say. My mind was too busy thinking to put the right words together.

'What shall we do? We could make our way there tomorrow, Ethan. That might give you more time to look for her once you get there.'

I couldn't concentrate. After all the wondering, the worrying and the chasing I finally knew of a place where my sister and I could be in the same spot at the same time. That knowledge caused a cluster of strange feelings inside me, feelings that seemed to muddle me up. The only thing I could clearly concentrate on was something that kept running around inside my head of its own will. If she was willing to tell any stranger who might wish to know where she was, why hadn't she told me? Didn't she want me to know where she was?

Elodie put her hand on my arm.

'Ethan,' she said softly. 'What should we do?'

I thought for a moment, trying to clear up the puddle of feelings in my head. 'Well, we've got a few days before the Full Moon Party. I think we should stay up here, do the loop and head down after. What do you think?'

'I'm happy to do whatever you're happy with. It would be fun to have a go at this trip.' She kissed me on the cheek. 'How exciting! We have a real chance to meet your sister! You must be so happy, Ethan.'

I was happy. I was.

I just wasn't as happy as I had thought I would be.

Part 4

---

*

"You won't find her. You'll only find yourself more lost than you already are." He paused and looked away from me into the garden. "She can't help you any more, Ethan. Replace your own life, not hers."

-o-

<u>Charlotte's Journal: Day 467</u>

I grew into life as I fell into beauty, but something's changed. I can't keep a hold of it now. I was getting somewhere, I was sure. Closer to the answer. I blinked in the lights of the truth of this moment and lost it all in there somehow. Where's it gone? Is it even there any more?

Do I have to let it break or try to fix it? Maybe some things need to be broken. What if the answers aren't there?

-o-

35

The road ran, leaping and bounding, beneath our wheels as the countryside strolled softly past us. I gripped the handlebars tightly and the bike and I were one. It was simply an extension of my self. Every bump, every puddle, every piece of soft and hard earth. It was my will that was exploring these roads; my mind that was running over and over on the world's surface. The bike brought that will to life and awoke that opportunity.

Elodie's arms wrapped around my waist as we drove. The sea wrapped around an island. Space wrapped around the earth. I had been unsure on the bike to begin with, taking a while to get comfortable with the controls. But she had never made me feel unsafe. Whenever I had struggled, she had said nothing. She had a simple, unexplainable way of giving me the confidence to keep going.

36

Our bike was a Chinese-made, burgundy scooter with a dented exhaust pipe and two buckled wheels. One of the foot pedals was bent in on itself and it only had one wing mirror. There was rust on its chassis and the rubber, brick-shaped seat had patches of its leather cover missing, revealing a stale, yellow-coloured foam underneath. It stood at a strange angle due to the kickstand, which didn't quite kick as it should. It was beautiful to me, though. It had more character and personality than a lot of people I had met in the past.

We had found it at the last place we had looked, having been close to giving up after a morning-long search that had been almost fruitless. The important thing, however, as the owner of the shop had demonstrated to us and was keen to point out, was that we had found a bike and that the engine and brakes worked fine.

I had watched the owner's demonstration closely, paying attention to which pedal and handlebar did what, trying to make mental notes of how he changed gear and accelerated. It was basic stuff that I hadn't known how to do and I wished I had. I had wanted to ask a whole raft of questions, but the owner had spoken no English so I had been forced to learn what I could through gestures and actions. He had used his fingers to indicate how much the bike would cost and Elodie and I had agreed simultaneously without the need to confer.

After we had handed over our deposits I had climbed on and nervously started the engine for the first time. The bike vibrated though my legs and up my thighs. It had been heavier than I had imagined a motorbike to be. I had adjusted myself on the seat and gripped the rubber handlebars tightly. When we were both on and I had wheeled the bike out of the garage and onto the road, Elodie had put her arms around my waist.

'Don't laugh,' I had said as I twisted my hand and we had jumped forwards and away.

37

Our beautiful bike had only survived for a short time before it started making unusual noises. As we wove our way out of the narrow streets in Thakhek, the roads had opened up and become wide gravel tracks, twice as wide as anything in the town itself. Dust had risen up from the road in orange clouds and hung, metres above the ground, as it had done in Cambodia. It had swirled and snarled each time a giant truck grumbled its way towards us, their wheel sizes alone revealing why the roads were so wide. Factories had popped up in the distance on each side of the road, chugging out smoke from huge chimneys that bellowed into the otherwise clear blue sky.

As we had approached yet another factory, far in the distance, and I had started to question whether there was any real countryside in Laos, the bike's noises had changed instantly from a grizzle to a clunk and the back wheel had locked. In a split second we had nearly skidded off the road and I had fought to keep the bike upright, grappling with the handlebars as the front wheel had kept on spinning and the back one had stopped.

The bike had wobbled angrily and Elodie had fallen

off behind me before I finally regained control and pulled on the brakes. Leaping off the bike, which fell to the floor, I had run the couple of metres down the road to where Elodie had fallen. She had been sitting by the side of the road, her legs stretched out in front of her. There had been a nasty graze on one of her knees and blood had been trickling down from it.

'Are you okay?' I had asked, crouching down beside her.

'Yeah, I'm fine. It's only a graze,' she had said, smoothing her hand up and down her leg.

'Are you sure?'

'Yeah, I'll be fine. It looks bad because of the blood. How's the bike?'

'I don't know. I think we broke it.'

'Oh God, I hope not.' Neither of us spoke for a minute or so.

Elodie had voiced the obvious question. 'What are we going to do?'

'I'm not sure. We need to get help from somewhere. Maybe we should wait by the side of the road and flag someone down.'

'We haven't passed anyone in a long time now,' Elodie had replied.

She was right. It had been a good half an hour or so since we had passed a truck or another bike. I had ruffled my hand through the hair on the back of my head before standing up and looking around. My feet had grated on the gravel of the road as another drop of perfectly circular crimson blood oozed out and crawled down Elodie's leg.

'Let's wait, for a little while, and see if anyone comes past,' I had suggested.

Fifteen minutes, half an hour, an hour had passed. The sun had stayed static in the sky. Nothing on the roads. An hour and a half. We had drunk the water from our bottles and it had escaped out of our skin, salty, moments later. Still nothing.

Castes that had just been visible in the far distance wobbled in the shimmering heat. I had kept checking my watch as I sat, before standing up and wandering out into the road to peer at the horizon. Nothing. Elodie's leg had still been bleeding, but the graze had turned scarlet and begun to congeal. The skin on my face and neck had felt hot and tight. I had started to pace up and down.

'Sit down,' Elodie had said. 'Acting like a caged animal won't make any trucks come quicker.'

'Well we've got to do something,' I had said.

I had watched a column of smoke plume out in the distance. It escaped into the huge vast sky for a couple of minutes before I had an idea.

'Why don't I run over to that factory and ask someone for help?'

Elodie had twisted her head.

'Over there? That's a long way away, Ethan. It'll take you ages to get there.'

'That's okay. We're not exactly going anywhere in a hurry, are we?'

'I guess not.'

'We can't stay here much longer.'

I had dropped the bike keys onto the floor by her bleeding leg and it had made me think. 'Will you be okay here on your own?'

'I'll be fine.'

'Maybe it's best if you don't stop anyone,' I had said, thinking that it wouldn't be well received.

'I can handle myself, Ethan. I'm not a damsel in distress, okay?'

'Okay, okay.' I had run my hand through her ponytail. 'I'll be as quick as I can.'

She had looked up at me and taken my hand. 'Just be careful, yes?'

'Yeah, you too.'

I had started running. Things in the distance are often closer than you think, I had told myself. But after fifteen minutes, as I had gradually begun to feel the burn in my legs, I had started to realise that maybe the opposite was true in this instance. Slowing to a fast walk, I hadn't felt any closer to the factory at all; in fact, it had felt as though it was moving away from me as I ran. In the other direction, Elodie and the bike had been dots, small flecks of light on my retina. Everything had been so far apart. I hadn't been able to tell what was close or far away.

I had often run back at home. It had been a way to escape the house and clear my mind, especially once Charlotte had gone. One summer when I was home from school I had gone running four or five times a week. I had a route I would follow that took me up the hill behind our village, out and away from any people or buildings.

I had run the tracks that stretched through open green fields and thick yellow crops of rapeseed. I would pass oast houses and old railway bridges that were no longer in use. Listening to music, I had forgotten as much as I could and just run. It had been a new mode all of its own. I had enjoyed it, and the silence and energy that had come with it. It had often been my favourite part of the day. But this running, in this heat, with all my heavy, sweaty clothes, had been different. I hadn't enjoyed this at all.

I had lingered for a moment, turning my head between the smoke and the flecks of light. Claudia's words had entered my mind and soon enough a picture of her face had joined them. All tight and drawn, and clouded in a haze of yellow smoke, it had begun to laugh at me.

'You're not exactly Charlotte, are you?' she was saying as she cackled loudly and took another hit from her hand-carved, authentic-fake Laotian bong.

My parents were also looking at me. They weren't laughing. They were staring – my father over the top of his glasses – in silence. They were giving me *that* look.

Wiping the sweat off my forehead, I had pivoted on my left foot and started running again.

38

It had been an hour before the factory had been close enough to smell. I had been gulping in huge lungfuls of air by this point, and with each giant, sickly breath I had known I was getting nearer. Burnt oil and smoke were the two things that had stood out the most, along with some kind of chemical smell I hadn't recognised. Hitting a thick, invisible wall, the smell of these things had struck me all at once. This foul, unnatural concoction had burnt through each corpuscle it touched, tarring my insides. I hadn't been able to catch my breath properly.

I had walked from that point on and within another quarter of an hour I had reached the perimeter of the factory. The main part of the factory consisted of a collection of huge, box-like concrete buildings. There were five of these clustered around the giant chimney that stood towering into the sky, bellowing its smoke into the atmosphere. Trucks and pickups had been driving around between the concrete boxes, each chugging out more black smoke from their exhausts. The noise of the place had been incredible; a complex collection of the clinking and clanking of machinery, the rumble of the trucks' huge tyres and the buzzing of saws. The whole place had felt alive, as if it were a giant automata.

I had thought back to a mechanical toy I had made at school once. It was a bird with a beak and wings, which had been glued from its breast to a stick that was in turn glued to a big, rectangular, wooden box. There was a handle on one side of the box and when you turned it the bird's wings had flapped up and down in a slow, stop-start manner, as if it were flying somewhere. The mechanisms that made it work had been hidden inside the box and I remember thinking how clever this was at the time.

I had wondered where the handle that was making everything in this factory move might be. I had pictured a giant, complicated system of pulleys and cams and shafts beneath the ground turning and rotating and making the whole thing work.

When I had regained my breath I began scanning the factory for someone I could ask for help. After some searching, I had managed to spot a small group of workers not too far from me. They were smoking and appeared to be on a break. I had rubbed the back of my neck and breathed in a heavy gulp of toxic air before walking in their direction.

I might as well have been wearing a clown costume from the way they had looked at me when I first approached. There were five men and each of their faces had risen to look at me in turn, their eyes fixed and wide open. They had been talking and laughing, but once I came into view they had all fallen silent and stared. I don't think I had ever had that kind of reception before. It had reminded me of the lesson I had taught with Elodie at the school.

I had stopped in front of them and smiled and waved hello before putting my hands in my pockets. They had continued to look at me and I quickly realised if I didn't speak we could have stayed that way forever, solidified by the smog in the same position until someone had discovered us as fossils one day far into the future. I had tried to speak, but my throat was dry and the words crackled out.

'Hello. Er… Does anyone speak English?'

The faces had continued to stare at me. I had been forced to try again.

'My name is Ethan. I'm English and my moto has broken down on the road.' I had turned and pointed. 'Over there.'

There had been a brief moment of silence and we had solidified a little more before one of the men spoke.

'Moto?' he had said in a gruff, non-crackly way.

'Yes, yes!' I had said, getting excited. 'Moto! Over there! My moto has broken.'

My hand gestures had given the international sign for *not right* as I spread out my palms and crossed them over each other a few times.

The man had pointed over towards the road and said 'Moto?' again.

It was then that the other men had sparked into life and started talking to each other. They had been gesturing towards me and the road, and I heard the word 'moto' used many times, though I hadn't been able to understand anything else.

The man with the gruff voice had seemed to be disagreeing with one of the other men about something, but it was short-lived. One of the group had stood up and walked off towards the factory and the gruff man had made the international gesture for *stay here* by opening his hands and pushing them towards the ground.

We had stood around for a few minutes, with only the odd smile to fill the awkward gap that had opened up. One of the men had tried to talk to me at one point, but I had only been able to nod in return and he had soon realised I didn't understand anything he was saying. I had been looking back towards the road, with Elodie and the bike out of sight, and beginning to wonder whether we were ever going to get out of this situation, when a rumbling noise approached.

I had turned to see a small truck pulling up next to us. A head had leaned out of the cabin window. It was the man who had left several minutes earlier. He had waved me towards the truck and nodded in the direction of the road. Along with two others and the gruff man, I had got into the truck and we had rumbled away. I hadn't been able to stop myself smiling and grabbing the hand of each man and shaking it. They had all begun to laugh, and as each one shook my hand my smile had passed down through my arm, up theirs and into their faces.

I had read once that we have things called 'mirror neurons' in our brains that fire when we see someone do something in the same way, as if we were doing it ourselves. Apparently, that's where empathy comes from. My smile caused a biological reaction in the men's brains, which caused them to smile in turn. They had no choice but to do it.

39

Two men had stood around our bike, while another two had knelt on the floor beside it, their fingers black with grease. The standing men had placed their hands on their hips and cocked their heads to one side. The gruff-voiced man was one of those kneeling on the floor. He had placed his hands inside the bike and had a deep furrow in his brow, as if he were trying to birth a calf.

The chain of our bike had hung loose, snarled up between the cogs and the wheel at the far end. His fingers had been squeezing in between the cogs and sprockets and gears, trying to untangle the chain, which had lodged itself firmly in the wrong place.

Elodie had been standing. Her knee was still red and raw, but it had stopped bleeding. She had looked calmer, more still.

It hadn't taken us much time at all to return to the bike and the road in the truck. Elodie had stood up and moved away from the truck as it had arrived, but once she had seen me climbing out she had walked towards me and given me a hug. One of those hugs that lasts longer than you think it will and where time slows down while it happens. I had been a caveman bringing home a kill that was days late.

The men had turned their attention straight to the bike and, after giving Elodie a good look up and down, they had turned it over and begun to work on it. It hadn't been long before gruff-voiced man had removed his hands from its inner workings and spun the rear wheel with a look of satisfaction on his face.

Amid my happiness that the bike looked to be fixed, I had wished I could feel that kind of satisfaction, but I was aware that there were few things I could do with my hands. I didn't have any skills, and I wasn't sure I had ever thought about it before that moment.

I could describe how a plant photosynthesised or why people smiled when they saw other people do so, but I couldn't unblock a drain or fix a motorbike. I had wondered which things were more useful to know. Out here, these men who probably had little or no schooling knew much more than me. I had made a promise to myself that I would learn something useful once I got back to England.

The men had turned the bike back over and stepped away. I had climbed on, turned the key and twisted my hand on the throttle. The bike had roared into life and begun to growl even louder than before. Everyone standing around the bike had smiled, and for a brief moment that patch of road was the happiest place in Laos.

Elodie had said thank you to all the men and they had bowed and smiled some more before she had picked up our bags and climbed onto the back of the bike. She had taken out her wallet and tried to give the gruff man money several times, but he had kept on making the international gesture for *no* by pointing his palms at us and waving his hands.

Eventually Elodie had put her money away and placed her arms around my waist. I had nodded to the gruff-voiced man and, when he nodded back, all language, culture and difference had got lost in the small space that existed between us. I had pulled away and we had mounted the road again. Elodie had turned around and waved goodbye, and by the time she had finished waving we had been off into the orange dust once more.

The road submitted to our journey and as I gripped the handlebars I owned that bike. I could do anything on it. I could do anything in the world.

40

Standing in the shower, I watched an orange trail of dust wash away down the plughole. I held my head under the water and let my mouth and ears fill until all I could sense was the cool liquid that was running all over me. My forearms were sore and my neck was stiff. I stretched out and curled my fingers back several times before reaching for the bar of soap.

Elodie had had her shower first and had told me how good it had been. It was only a bucket hung from a hook with holes punched in the bottom, but it felt great.

It was seven o'clock in the evening and we had spent almost the entire day on the bike. The first day had only been riding; an escape from the city and an entrance into the world beyond. It hadn't taken us long to leave Thakhek and its surroundings, and after the breakdown we hadn't had any problems with the bike.

The ride had got better and the scenery had become something completely different as the factories and any last scraps of trucks and traffic had been left behind us.

The factories had been replaced by giant limestone castes, which towered out of the ground like skyscrapers.

I imagined them as the fingertips of some great being reaching out from under the surface of the earth and just managing to poke through. They dotted the landscape, their straight lines and crumbling surfaces dominating the horizon. The hot haze hung around them as they stood, ancient and united.

After our showers and a change of clothes we wandered out into the village to find something to eat. It was a fairly small place; a collection of houses and stalls huddled in the space between castes. The sound the village generated bounced around inside the castes and made the place seem much larger than it was. We found a stall selling food and after a little confusion managed to order something. We had a meal of omelette and rice and we both ate with intent, trying to refill our tired bodies as we sat on our plastic chairs by the side of the road.

A small crowd of onlookers came and went while we ate. There was curiosity, but not sheer amazement. It wasn't the same as the way the factory men had looked at me. We were worth a good glance, but nothing more. We didn't say much as we ate, both of us chewing and swallowing in the presence of our own thoughts, deep down somewhere in the cathedrals of our minds.

We slept at a guest house that night; the last recognised one that would be available to us before we returned to Thakhek. It was a small place; a house that had been converted into three separate bedrooms. We were the only guests staying there, but we were treated with routine and a degree of service that seemed to involve the least effort they could get away with. The room was dirty and the sheets hadn't been cleaned. Brown mould was growing on the windows. Still, it didn't matter. I was too tired to care.

After returning from our meal we went straight up to the room and collapsed onto our beds. I don't remember falling asleep; I remember having been on the bike so long that day that the bed was moving underneath me while I lay on it. It wasn't until the next morning that I realised I hadn't taken my clothes off or climbed under the stained covers.

41

The ride the following day was something else. We climbed and fell and climbed again on tracks no wider than walkways that took us deep into the Laotian countryside. The roads curved gently through the vast, open stretches of land that stretched as far as the eye could see. The earth around us was cut and stitched into different shapes and colours. The hillsides were steep and tiered, with contrasting brown and colourful cultivated areas of different sizes and depths.

They reminded me of a geography project we had done at school, where we had made a 3-D map out of cardboard to show the contours. As we rode further and further, everything became much greener and, softened by a haze of heat, the whole place was dreamlike; a fairy tale country that existed somewhere in the sky.

We moved through this fairy tale unseen and unheard, only the growling and groaning of our bike giving us away from time to time. Its age and condition began to show as it struggled and strained to carry us up some of the steeper climbing sections. We had to go right down into first gear at some points and inch our way up the windy pathways. We were almost completely alone, explorers of a wonderful new land, passing only two other bikes the whole day. These motos were carrying local families and both times they beeped and waved at us as they overtook. Big smiles followed them as they whizzed past. We waved back as we crawled up the hills in their wake.

We arrived at our destination for the second day in the late afternoon. It was another small village, even smaller than before, and as we scuttled our way in we weren't entirely sure if it was the place we had planned to stop at. We had been driving through rice fields for half an hour at that point, dipping and bumping our way through furrows of dried mud that carved their way between the fields. My forearms were sore.

At times, Elodie had had to get off and walk because the bumps were so big the bike couldn't get over them with the weight of both of us on board. I had navigated them at not much more than a mile an hour, but even so one bump had dropped so sharply I had been unceremoniously thrown off the bike and onto my backside. Elodie had laughed hard at this, creasing over and putting her hands on her knees in hysterics as I ran after the bike, which had been wobbling its way towards a rice field. Fortunately, it had toppled over just before it reached the edge of the track, and with only a slightly bent foot peddle for damage we had soon been back on the bike and off again.

The village was nothing more than a collection of maybe twenty or twenty-five huts, built high on stilts above the ground. These houses were different from those at ETP. They were higher up from the ground and smaller. They looked less sturdy as they perched, with only thin wooden poles holding them up. I imagined giving one house a giant push and seeing the whole village fall like dominoes.

When we reached a point that was somewhere near the middle of the village I stopped the bike and kicked up the stand. We both stiffly climbed off and stretched out our tired limbs. Putting the key in my pocket I had a look around. I couldn't see anyone at all. I looked through the open door frames and under the houses. Nobody. My eyes were drawn beyond the houses, back in the direction from which we had come. Several castes stood tall in the distance, the rice fields sitting quietly between us and them.

'Do you think this is the right place?' asked Elodie, twisting her back and pulling her arms behind her head.

'I think so,' I replied. 'We've been driving for about the right amount of time according to the instructions, maybe an hour more, but we did have to get off and on again for a while. And this isn't exactly the world's greatest motorbike, is it?'

Elodie laughed. 'That's an understatement. Still, she did all right today, didn't she? So maybe we should cut her some slack.'

I took a swig from the water bottle. 'Shall we take a look around and see if we can find anyone?'

'Yes, good idea.'

I closed the cap and we strolled off into the village.

Elodie put her arm around my waist as we walked. 'Do you know,' she said, 'that all this area was once underwater? That's why those weird castes are all over the place.'

'Really? When?'

'Oh, a long, long time ago now. Funny, huh?'

As we walked, I thought how strange what Elodie had told me was. I imagined the two of us swimming through the village, the sun's light fading into the deep blue in front of us. I imagined ancient turtles paddling past us, gently cruising between fields of minty green and charcoal black coral, meandering their way between the houses' stilts. I imagined shoals of fish darting around, black spots against the blue sunlight until they caught it and it reflected off their backs in flashes. I pictured coral in the shape of light brown vases and upturned lampshades clustered together on the seabed. Loitering just above this imaginary art-deco display there was a confetti of fish in a myriad of colours. A long trumpet fish swaggered past this flickering ticker-tape parade. As a cloud of tiny, colourful tetras swam across in front of me, I heard a voice.

'Hello! Hello! Excuse me!'

I turned around and looked into the blue to see a man shouting over from one of the houses to our right. He was leaning over the edge of his balcony and beckoning us towards him. With each wave of his arm the water washed away, leaving me standing on solid ground once more.

'Over here! Come, come this way! Oh goodness, this is a most wonderful surprise! My friends, come, come. Where are you from?'

42

Mr Kamvane had once been an English lecturer at the University of Vientiane. He was a slight man, with a good head of white hair and skin that creased into sun-beaten lines on his soft face. He had big, brown eyes that were magnified to an even larger size by a pair of thick plastic spectacles that sat on his nose and had to be pushed up repeatedly.

He had retired ten years previously and, having lost his wife and without any children of his own, he had decided to move out to live with one of his sisters in the countryside. She had never left the village they grew up in and still lived and worked in the rice fields he had known as a child.

Mr Kamvane explained how his father had invested all his savings in order to ensure that his only son received an education. He had sent him to a school in Vientiane when he was a teenager, leaving only his two sisters to help in the fields. This had been frowned upon by other families in the village, but his father had stuck to his convictions and Mr Kamvane had received an excellent education, learning academic subjects at one of the best schools in Vientiane.

He had had to work hard at a number of different jobs while he was studying in order to support himself in the city, and he spoke of times when he had had to go straight from school to work and back again without any time for sleep.

Deciding, when he finished his studies, that his education was something he wished to help pass on, Mr Kamvane had become a lecturer at the university where he had acquired his degree. He had made sure he sent money home to his sisters whenever possible because he was aware of the good fortune and opportunity he had been given by his father, who had since passed away.

These days, he was now supporting himself and his sisters with what could, in Laos, he said, be described as 'a comfortable way of life', drawing on his savings and the money his sisters' children made from the rice crops.

He was thrilled to have found a couple of English speakers and swiftly invited us to stay with him and his sisters for the night. Elodie and I felt we couldn't refuse and fetched our stuff as he turned and called to whoever was inside to begin organising supper.

That evening, we were given a feast of dishes that kept on appearing, one after the other. We ate fresh greens that had been cooked with peanuts and chilli. We had larp, a kind of spiced, minced deer meat. We ate rattan, which had been stewed or boiled in some way and had the strangest texture of anything I had ever eaten. We had handfuls of sticky rice, rolled into balls with a sweet chilli sauce.

When I thought we were finishing, Mr Kamvane's sister appeared with a huge dish. She placed it on the floor between us and took off the lid. The smell instantly filled my nose and mouth. Inside the dish was a whole fish, which apparently one of the grandchildren had run off to fetch from a neighbour soon after we arrived. It had been baked in mounds of garlic and chilli. It was moist and succulent. All this was washed down with strong homemade *lao lao*, a type of local rice wine.

Throughout the meal, members of Mr Kamvane's extended family joined us and sat at the edges of our small circle. Elodie tried to encourage them to come and join in, but they smiled and stayed where they were. Mr Kamvane said this was because we were their guests and we were to eat first. They would eat separately once we had finished.

I looked around at them while Elodie, Mr Kamvane and I were eating, wondering what they were thinking. All I knew was that whenever I accidentally locked eyes with one of them they grinned wildly and nodded me back towards the food.

I deliberately didn't eat as much as I could have, and when we were finished the feast that lay half-destroyed in front of us was moved out of our circle and placed in front of the others. As we sat there, letting our delicious dinner go down, the younger members of the family tucked into what was left, all the while keeping their eyes fixed on us.

Mr Kamvane took a big swig from his glass and cleared his throat to speak. 'Now that we are here and have eaten and our stomachs are warm and full, it is time for us to discuss,' he said.

He turned to me directly. 'You must tell me of your questions, Ethan.'

'My questions?' I replied, with five sets of eyes and chomping mouths facing me.

'Yes, your questions! Tell me of them, and then we may begin to talk about them.'

'I'm sorry. I'm not sure what you mean, Mr Kamvane. What do you mean by my questions?'

'The things that remain unanswered in your mind. Everybody has questions, Ethan. Some more than others, though I suspect you have many questions that you wish you knew the answers to. Many things are uncertain. Matters of life, matters of death, matters of the world. This world is a wondrous thing, a beautiful place, but it is very complicated, yes! So tell me, Ethan, what are your questions?'

I took a moment to think. There was only one immediate question, but it felt strange to discuss it with anyone else. 'Well, there is one question I've been trying to answer for a long time. Something my sister said to me before she left that I've never been able to figure out.'

'Excellent! This sounds very intriguing. Just the kind of thing I wish to hear! This is your question, Ethan. It defines you and how you live your life. Let us see if we, together, cannot try to help you in your thinking. Tell us, Ethan, what is your question?'

I took a deep breath in and out. Elodie gave the tiniest of nods in my direction.

'The question I can't seem to get my head around, I mean that I've been a bit stuck on, is: why are the stars so beautiful?'

'Ah!' Mr Kamvane clapped his hands together loudly and caught the sets of gazing eyes by surprise. 'What a question! This is a most excellent topic for discussion! Beauty, aesthetics. Fascinating! So, Ethan, we must begin. What have your thoughts been on this topic so far?'

'I don't know,' I said honestly. 'Every time I think I'm getting somewhere I change my mind. Nothing seems to give me an answer that satisfies my mind.'

'Why do you think that is?'

I paused and gave it some real thought. 'I'm not sure. I think maybe the problem is that I can't get my head around the idea of beauty. How can one thing be so different from person to person?'

Mr Kamvane opened his hands wide. 'Well, perhaps you are not thinking about this question in the right way, Ethan.'

'How do you mean?'

'Will you allow me to offer my point of view on this most interesting of thinkings?'

'Please, by all means.' I adjusted myself on the wooden floor.

'In essence,' he said, pausing, 'everything in nature is perfect. This is something you must understand. It is only our interpretations of things that lead us to what we see as things that are wrong or imperfections. When we experience beauty, Ethan, this is when we are aware of the perfection of nature. This can be caused by something we see, like the stars, or another person.' He looked at Elodie before carrying on. 'Or by an awareness of something within yourself. For you are a part of nature, Ethan, and this means that are also a part of perfection.'

Mr Kamvane ended his speech and looked to me for a response. The eating continued around us, everyone waiting for someone else to speak. I looked at Elodie.

'I don't understand what you mean when you say that everything in nature is perfect. How can it be?' said Elodie, knowingly entering into the discussion. I was surprised to hear a note of tension in her voice.

'Well, my dear, matter and energy are what essentially construct the universe, and neither of these things can be destroyed; they are merely transformed. It is true, matter can be torn up and shredded and ripped apart, but what exists inside the atoms is still there, just in a different form. If perfection is the best thing anything can attain to, then this means, in some way, that what constructs the universe is perfect. For, can you create anything better than something that is infinite? Could the human mind even begin to design something like this? You only have to look around you to realise that the universe is a truly wondrous place. And sometimes, when you see something, this is what makes you aware of this marvellous nature of the universe. Perfection is good, so beauty is good because it is an awareness of the perfection of the universe. So, why are the stars so beautiful? My answer would be because nature is perfect and seeing the stars awakens an awareness of this within you. What do you think?'

Mr Kamvane took another swig of his *lao lao*, reached inside his shirt and scratched his back. Elodie was turning a glass around between her fingers. She was frowning.

'How do you explain why beauty is different for different people in your theory?' she asked.

'Ah, this can be easily explained,' he said, smiling, as if he had known the question was coming. 'It doesn't matter that people find different things beautiful. It only matters that they find *something* beautiful. There is something out there that makes each person aware of the perfection of the universe. Some people see it in more things than others. Different things trigger this awareness in different people, but it is always a realisation of the same truth.'

'It doesn't seem to be a perfect universe to me,' said Elodie, raising her eyes from her glass. 'Matter and energy are one thing, but the human being and what it is capable of is something else.'

'Ah, but you and I are part of this whole, this matter and energy, as everything else is. You must see this. Because we have developed so much, we *think*,' Mr Kamvane pointed to his temples. 'We lose touch with our basic natural make-up. Our construction as physical objects. It's all the same system, and it works so well as a system, my dear. But we have developed out of its basic structure. The human being can be a terrible thing. We think we aren't part of it any more. We abuse it, we ignore it, we set ourselves above it, we disconnect ourselves from it. It is this that makes us feel ill at ease, incomplete, unhappy. This is why the human race is so discontented. We are breaking down the system that has been here since creation and built up over billions of years.

He paused. 'But we are still part of this whole, made of the same stuff, aren't we? It's only at certain times that we realise it; this natural connection to everything that exists. A life running through everything. This is the case when we see the stars. There's a force connecting all that exists, which, when felt, makes you feel right again, as you should without all the human fading things and designs we bring into the world. This is permanent, running through our very beings. This won't disappear. This is everything. This is *you.*'

He reached out and took Elodie's hands and she looked up.

'*You* are everything, my dear,' he said.

Elodie smiled at him, before withdrawing her hands and reaching for her glass again. We all sat digesting our food and Mr Kamvane's words.

Before I had the chance to think it all through, he continued. 'Mademoiselle, I sense you are not contented by my answer. Perhaps we should try another line of thinkings. What question would you like to propose to our discussion?'

I turned to look at Elodie, who was looking out over the balcony. The sun had set and the sky was a purple green colour, not yet black. The early evening was clear and the castes stood silhouetted in the distance. I thought of the bike briefly and hoped it was still sitting where we had left it.

'I don't think I have any questions to discuss,' said Elodie as she looked back in towards us.

'Come now. I can see your questions in you, my dear. They're obvious. They're satellites orbiting, spinning around your head.'

He twirled one of his old, leathery fingers in the air and smiled at her. 'Just release one. Try it. Let the gravity go and maybe you'll feel a little lighter.'

I watched Elodie as she looked into space and imagined her trying to spot one of her satellites.

'I don't see questions as important. I'm sorry, I don't,' she replied.

'May I ask why?' asked Mr Kamvane.

'Any questions I have – about big stuff that has no accepted answer – have been invented by me, so I don't think they have an answer. I don't even know if they are truly meaningful, in the same way, to anyone else. Any questions you have will have come from you and your mind, and any answers will come from the same place. Even if we *think* we are answering the same questions, they really mean something different in each of our minds. I honestly don't think anyone can fully understand what I want to know but me, by the simple nature of my mind being different from yours.'

'This is a very interesting point, but I must disagree with you. Surely, you must admit that in some way there must be *an* answer out there in the world? Something that is ultimately *true*. An explanation for all of this.' His hand waved out into the cool air. 'It can't all depend on you, my dear.'

'I'm afraid *I* disagree. I don't see an answer; a point to this universe. It's just here, that's all. What you do with it, how you see it, gives it a meaning. A point, I suppose. I see the stars as what I make of them; a sparkling piece of nature I enjoy looking at. Nothing more.'

'Your answers seem to be lacking something, my dear. The *human condition* is to question, is this not true? If there is no questioning, we are not human. When a hollow shell cracks, nothing comes out. Remember, you need the darkness if you want to see the stars.'

Elodie frowned again, harder this time. 'Ask questions, that's fine. Just don't expect any answers that can be agreed upon other than scientific ones.'

She tightened her ponytail and put her hand down in order to stand up. She quickly grabbed her bag from the edge of the balcony and put it on her back. 'I'm afraid I'm tired now and would like to go to bed.'

Once we had cleared the food away and retired to the floor in Mr Kamvane's living room I couldn't get the conversation out of my head. I kept on turning over the words in my mind. I wanted to let what Mr Kamvane and Elodie had said melt into my thinking and flow around in the chemicals inside my brain. I wanted to be able to pick a side in their debate.

I wished I had said more. There were things I had wanted to say.

The whole experience had been like another of my strange dreams. Something from the movies. As if it had been something that I had always wanted to do but didn't know it until then.

43

The next day we woke up with the sun. Its bright light filled the open room we were sleeping in. Shadows from the windows and walls stretched across the bamboo floor, dividing the light into oblong shapes. For once I was awake before Elodie. Rubbing my eyes, I looked at her sleeping in the sunshine. Her hair hung loose over her shoulders. Her chest was rising and falling slowly with every breath of sunny morning air. Curling up next to her, I gently wrapped my arm around her middle and lay there, watching her sleep. It was entirely quiet and all I could hear was the sound of her breathing.

I concentrated on it and pictured myself as the air that was being inhaled and exhaled from her lungs. As an oxygen particle that had made it down her oesophagus and had been picked up by one of her alveoli, becoming a part of her being. I began to swim through her bloodstream and got swept up in the journey through the veins around her body.

It wasn't long before she awoke and my journey came to an abrupt halt. When she opened her eyes and saw me, she smiled.

Soon the village awoke and we were invited out to join Mr Kamvane again. After a quick breakfast of an omelette and coffee, eaten without an audience, Mr Kamvane had taken us downstairs and introduced us to a moustached friend of his.

This friend had offered to take us on a trip through the underground river my sister had mentioned in the guest book back in Thakhek. We had asked about it that morning and immediately Mr Kamvane had taken it on as a personal mission to ensure that we got there.

'You must go,' he had said. 'It is a wondrous place!'

As we ate, various members of his family had begun to run back and forth around us, in and out of the house, in order to get the trip organised while we sat on raised stilts above it all. Elodie and I had offered to help on several occasions, but each time had been dismissed and told to sit and wait.

After an hour or so, the thin, middle-aged man with a tiny moustache arrived on a moto. He had pulled up outside Mr Kamvane's house, nodded and smiled to us and gone in to talk to Mr Kamvane.

It would have taken less than a minute to pluck out his moustache. I had imagined his wincing face as each hair was pulled out. After not much more than a minute, they had both come out of the house together, moustaches intact.

'My friends,' said Mr Kamvane. 'This is Mr Sok. He will be taking you down to the river today. Please follow him. You must go soon or you will not have enough time to reach your next stop before dark.'

Mr Sok bowed to us and we both bowed back. He was

promptly dismissed towards his bike, which he climbed onto, starting the engine noisily.

I stood up and turned to Mr Kamvane as Elodie began to pick up her stuff.

'Thank you so much for looking after us,' I said, reaching out to shake his hand.

'Yes, thank you,' agreed Elodie.

'And thank you for the conversation last night. It was very interesting,' I added.

'It was my pleasure to enjoy your company.' Mr Kamvane shook our hands firmly and gave a wide grin as he spoke. 'You must come back and visit me again. I feel we did not finish our discussion, mademoiselle!'

He laughed loudly at this point and a nearby dog started barking, which made Elodie jump.

'Off, off you go. Drive carefully and enjoy the cave. And remember, Ethan, be aware of the universe! You can't miss it if you keep an eye out!'

After waving goodbye to Mr Kamvane and his family, we walked towards our moto and refuelled it using the Coke bottle filled with petrol Mr Sok had given us. We climbed on, and as Elodie put her arms around my waist again we set off. We followed closely behind Mr Sok, slowly bumping our way through several rice fields and desperately trying to keep up as he manoeuvred his way expertly over all the ups and downs before reaching a small group of trees and leafy shrubs. We came to a halt just before the trees and Mr Sok kicked up his bike and gestured for us to follow him. As we made our way through the green leaves we embarked upon a gradual descent and could soon hear the sound of running water.

Rounding a corner, I caught my first glimpse of the river through the trees. It was the most perfect turquoise; a cut topaz sparkling in the sun. Flecks of light flicked in and out of existence on its surface. Hints of green and blue jumped about under the light as if they were subatomic particles, appearing and disappearing, ordered in their randomness. Elodie squeezed my hand before running down the slope towards the seed-shaped boat that was moored where Mr Sok was standing.

We climbed in and bobbed for a moment before Mr Sok untied the rope and pushed off. The cave was in front of us and in the bright morning sun it was black as black inside. Mr Sok had a long stick, which he was using to punt us along the river towards the cave. The sparkling surface of the water disappeared as we floated into its mouth.

Darkness is only an absence of light.

The minute we were inside the cave, the heat went away and the air was cold and damp and lost its colour. It became oddly silent. The only noise we could hear was the occasional push of Mr Sok's pole as he punted our boat along.

After a couple of minutes our guide switched on a large, round torch that was fixed to the front of the boat. The whole cave became illuminated, casting strange shadows and patterns of light around us. A huge domed roof was revealed above the boat. Large stalactites and stalagmites hung from and grew out of the ceilings and floors. Lots of little ledges led to tiny sections of rapids that echoed around the blackness. Other than this section, the water was perfectly still and in the torchlight complete, untouched, crepe paper reflections of the cave walls lay on its surface. How long had it been since the stone inside this cave had seen natural light?

We pushed our way on through the silence, turning the torch to focus on the different parts of the cave. At one point a tiny sandy beach appeared on one side of the boat. The antithesis of any other beach I had seen, it seemed to serve no purpose. It simply sat there. Some sort of punishment from the Greek gods, I pictured grey, sun-starved bikini wearers lying on the sand, tortuously turning over to invite an all-over bronzing effect they would never achieve.

This environment was so foreign and so fascinating to me that our twenty-minute trip was over in an instant. As we continued to punt our way through, the tiny dot of daylight that had appeared at the far end of the tunnel gradually grew until it was big enough to make me squint. I watched the light approach as we edged our way towards the exit and I narrowed my eyes. It looked brighter than anything I had ever seen before.

When we eventually came out the other end and my eyes had readjusted to the light, I looked up. The sun seemed different somehow from when we had gone in. It was still high in the sky, still perfectly round, still incredibly hot, still still. I cocked my head to look at it. Something was different. It had been switched off and on again while we were in the dark. Someone had pulled away the sky, peered in and pushed a giant reset button. I looked at the trees and the boat and the water and I looked at Elodie, and after the dark of the cave, and in this new sunlight, it was as if I hadn't seen them for a long time. I put my arm around Elodie and kissed her.

'I'm really glad you're here,' I said.

She looked at me. After all that darkness, her green eyes were leaking light.

'Thank you for coming with me,' I said.

She smiled and kissed me back. 'It's been my pleasure,' she said.

The sun shone its new shine and the world grew a little brighter.

44

On the final night of the loop, after another day's riding, we stayed in our own wooden house on stilts. We were in another village, a bit bigger and closer to civilisation than the place we had stayed at with Mr Kamvane, and had found a room to stay in after seeing a sign in the window. The owners weren't as interested in us as the family from the previous night had been and we had no audience or banquet or great philosophical discussion. We were merely shown where we were staying and pointed towards a stall where we could get something to eat.

The ride had been good that day. I had had no problems with the bike and had focused less on the handlebars and controls, which had given me more time to look at the scenery around us. After the cave, the sun had continued to shine brightly, lighting up the world in a new way. We had left the rice fields within an hour and had found ourselves back on designated tracks, which had provided a much smoother overall ride. Our backs and my arms had been grateful. The roads had begun to open up again towards the end of the journey and a sense of nearing completion had entered my head.

That evening, after dinner, Elodie and I sat out on our wooden balcony and talked into the night. We had bought a bottle of local rum from a stall in the village and decided to drink it, taking it in turns to knock back swigs and grimace. It tasted of pure alcohol. We would take a gulp, swallowing it quickly and loudly before it had the chance to spend too long burning our taste buds.

As the night wore on and the rum bottle emptied, we talked about all sorts of things. Almost inevitably, the conversation turned to Charlotte.

'Do you miss Charlotte?' Elodie had asked, still grimacing from another shot of the rum.

'To be honest, I don't know any more.'

I picked up the bottle and swilled around the last remaining dregs to see how much was left.

'It was odd, her disappearing. It took a long while before I realised how much I would miss her. I had got used to not having her around. So it wasn't any different when we first thought she might have gone missing. She still wasn't at home, like always.'

I drank the last of the rum from the bottle and coughed as it went down.

'It was only when the time started to pass that it hit me that I might never see her again. And I started to miss her. I hadn't seen her for a couple of years, and it hadn't bothered me too much before. It was normal. But when the phone calls started coming back with no news, something clicked.'

I looked down at my hands. 'That was the hardest time.'

'It must have been awful.'

'It was bizarre. Surreal rather than awful. It didn't feel like it was happening. It still doesn't in a way. This whole trip doesn't feel real.'

I breathed in deeply and sighed, shifting my position in my seat.

'Do you miss your family? It's been a few months since you've seen them, hasn't it?' I asked.

'No, I don't miss them. I never do. I miss my best friends from back home. I really miss them.' Elodie paused briefly, rubbing her thumb over and around her wrist. 'But my parents? No.'

'What are they like, your parents?'

'Oh God.' She sighed, filling her cheeks with air. 'My parents? Do you really want to know?'

'Yes, I do.'

She flicked her eyes up to the sky. 'Okay. My dad used to be a diplomat when we lived in France. He's a big man, overconfident and outspoken on most issues. A real *storyteller*. He moved to England to further his business idea and set up his marketing company with diplomatic contacts he had in London. That's as much as he tells me about his work. He never talks to me about it. He'll happily talk about it for hours with his colleagues on work functions and nights out on the town, but he never involves me. He spends very little time with me, in general. I'm sure there was a time when we used to do things together, but it's not a time I can remember well. I don't think he knows much of me at all.'

She sighed. 'He will once I go and work there myself, of course.' She flashed a smile and it was gone.

'What about your mum?'

323

'My mum, there's not much to know. She's a socialite. She goes to parties and entertains and drinks cocktails for a living. She loves the glamour of it all: dressing up, make-up, that kind of thing. She's still a child in some ways. She and Dad met at some international dinner in Paris a year or so before they had me. They don't talk about it, but it's obvious I was a mistake. They were only together for a year at most before my mum fell pregnant. They married before I was born. A whirlwind romance, they call it. Star-crossed lovers, fated to meet. A drunken fumble and a mistaken wedding, more like. Whenever they have their high-society, fake guests over and they tell the story of the night they met I always want to ask my mum if she was only easy for my father.'

I looked up.

Elodie looked back at me and frowned. 'I know it sounds harsh. I know it does. But you should hear them talk about it. It's as if it were the most important, glamorous, decadent evening and encounter known to man. Their sense of self-importance is so high I can't stand it sometimes. I can't stand that kind of fake person who thinks they've got everything under control. The kind of person who pretends to be happy all the time when they're obviously not. Why can't people be honest and admit that they fill up their time with so much crap because if they had any spare moments they might realise how unhappy they are?'

'Are you happy, though?' I asked hopefully, trying to change the subject.

'I feel like I am sometimes, but it never seems to last. I've always had this big hole in me. A space that grows

324

whenever I think about it. When I feel it, it's hard to describe. It's almost beautiful in its intensity. And not because it's *perfect*, just because… it's so sad that I can't feel anything else. A mind full of sadness takes over at the strangest of moments.'

I thought of all the sadness I had ever felt and wondered if it was in any way the same as hers.

'And for a long time I couldn't work out why. Why was I feeling so sad? It wasn't until I left home that I realised… I had nothing to love.'

She looked at her hands and rubbed her fingers with her thumbs.

'I so want to care for something. To find that genuine thing that fills this well of sadness that I have and block it up for good. It seems as though everything lets me down. I don't know if I know what love is, but I know that I want it more than anything else. I want to fall in love and spiral up to the stars and fly off with the clouds and climb the constellations. And I couldn't ever do that on my own. I think I need someone to save me, because I'm fed up with saving myself.'

She put her hands over her eyebrows. 'I'm sorry… I'm drunk. I'm sorry.'

I waited until I could find the right thing to say, but it didn't come. A little piece of the dark quiet from the cave returned and I didn't know what to do with it.

'I wish I could save you,' I said, looking at the floor by my feet.

It was quiet again for a while, both of us looking at the floor.

Elodie breathed in and breathed out. 'Oh, Ethan,' she

said, putting her hand on my arm. 'I think maybe you already have.'

And with that, the quiet piece of cave melted away into the night sky.

45

That night, Elodie silently left her bed empty and climbed into mine. After a minute or so her head moved towards mine on the pillow. I could feel her breath. She whispered something in my ear. Her words were warm, moist and soft. They trickled their way through the internal workings of my head, warming every firing synapse and flowing molecule until they finally nestled in a tiny part at the far corner of my brain. The part that feels love. The part that had been used so little before. I held them there, the words, squeezing them tightly in that moment while finding a safe place in my cathedral to store them. A place where I could lock them away forever. Mine to keep. Mine to treasure. Mine to turn to whenever the world was too much and I needed that warmth again.

I kissed her and whole galaxies were created around us, bursting with stars and energy. As they exploded and imploded and fired out into space, her words became a part of my past, etched into my memory. Tangible things to exist as long as I did. Gradually, everything in our galaxies slowly began to cease to expand and started to shrink back together again. In the films this was always the time that the next thing happened. Fade out as the covers begin to move. Build up stirring but soft music. Cut to morning.

But it didn't feel right. I didn't want to ruin this moment. I didn't want to get it wrong. Seija was still in the back of my mind. Things were almost perfect the way they were. Elodie was too much to put in that thing's powerful hands. I kissed her again and closed my eyes. This, where we were now, was right. I could feel it. It was different. Not the spectacle it had been with Seija, but something so much more. Not fireworks, but waterfalls. This was what how it was supposed to be.

As my eyes closed, I turned to those words and let them flow through my mind once more. We both fell asleep, our bodies curled up. Two pieces of the same puzzle.

Charlotte's Journal: Day 183

As I sit here, green leaves brush the sky. The chill of blue blows silently past. Chocolate sculptures stand on the horizon. They refuse to melt as the sugar falls around them.

All becomes sweet.

Everywhere I look, animation reveals the life. The hiss of invisible hands through the trees. The sound of wind-up birds that never runs out. The cotton swirls down from the sky.

All becomes me.

Through the window, outside gently glides to the inside, the boundaries lost somewhere between. Formless lines that hang and give visible shapes. The endless curls settle in my eyes.

All dissolves me.

I am the world.

-o-

Part 5

One morning back home, as we were eating breakfast a few weeks before Charlotte left, she had told me of a dream she had had. I didn't understand it then, but its black-and-white images had stayed with me. From the way she had told me, I had felt as though I was there, her voice stinging and looping and falling and climbing with each word. Looking back, maybe it should have been obvious that she was going to get out. Out of life as I had thought it was, that is. Out of life as most people see it.

But when she had told me her dream that day, as I ate my cereal and drank my juice, it had seemed normal, another of Charlotte's stories that my parents had ignored and I longed to understand. I don't know what she had hoped to get out of telling me, maybe telling someone alone had been enough. Maybe she had wanted me to grab her and shake her and say, 'Snap out of it!' Maybe she had wanted me to tell her to go as far away as she could. Maybe she had wanted me to ask her to explain exactly what she had meant. Maybe she had wanted me to tell her everything was going to be okay. As it was, I had done none of those things.

And I so wished I had.

'I opened my eyes and a street opened out in front of me,' she had begun. 'I looked at my feet. Fake cow skin cut, stitched and tied over a pair of thick polyester socks. I moved my toes and the synthetic fibres scratched. I realised I was standing on a traffic island. It was still. Motionless, cold concrete built upon more motionless, cold concrete. I didn't need to look... I knew. The whole city was dead.

'I lifted my eyes from my feet and looked around. The road was empty but for its toxic paint in dots and boxes and arrows that scattered in different directions. They were useless; there was nothing to instruct. I remember thinking it was odd that the road should be empty at that time of day. The pavements to my left and right were emptier still. Their different shades of tarmac were a patchwork of spills; a succession of accidents and mistakes covered up without subtlety. Gaping holes stuffed with temporary solutions.

'The buildings that framed the road rose high into a blazing blue sky. Miles of manmade grey and glass blocking out the sun. The whole street was in shadow. The sky looked blue and clear, but a cold lack of colour and warmth smothered the clean, geometric lines of the walls I was trapped between. On my island.

'Looking down the street I saw a flicker of light. At the far end of the road, two street lamps – one on the left-hand side and one on the right – clicked into life. I could hear the sound of electricity, an almost unperceivably high hum that stung and tingled in the air, bouncing off the walls. But there was only me there to hear it, and it knew that somehow.

'The lights began to turn on, two by two, from the end of the street in my direction. Pairs of unnatural, synthesised lights that would survive anything, even a divine flood, due to their chemical waterproofing and manmade materials.

'Standing there, the street was approaching me with every flicker. It grew closer and closer, but as I tried to move, my island remained still. The walls lit up behind the lights and grew taller and bolder, bigger and heavier. The sky was disappearing.

'The lamps were racing, flicking on almost instantly, one after the other. When they reached me and I felt the cut of the harsh, clinical light immediately and completely, all I could smell were the burning fumes of rubber and exhaust.

'My feet were damp and I looked down. The island I was on had become a melting mass of black, all viscous and thick, like oil. I began to sink into it as it bubbled in the artificial light. I froze as I sank, my arms as grey as the buildings around me, and eventually I felt nothing but sticky, stifling black.'

I had swallowed another glassful of juice after she had finished talking and sat staring at the tablecloth. A car had driven past the house. The radiator next to me had clunked and gurgled.

Charlotte, I'm sorry.

If I ever find her, that's what I'll say.

46

I awoke early, carefully pulled my arm out from under Elodie and looked out towards the window. The sun was shining through the square frame in perfect, straight lines. In the dark of the rest of the room it shone through. It was a block; a prism of heavy, solid light that would crush anything underneath it. Colourful air was trapped, hot and glowing inside, bursting to get out.

Seeing it there the way it was, I wanted to dive into it and let it break and smash all over me, the golden shards of light cutting into my skin and embedding in my body. The sun would be me and I would be the sun and I would dance around the room dropping pieces of golden light everywhere. I would kiss Elodie and pass some of it into her mouth and watch her glow like me. We would hug and move and get lost in the warmth and mirage of our own burning gases, and it would be completely beautiful.

I looked at my watch to check the date.

It was the day of the Full Moon Party.

We had arrived into Ko Pha Ngan late the night before after another long day travelling down from Thakhek. On the final day of the loop I had been the most at home on the bike I had ever been, no longer having to think about the little things I had been forced to concentrate so hard on at the beginning. Pulling back into Thakhek, the sun had been shining and we had climbed off the bike for the last time before handing it back to its owners.

The act of handing the bike back had reminded me that the night of the Full Moon Party was only two days away. I had barely crossed my mind over the four-day journey, but at that point it had seemed very real.

We had decided to get an early night after we finished the loop and had left at six the following morning. I had slept for a large part of the journey and, on the whole, crossing between Laos, Cambodia and Thailand had gone quickly.

The last stretch on the boat from the mainland to Ko Pha Ngan itself had been the highlight of the journey. Out on deck, the cool air that rippled off the sea had blown and left me feeling fresh and eager to arrive. As we approached the island, the lights from the town had been flickering on the surface of the water, dancing with me as I looked on. The sparkling sea had mirrored the clear night sky, as if each one was trying to outdo the other. In all their vastness, it was the flecks of light they had been competing with.

I had wondered what would happen if all the darkness in the universe became light and all the light became darkness. I had never been able to work out why there was so much darkness. It hadn't seemed to serve any real purpose. It had seemed to me that the universe would be a much better place if it were the other way around. Still, I had begun to think as I stepped off the boat and onto the island that maybe the universe wasn't so bad as it was.

47

The morning of the party raced by. Once I had woken Elodie and we had washed and dressed, we had a delicious breakfast of fresh fruit from a local stall. We had a look around the local market and went back to the hostel to grab towels and books to take down to the beach.

Elodie had said that the market reminded her of Bangkok, and as she said this I thought back to Charlotte's first journal entry, remembering how I had felt when I read it. It did demand attention. It was a collection of narrow streets, each lined with stall after stall. The stalls were nothing more than patches of floor space that had been covered in goods, or wooden planks that had been used as tables to sell anything and everything: T-shirts, jewellery, sarongs, sunglasses, wallets, watches, bongs, flip-flops, orange juice, noodles and fruit. It was bursting with colour and activity and people.

It had been impossible to browse quietly without being pounced on by one of the street vendors. We had split up for a while to try to cover it all, but it had still taken us a good hour or so to make our way around a small area of narrow lanes.

It was another perfect day as we left the hostel after the market and set off for the beach. I stopped on the steps that led out of our building and looked up.

A searing sun in a bold blue sky.

I paused for a moment in time that seemed to take longer than the watch on my arm indicated. As time moved slowly, I thought of Phnom Penh and Jon-Paul and Jacob and Charlotte. I thought of Tee and Davi and the cafes and the motos. I thought of Lucio's and happy pizzas and Sunshine Happy Guesthouse and Bjork. I thought of the lake and how it was as green and still as before. I thought of Mr Kim and Sunita and the kids. I thought of Claudia and the waterfall. I thought of Mr Kamvane and perfection and the village that was underwater. I thought of the cave and the sparkles of light. I thought of my parents and my house and my bike and the honeysuckle bush. I thought of the phone on the table and the worn-out leather chair. I thought of the deep-set trenches and the thin grey lines. I thought of the garden and the piles of leaves. I thought of the tears and the arguments. I thought of the park and the grass and the night sky. I thought of the stars.

I thought of Charlotte.

Standing there in the sunshine, caught up in my moment in time, I heard a voice call out to me that I was sure I recognised.

'Hey, look who it is! Ethan! Elodie! Hey! What are you doing here?'

'Oh my God! Fillip! Mimi! Hey!' Elodie's voice was high-pitched and excited. I looked out in front of us and saw them on the beach grinning wildly.

'Wow! What a great surprise!' said Fillip. 'We're here for the Full Moon Party. You?'

'Yeah, same!' Elodie said.

'Oh, that's ace!' said Fillip, making a fist and giving an air pump. 'Where have you been? What have you…?'

Mimi interjected, giving Fillip a harsh frown. 'Fillip! What he means to say is, have you found your sister yet?'

'No, not yet. But she's supposed to be here, for the party, so hopefully I'll be able to find her tonight.'

'That's excellent news!' said Fillip. 'Another reason to party!'

'Yes!' I said, unsure what else to say.

We all smiled and nodded, followed by an awkward moment of silence.

'Well, what are you up to now?' asked Elodie.

Mimi pointed towards a collection of buses down the road. 'We're going out of the village to find a great market we've heard about. You?'

'Just going down to the beach to have a look around. See if we can see Charlotte. Then hopefully we can relax for a while before tonight.'

'Oh, okay. Sounds like fun!' Mimi said.

There was another little awkward silence.

'Shall we see you tonight, then?' asked Elodie.

'Yes, yes, that would be great! Where? What time?' asked Mimi.

'How about back here at, say, half seven?' I suggested.

'Perfect!' said Mimi. 'See you then. And good luck finding your sister!'

Mimi and Fillip walked off and were soon deep in their own animated conversation. Elodie turned to me and handed me something. It was rectangular and wrapped in soft tissue paper.

'Here, I got you a present.'

'What is it?' I asked, holding it in both hands.

'Open it and find out!'

I found the seal and carefully unwrapped the paper, taking care not to tear it. Once I had separated the two sheets, I lifted out what was inside. It was a book. It was bound in green leather and had a string attached to its spine. I opened it to the first page. It was blank white paper.

'It's a journal,' said Elodie. 'It's time to write your own story, don't you think?'

I looked at the journal and turned it over in my hands as I took in her words.

'Thanks Elodie. Yeah, I guess you're right.' I drew my palm across its smooth front and looked up at her face. 'I wouldn't know where to start.'

'How about starting with today? Let's go down to the beach and you can write your first page.' She was smiling at me.

'Okay, sounds good.'

'You'd better write something nice about me in it, though!'

Elodie laughed as she turned towards the beach. I saw the soft curves of her shoulders twist and bend and that small part of my brain where I had locked those words expanded and grew.

Charlotte's Journal: Day 570

Deep feelings of love and connection slide into my experience of the world unannounced. They give me a fulfilling sense of contentment and clarity. And at the same time they still confuse the hell out of me. It's a forked movement that takes my body in one way and my thoughts in another. I am aware of the intrinsic link between the two; of my thoughts as an offshoot of my physical experiences. But there seems to be a sense that I can feel real satisfaction, clean, open and alive, without any reference to my thoughts. In fact, it's almost due to the absence of my thoughts. With my thoughts come questions, and with questions comes confusion. And confusion doesn't deeply satisfy unless one finds an answer. And I'm beginning to wonder whether that is possible.

My feelings of the world seem to come pre-packaged with the answer; I'm just not sure what that answer is.

48

The music was starting to make my legs move of their own accord, my feet lifting rhythmically up and down in my flip-flops. It was early evening and we had been out on the beach for an hour or so, drinking, talking and laughing.

I looked out to sea. The sun was well hidden behind the horizon and the sky was a beautiful deep blue and red; the last tinges of colour before the day was gone. The air around me was quickly cooling and I could feel the evening approaching. I breathed in deeply and held it inside. The air tasted of anticipation. Everyone on the beach was in a good mood, ready for something great.

I had wandered up and down the beach several times that morning and afternoon. Elodie and I had given up for a while, having a lie down on the hot sand while it was still early. I had even managed to have a go at starting my new journal. As the afternoon had gone on, more and more people arrived on the beach. I hadn't realised how massive an event the Full Moon Party would be. Bars lined the front, one after another, each with a big dance floor and people spilling out onto the sand. Fire dancers – twirling patterns of heat and light – were dotted along the beach.

There were groups of people arriving from neighbouring islands wearing coloured name tags so they would know how to get back in the morning.

As the day drew on I kept looking out across the sand for Charlotte. Whenever I had a free moment or if the conversation slowed down I would go for a quick wander, but the beach was teeming with more and more tourists, all drinking buckets full of rum and Coke with a strong, local, fake Red Bull thrown in. My quick wanders were starting to take half an hour, and that was only around the little section of beach we were on. It was a confusing place and with so many people there it was easy to get lost. As the sound of the music grew and the club lights switched on I began to realise how much of a task I had on my hands. Finding a group of people on this beach would be hard enough to do, let alone one person. Whom I might not even recognise.

In my breaks between searches, Elodie, Mimi, Fillip and I talked about all sorts of things. After several drinks, the alcohol was beginning to run freely in our bloodstreams and any remnants of the awkward silences we had shared earlier were well and truly gone. The buckets were strong and I could feel the effects of the alcohol teasing its way into my brain.

Having told the story of the loop and our adventure, Elodie asked about ETP and what had happened after we had left. The conversation turned to the place that was now a distant memory to me, from before the time the sun had been reset.

After he had updated us on Mr Kim and the children, and how everything had gone since we had left, Fillip leaned into me and gently nudged me on the shoulder. He was wobbling a little as he spoke.

'So, Ethan. You've got to tell me how you did it, man!' he said attempting to whisper, but failing.

I smiled. 'Did what?'

Mimi and Elodie could easily overhear his words and looked on, intrigued.

'Seija, man!'

I stopped smiling. 'Huh?' It was the only noise that would come out of my mouth.

'I saw you go into the orphanage with Seija that night after the wedding, creeping out of your sleeping bag! There's only one reason anyone goes into the orphanage instead of the house at night, and it's not sleeping, if you know what I mean! So how did you do it, man? That Seija is a fox!'

Filip patted me on the back and grinned expectantly. Mimi poked him in the ribs, frowning as he spoke, but it was too late.

Elodie looked at me, all elemental; fire and water. 'Is that true, Ethan?'

I shifted my weight from foot to foot and rubbed the back of my neck. 'Well, yeah. We went into the orphanage that night. Yes, that's true.'

'Come off it, Ethan, you know what I mean. Why did you go into the orphanage with her?'

'We just did. It was the end of a long night, we were drunk. That's all.'

'That's *all*?' Her eyes were burning.

'Yeah, it was nothing.'

She looked down and drew a line in the sand with her toe before asking, 'Did you sleep with her?'

'Don't do this, Elodie. It's no big deal.'

I looked across at Filip. He had stopped smiling.

'Answer the fucking question!'

'Elodie, please. It was a long time ago. It doesn't matter.'

'It *does* matter! It matters to me! It matters! Just tell me, Ethan. Did you sleep with Sieja?'

'Yes, but…'

'I knew it!'

She slapped me. 'You're an arsehole, Ethan Willis. A fucking arsehole! It had to be her, didn't it? Everything I hate. I fucking knew it!'

'Elodie, please. It was a mistake, something silly before we got together. Before I knew what would happen with you and me.'

'There isn't any you or me. I don't want to see you again. God, I can't believe you did that!'

She was shaking her head. 'I thought you were different.'

'I'm sorry…'

'I don't care about you or your stupid sister any more, Ethan. I hope you never find her! You don't deserve to!'

Elodie turned and ran off across the sand. I watched her go for a moment and she disappeared into the crowd, becoming just one of many. I clenched my teeth and ran my fingers through my hair.

'Shit, I'm sorry bro. I didn't….' Filip looked at me, the fun gone from his face.

'Don't worry about it.' I stared at the sand. 'It's my fault. Look, I'll see you around, okay.'

I walked off into the crowd but couldn't see Elodie anywhere. There were too many people. The anger and

346

resentment and frustration and hurt tore up through me and I roared 'FUCK!' into the night. The night gave no response.

I was alone. The darkness came out.

For the next hour or so I wandered in and out of clubs and bars. I forced a path through people, pushing them out of the way. I walked the length of the beach I don't know how many times. The music, the dancing, the alcohol inside me all fell into the same place. The pit of my stomach. Nothing felt good any more. I was lost. Why had I even come here? How could I expect to find Elodie, let alone my sister, in all this? I had been so naïve. It had been all so *predictable* of me. My time here hadn't changed me. I wouldn't find her. And Elodie was right; I didn't deserve to.

I stopped at a quieter point on the beach between two clubs. Bottles and litter scarred the sand around me. The sea rolled in to collect people's piss and rolled out again, dirty and sick. The moon had gone behind the clouds, leaving a grey sky that slumped onto the world, fading everything. I put my head in my hands.

'Hello, my friend. You want some ecstasy, mushrooms, coke?'

'Huh?'

A small man was standing next to me. He spoke quietly in my ear, the peak of his greasy cap brushing the hair on the back of my head.

'I have ecstasy, my friend. Best kind at party. Good price for you. Cheap.'

I looked at him. His eyes were facing away from me, his hands in his pockets. Another drug dealer. How many must there be on this island? I looked at all the people around me. How many of them had paid a man like this?

'You want?'

I wanted lots of things at that moment. I wanted to forget. I wanted to love. I wanted to hate. I wanted to wipe away time. I wanted to release. I wanted to tear out my insides. I wanted to say, 'Fuck you!' to the world. 'Look where you've got me.' I wanted to say, 'This is the sum total of my life. I'm fucking nowhere, nothing. Lost. Alone.' Yes, I wanted.

'Yeah, pills. I… I want pills.'

Pills for my disease, pills for my loss.

'Ok, five for forty baht.'

I didn't even haggle. I paid him and took them, palm to palm. And with that he was gone.

I looked at them in my hand, rolling them in my fingers. So small, so white. So perfectly circular. I found a half-drunk bottle of beer in the sand and put the pills in my mouth. All of them. Fuck it. The darkness could win. I wanted to feel something. Anything other than this. I wanted to be a part of my sister's life in some small way. I wanted to make this whole wretched journey worthwhile.

I wanted to destroy.

I poured the warm beer into my mouth and the spiders washed down the plughole. I sat down and stared out to sea.

It was done.

It wasn't long before the world started to change. Images began to detach from their objects, the light slightly delayed. The cool air around me became warm and sticky. For some reason I started to run. I pumped my arms and legs mechanically. My blood was racing, pulsing, surging around my body, and with it raced questions and answers. Questions and *answers*. So many questions and *answers*. So many beautiful truths I had never seen before. So much modeless, effortless content and meaning. I loved that sensation of knowledge.

I loved how the beach finally made sense to me.

I found myself in a club, moving on the dance floor. I had become one with the music. It beat my heart and moved my limbs. My eyes were wide and full of colours. The lasers and lights shone beauty onto myself and the other mortals below. I danced and danced. Happiness leaked into my brain in large drops and drowned everything else out. Euphoria felt like this, I was sure. Time adjusted itself to my clock and for a few immeasurable moments everything was bliss and nothing else mattered.

It didn't matter about my sister, or Elodie, or Seija, or the truth, because everything was *okay*.

Then the lights began to swirl. They swirled in a pattern that didn't match my design. The colours had begun to change. The club was no longer my perfect building. It was becoming a foreign landscape; stuttery and jagged. The music slowed, beating irregularly like my heart. My head didn't stop when I did. Everything kept blacking out.

I somehow made it onto the beach outside the club. I had a strong, bitter, chemical taste in my throat. Something started to dribble from my mouth. I wiped it with my hand. It was foam. The foam of a violent wave that had crashed inside me. The crowds of people spun and swirled. I choked. I put my hands to my forehead but they slipped off in the sweat. Everything fell apart.

I collapsed.

When I hit the sand, it was cool. Its grains stuck to the sweat on my head and neck. I could hear shouting and see disjointed faces standing over me. They were possessed with a madness and horror I couldn't recognise. The wave kept on crashing and my mouth continued to fill. It dripped down over my cheeks and dissolved into the sand. I couldn't make sense of anything any more. What were those questions? What were the answers? They had been so beautiful and clear, but now I could only remember one.

I desperately tried to find the words Elodie had said to me, the ones I had locked up safe and warm, but I couldn't. They were covered in darkness. I couldn't concentrate. Where were they? I felt hot. I was melting. Where was I? *What* was I? The shouting and faces above me had become one and I was somehow lost in the midst of it all.

And then, out of the crowds and the heat and the swirling and the madness came one voice. One voice that I knew in an instant.

'Ethan? Ethan? Is that you? Oh my God! What are you doing here? How did you find me? Ethan? Ethan, what's wrong? Fuck! What have you taken? Ethan, talk to me! Open your eyes! What have you taken?'

'The stars.'

'What?'

It was the only answer that made sense to me.

'The stars.' My mouth fizzed and bubbled and foamed. 'You wanted to know why they're so beautiful.'

I choked and coughed. 'They're so beautiful because they're perfect, they're... infinite, they're untouchable. Out of my reach. They can't be spoilt or ruined or messed up.

Like sunsets or... mountains or the sky. Everything else just... Why do I fuck everything up? Why? If the world is so amazing, why do I have to ruin everything?'

'Oh Ethan,' her voice crackled. 'What have you done? We can talk about all this. You can tell me everything. I've got so much to say, Ethan. I bought my plane tickets home. I was coming to see you.'

Her hands ran through my hair. 'I'm sorry, Ethan. I'm sorry I left you. I was searching for answers on some things and it took me a long time. I thought I had found them, but every time it wasn't right.'

My eyelids wanted to rest. I was losing them to gravity.

'Keep listening, Ethan. Stay with me. The reason I never found any answers is because there *are* no answers. There are only questions. I realise that now. I was so stupid. I talked about this stuff, but I don't think I ever truly *got* it; I couldn't let go of the idea of seeing the whole statue. I needed to learn for myself, I think. But I know now. That's why I'm ready to come home. There are no answers, Ethan, so you're wrong about the stars. You're wrong. We don't fuck everything up. There are good things out there. You're going to be okay... You're going to be okay. Just hold on a bit longer. Is someone coming? For God's sake! Hold on, Ethan, hold on.'

'I want to... I wish I could. I'm sorry...' My mouth tasted of bleach and chemicals and fire. The foam from my wave flowed into my throat like an oil spill.

'You can, Ethan, just concentrate. Come on! Fuck! Can somebody help me? Don't worry, Ethan, I'm not going to lose you. Not you... not you.'

For a moment the clouds cleared and I could see

the starlight above me. It filled my eyes. Like travelling through time, all I consisted of was ancient light. Bright, pure and perfect. Infinite and invincible. And the images faded away. The world went dark. The beautiful echoes of a faint voice slowly left my ears. And everything stopped.

Ethan's Journal: Day 1

I've been lying on the beach here on Ko Pha Ngan for a couple of hours now. It's the morning of the Full Moon Party and I've been trying to write something in this new journal Elodie bought me.

The problem is, I can't think what to write. I can't work out how to start it off. I don't know if I can write like my sister. I don't know anything about poetry or style. You see, I think I could easily sit down and write and stuff would come out, but it would be a waste of time. I realise that lying to myself is often the easiest lie of all. What is the point in writing lies? So I thought, no lying, no pretence, just the truth. What is it I want to say? Right now, this is it.

The world is an amazing place, I know this now. But it's so easy to forget this simple fact that I do it all the time. I've got to keep reminding myself that it's true. It only takes something small, some piece of nature, to remind me. And I must be reminded, because that's what keeps the world beautiful.

Stay amazed by it. Don't lose its wonder to the suck of everyday life. This would take away a vital part of my existence, and one that I need to be happy. Certain people have helped me see this and will help me see it in future. (Elodie, that's for you!)

Be amazed, it's so easy.

Because the world is amazing; in its detail, its intricacy, its perfections, its mannerisms, its character, its performances, its life forms, its beauty. However this is all possible, however it all came about, whatever – if anything – lies behind it, it's amazing. And that is always certain and cannot be taken away.

I must remember.

It needs to be remembered.

It's so easy. I just have to allow it to be.

Life isn't a movie, I know that. But it often feels that way. And too often I have wished that it was that way. Enough time-wasting Ethan. You've got to get on with your <u>real</u> life.

49

I woke up and there she was, sitting at the foot of my bed. I couldn't believe it. And yet I could in a strange way. She was grinning wildly.

'Finally! You're awake!'

She jumped off my bed and pulled the duvet from over me.

'Hey!' I said, instinctively wrapping my arms around my shoulders. 'It's cold!'

'Oh, don't be such a girl! Come on, get up!'

I was excited. It made sense that I was excited, but I couldn't work out why. There was a faint light in the room from a street lamp that shone outside. The shadows looked familiar. I rubbed my eyes and sat up in bed.

'I brought my pillow case in so we can open everything together!' she said.

I peered over the edge of my cabin bed and saw her bundle of presents on the floor. They were inside an old, cream-coloured pillowcase that I instantly recognised. The jagged angles of the presents gave the pillowcase an odd geometric shape. It looked similar to one of Daddy's funny cubist works of art.

I reached up to my shelf and picked up my glasses.

They were brand new, shiny and metal-framed – a special pair from the man at the opticians to help with my funny eye – and I still enjoyed wearing them. I still hadn't told Mum and Dad that they had fallen off when I was playing football the previous week. The glasses sat slightly askew because of this, but no one seemed to have noticed so it looked as though I wouldn't get in trouble.

With my glasses on, I could see properly around the room. I saw the bookshelves filled with all my favourite books. They stood neatly in line, propped up by Charlie the wooden elephant at one end. I saw my collection of soap animals, perching, crawling and prowling on my desk. I saw my favourite cuddly toys lined up and colourful on my windowsill. Even Ginger the dog was there. I thought I had lost him.

This was my bedroom.

I ought to be surprised by this, and yet it seemed perfectly normal. I climbed down off my bed and sat cross-legged on the floor next to Charlotte. The bed was a strange distance from the floor. Charlotte handed me my pillowcase. It was heavy; I could only just lift it.

'Let's open them at the same time, okay?' Charlotte looked at me, her eyes wide and bright. She was happy.

'Okay.'

'You get one out and then I'll get one out. You go first.'

I reached in and took out the biggest present I could find. It was enormous in my hands as I lifted it out of the pillowcase. The paper it was wrapped in had snowmen throwing snowballs on it. They were all smiling and had carrots for noses. I thought how funny it must be to have a carrot for a nose.

Gently, I held the present in my hands and looked towards Charlotte. Charlotte plunged into her pillowcase and pulled out the first present she got her hands on.

'Ready?' she asked, her fingers poised.

'Ready.'

'Let's go!'

We both tore open the paper and within seconds it was off. Charlotte whooped with glee as she looked at her beautiful purple diary with its matching pen. The diary was spiral-bound and hard-backed. The pen was fluffy and covered in gold stars. She ripped open the plastic around the pen and began to write with it immediately. She wrote her name several times in beautiful blue ink.

The box my present came in had wonderful colours too: bright reds, greens and yellows. I smiled when I read the bold lettering on the box. *Screwball Scramble* was what I had wanted.

I slipped the lid off carefully and pulled the game from its thin plastic sleeve. A ball bearing was sellotaped to the inside of the lid. I peeled it off and placed it on the board. I pushed the buttons and it clunked and clicked into life.

How wonderful this thing was! How did it all work? The amazement of it drew all my concentration.

It was only when my parents spoke that I realised they had come into the room.

'Happy Christmas, you two! How are the presents?' our mummy asked.

'Brilliant!' shouted Charlotte, having already opened two more. 'I love them!'

'And you, Ethan?'

'It's great! Thanks Mum! Thanks Dad!'

'That's not a problem. There are more in there to open yet! We are going to make a cup of tea. Come down when you're ready and we'll have breakfast.'

My father was smiling. He ruffled my hair. My mother had her hands around my father's waist. I reached out and gave them both a hug. As I closed my eyes it was as though I had been here before, but I couldn't remember when. Hadn't I already had a *Screwball Scramble* for Christmas?

I couldn't concentrate on the question. All I could feel was the hug. All I wanted to think of was this moment with my parents, the pure good it contained. Charlotte joined in and hugged Mum and Dad through me. It was soft yet strong. We were one thing, breathing together.

I was glad to be at home. I was happy. The hug was warm and beautiful and felt like it would last forever.

In this one hug, I experienced the warmth and the goodness and the glow and the perfect memories of everything and everyone, all happening at the same time.

Everything I can remember happening at once.

I feel my mother's arms squeeze me more tightly and my sister's heart beating by my side.

I feel Charlotte put her hand on my cheek.

'Ethan?' she says in a strange voice. 'Can you hear me?'